William Shakespeare

THE TAMING
OF THE SHREW

Edited by Robert B. Heilman

The Signet Classic Shakespeare
GENERAL EDITOR: SYLVAN BARNET
Revised and Updated Bibliography

A SIGNET CLASSIC
NEW AMERICAN LIBRARY
TIMES MIRROR
NEW YORK AND SCARBOROUGH, ONTARIO

SIGNET CLASSIC TRADEMARK REG. U.S. PAT. OFF. AND FOREIGN COUNTRIES
REGISTERED TRADEMARK—MARCA REGISTRADA
HECHO EN CHICAGO, U.S.A.

SIGNET, SIGNET CLASSICS, MENTOR, PLUME, MERIDIAN AND NAL
BOOKS are published *in the United States* by
The New American Library, Inc.,
1633 Broadway, New York, New York 10019,
in Canada by The New American Library of Canada Limited,
81 Mack Avenue, Scarborough, Ontario M1L 1M8,

First Signet Printing, May 1966

13   14   15   16   17   18

PRINTED IN THE UNITED STATES OF AMERICA

Contents

Shakespeare: Prefatory Remarks

Between the record of his baptism in Stratford on 26 April 1564 and the record of his burial in Stratford on 25 April 1616, some forty documents name Shakespeare, and many others name his parents, his children, and his grandchildren. More facts are known about William Shakespeare than about any other playwright of the period except Ben Jonson. The facts should, however, be distinguished from the legends. The latter, inevitably more engaging and better known, tell us that the Stratford boy killed a calf in high style, poached deer and rabbits, and was forced to flee to London, where he held horses outside a playhouse. These traditions are only traditions; they may be true, but no evidence supports them, and it is well to stick to the facts.

Mary Arden, the dramatist's mother, was the daughter of a substantial landowner; about 1557 she married John Shakespeare, who was a glove-maker and trader in various farm commodities. In 1557 John Shakespeare was a member of the Council (the governing body of Stratford), in 1558 a constable of the borough, in 1561 one of the two town chamberlains, in 1565 an alderman (entitling him to the appellation "Mr."), in 1568 high bailiff—the town's highest political office, equivalent to mayor. After 1577, for an unknown reason he drops out of local politics. The birthday of William Shakespeare, the eldest son of this locally prominent man, is unrecorded; but the Stratford parish register records that the infant was baptized on 26 April 1564. (It is quite possible that he was born on 23 April, but this date has probably been assigned by tradition because it is the date on which, fifty-two years later, he died.) The attendance records of the Stratford grammar school of the period are not extant, but it is reasonable to assume that the son of a local official attended the school and received substantial training in Latin. The masters of the school from Shakespeare's seventh to fifteenth years held Oxford degrees; the Elizabethan curriculum excluded mathematics and the natural sciences but taught a good deal of Latin rhetoric, logic, and literature. On 27 November 1582 a marriage license was issued to Shakespeare and Anne Hathaway, eight years his senior. The couple had a child in May, 1583. Perhaps the marriage was necessary, but perhaps the couple had earlier engaged in a formal "troth plight" which would render their children legitimate even if no further ceremony were performed. In 1585 Anne Hathaway bore Shakespeare twins.

That Shakespeare was born is excellent; that he married and had children is pleasant; but that we know nothing about his departure from Stratford to London, or about the beginning of his theatrical career, is lamentable and must be admitted. We would gladly sacrifice details about his children's baptism for details about his earliest days on the stage. Perhaps the poaching episode is true (but it is first reported almost a century after Shakespeare's death), or perhaps he first left Stratford to be a schoolteacher, as another tradition holds; perhaps he was moved by

> Such wind as scatters young men through the world
> To seek their fortunes farther than at home,
> Where small experience grows.

In 1592, thanks to the cantankerousness of Robert Greene, a rival playwright and a pamphleteer, we have our first reference, a snarling one, to Shakespeare as an actor and playwright. Greene warns those of his own educated friends who wrote for the theater against an actor who has presumed to turn playwright:

There is an upstart crow, beautified with our feathers, that with his *tiger's heart wrapped in a player's hide* supposes he is as well able to bombast out a blank verse as the best of you, and being an absolute Johannes-factotum is in his own conceit the only Shake-scene in a country.

The reference to the player, as well as the allusion to Aesop's crow (who strutted in borrowed plumage, as an actor struts in fine words not his own), makes it clear that by this date Shakespeare had both acted and written. That Shakespeare is meant is indicated not only by "Shake-scene" but by the parody of a line from one of Shakespeare's plays, *3 Henry VI:* "O, tiger's heart wrapped in a woman's hide." If Shakespeare in 1592 was prominent enough to be attacked by an envious dramatist, he probably had served an apprenticeship in the theater for at least a few years.

In any case, by 1592 Shakespeare had acted and written, and there are a number of subsequent references to him as an actor: documents indicate that in 1598 he is a "principal comedian," in 1603 a "principal tragedian," in 1608 he is one of the "men players." The profession of actor was not for a gentleman, and it occasionally drew the scorn of university men who resented writing speeches for persons less educated than themselves, but it was respectable enough: players, if prosperous, were in effect members of the bourgeoisie, and there is nothing to suggest that Stratford considered William Shakespeare less than a solid citizen. When, in 1596, the Shakespeares were granted a coat of arms, the grant was made to Shakespeare's father, but probably William Shakespeare (who the next year bought the second-largest house in town) had arranged the matter on his own behalf. In subsequent transactions he is occasionally styled a gentleman.

Although in 1593 and 1594 Shakespeare published two narrative poems dedicated to the Earl of Southampton, *Venus and Adonis* and *The Rape of Lucrece,* and may well have written most or all of his sonnets in the middle nineties, Shakespeare's literary activity seems to have been almost entirely devoted to the theater. (It may be significant that the two narrative poems were written in years when the plague closed the theaters for several months.) In 1594 he was a charter member of a theatrical company called the Chamberlain's Men (which in 1603 changed its name to the King's Men); until he retired to Stratford (about 1611, apparently), he was with this remarkably stable company. From 1599 the company acted primarily at the Globe Theatre, in which Shakespeare held a one-tenth interest. Other Elizabethan dramatists are known to have acted, but no other is known also to have been entitled to a share in the profits of the playhouse.

Shakespeare's first eight published plays did not have his name on them, but this is not remarkable; the most popular play of the sixteenth century, Thomas Kyd's *The Spanish Tragedy,* went through many editions without naming Kyd, and Kyd's authorship is known only because a book on the profession of acting happens to quote (and attribute to Kyd) some lines on the interest of Roman emperors in the drama. What is remarkable is that after 1598 Shakespeare's name commonly appears on printed plays—some of which are not his. Another indication of his popularity comes from Francis Meres, author of *Palladis Tamia: Wit's Treasury* (1598): in this anthology of snippets accompanied by an essay on literature, many playwrights are mentioned, but Shakespeare's name occurs more often than any other, and Shakespeare is the only playwright whose plays are listed.

From his acting, playwriting, and share in a theater, Shakespeare seems to have made considerable money. He put it to work, making substantial investments in Stratford real estate. When he made his will (less than a month before he died), he sought to leave his property intact to his descendants. Of small bequests to relatives and to friends (including three actors, Richard Burbage, John Heminges, and Henry Condell), that to his wife of the second-best bed has provoked the most comment; perhaps it was the bed the couple had slept in, the best being reserved for visitors. In any case, had Shakespeare not excepted it, the bed would have gone (with the rest of his household possessions) to his daughter and her husband. On 25 April 1616 he was buried within the chancel of the church at Stratford. An unattractive monument to his memory, placed on a wall near the grave, says he died on 23 April. Over the grave itself are the lines, perhaps by Shakespeare, that (more than his literary fame) have kept his bones undisturbed in the crowded burial ground where old bones were often dislodged to make way for new:

> Good friend, for Jesus' sake forbear
> To dig the dust enclosèd here.
> Bless be the man that spares these stones
> And cursed be he that moves my bones.

Thirty-seven plays, as well as some nondramatic poems, are held to constitute the Shakespeare canon. The dates of composition of most of the works are highly uncertain, but there is often evidence of a *terminus a quo* (starting point) and/or a *terminus ad quem* (terminal point) that provides a framework for intelligent guessing. For example, *Richard II* cannot be earlier than 1595, the publication date of some material to which it is indebted; *The Merchant of Venice* cannot be later than 1598, the year Francis Meres mentioned it. Sometimes arguments for a date hang on an alleged topical allusion, such as the lines about the unseasonable weather in *A Midsummer Night's Dream*, II.i.81–117, but such an allusion (if indeed it is an allusion) can be variously interpreted, and in any case there is always the possibility that a topical allusion was inserted during a revision, years after the composition of a play. Dates are often attributed on the basis of style, and although conjectures about style usually rest on other conjectures, sooner or later one must rely on one's literary sense. There is no real proof, for example, that *Othello* is not as early as *Romeo and Juliet*, but one feels *Othello* is later, and because the first record of its performance is 1604, one is glad enough to set its composition at that date and not push it back into Shakespeare's early years. The following chronology, then, is as much indebted to informed guesswork and sensitivity as it is to fact. The dates, necessarily imprecise, indicate something like a scholarly consensus.

PLAYS

1588–93	*The Comedy of Errors*
1588–94	*Love's Labor's Lost*
1590–91	*2 Henry VI*
1590–91	*3 Henry VI*
1591–92	*1 Henry VI*
1592–93	*Richard III*
1592–94	*Titus Andronicus*
1593–94	*The Taming of the Shrew*
1593–95	*The Two Gentlemen of Verona*
1594–96	*Romeo and Juliet*
1595	*Richard II*
1594–96	*A Midsummer Night's Dream*
1596–97	*King John*
1596–97	*The Merchant of Venice*
1597	*1 Henry IV*
1597–98	*2 Henry IV*
1598–1600	*Much Ado About Nothing*
1598–99	*Henry V*
1599	*Julius Caesar*
1599–1600	*As You Like It*
1599–1600	*Twelfth Night*
1600–01	*Hamlet*
1597–1601	*The Merry Wives of Windsor*
1601–02	*Troilus and Cressida*
1602–04	*All's Well That Ends Well*
1603–04	*Othello*
1604	*Measure for Measure*
1605–06	*King Lear*
1605–06	*Macbeth*
1606–07	*Antony and Cleopatra*
1605–08	*Timon of Athens*
1607–09	*Coriolanus*
1608–09	*Pericles*
1609–10	*Cymbeline*

1610–11   *The Winter's Tale*
1611   *The Tempest*
1612–13   *Henry VIII*

POEMS

1592   *Venus and Adonis*
1593–94   *The Rape of Lucrece*
1593–1600   *Sonnets*
1600–01   *The Phoenix and the Turtle*

Shakespeare's Theater

In Shakespeare's infancy, Elizabethan actors performed wherever they could—in great halls, at court, in the courtyards of inns. The innyards must have made rather unsatisfactory theaters: on some days they were unavailable because carters bringing goods to London used them as depots; when available, they had to be rented from the innkeeper; perhaps most important, London inns were subject to the Common Council of London, which was not well disposed towards theatricals. In 1574 the Common Council required that plays and playing places in London be licensed. It asserted that

> sundry great disorders and inconveniences have been found to ensue to this city by the inordinate haunting of great multitudes of people, specially youth, to plays, interludes, and shows, namely occasion of frays and quarrels, evil practices of incontinency in great inns having chambers and secret places adjoining to their open stages and galleries,

and ordered that innkeepers who wished licenses to hold performances put up a bond and make contributions to the poor.

The requirement that plays and innyard theaters be licensed, along with the other drawbacks of playing at inns, probably drove James Burbage (a carpenter-turned-actor) to rent in 1576 a plot of land northeast of the city walls and to build here—on property outside the jurisdiction of the city—England's first permanent construction designed for plays. He called it simply the Theatre. About all that is known of its construction is that it was wood. It soon had imitators, the most famous being the Globe (1599), built across the Thames (again outside the city's jurisdiction), out of timbers of the Theatre, which had been dismantled when Burbage's lease ran out.

There are three important sources of information about the structure of Elizabethan playhouses—drawings, a contract, and stage directions in plays. Of drawings, only the so-called De Witt drawing (c. 1596) of the Swan—really a friend's copy of De Witt's drawing—is of much significance. It shows a building of three tiers, with a stage jutting from a wall into the yard or center of the building. The tiers are roofed, and part of the stage is covered by a roof that projects from the rear and is supported at its front on two posts, but the groundlings, who paid a penny to stand in front of the stage, were exposed to the sky. (Performances in such a playhouse were held only in the daytime; artificial illumination was not used.) At the rear of the stage are two doors; above the stage is a gallery. The second major source of information, the contract for the Fortune, specifies that although the Globe is to be the model, the Fortune is to be square, eighty feet outside and fifty-five inside. The stage is to be forty-three feet broad, and is to extend into the middle of the yard (i.e., it is twenty-seven and a half feet deep). For patrons willing to pay more than the general admission charged of the groundlings, there were to be three galleries provided with seats. From the third chief source, stage directions, one learns that entrance to the stage was by doors, presumably spaced widely apart at the rear ("Enter one citizen at one door, and another at the other"), and that in addition to the platform stage there was occasionally some sort of curtained booth or alcove allowing for "discovery" scenes, and some sort of playing space "aloft" or "above" to represent (for example) the top of a city's walls or a room above the street. Doubtless each theater had its own peculiarities, but perhaps we can talk about a "typical" Elizabethan theater if we realize that no theater need exactly have fit the description, just as no father is the typical father with 3.7 children. This hypothetical theater is wooden, round or polygonal (in *Henry V* Shakespeare calls it a "wooden *O*"), capable of holding some eight hundred spectators standing in the yard around the projecting elevated stage and some fifteen hundred additional spectators seated in the three roofed galleries. The stage, protected by a "shadow" or "heavens" or roof, is entered by two doors; behind the doors is the "tiring house" (attiring house, i.e., dressing room), and above the doors is some sort of gallery that may sometimes hold spectators but that can be used (for example) as the bedroom from which Romeo—according to a stage direction in one text—"goeth down." Some evidence suggests that a throne can be lowered onto the platform stage, perhaps from the "shadow"; certainly characters can descend from the stage through a trap or traps into the cellar or "hell." Sometimes this space beneath the platform accommodates a sound-effects man or musician (in *Antony and Cleopatra* "music of the hautboys is under the stage") or an actor (in *Hamlet* the "Ghost cries under the stage"). Most characters simply walk on and off, but because there is no curtain in front of the platform, corpses will have to be carried off (Hamlet must lug Polonius' guts into the neighbor room), or will have to fall at the rear, where the curtain on the alcove or booth can be drawn to conceal them.

Such may have been the so-called "public theater." Another kind of theater, called the "private theater" because its much greater admission charge limited its audience to the wealthy or the prodigal, must be briefly mentioned. The private theater was basically a large room, entirely roofed and therefore artificially illuminated, with a stage at one end. In 1576 one such theater was established in Blackfriars, a Dominican priory in London that had been suppressed in 1538 and confiscated by the Crown and thus was not under the city's jurisdiction. All the actors in the Blackfriars theater were boys about eight to thirteen years old (in the public theaters similar boys played female parts; a boy Lady Macbeth played to a man Macbeth). This private theater had a precarious existence, and ceased operations in 1584. In 1596 James Burbage, who had already made theatrical history by building the Theatre, began to construct a second Black-friars theater. He died in 1597, and for several years this second Blackfriars theater was used by a troupe of boys, but in 1608 two of Burbage's sons and five other actors (including Shakespeare) became joint operators of the theater, using it in the winter when the open-air Globe was unsuitable. Perhaps such a smaller theater, roofed, artificially illuminated, and with a tradition of a courtly audience, exerted an influence on Shakespeare's late plays.

Performances in the private theaters may well have had intermissions during which music was played, but in the public theaters the action was probably uninter-rupted, flowing from scene to scene almost without a break. Actors would enter, speak, exit, and others would immediately enter and establish (if necessary) the new locale by a few properties and by words and gestures. Here are some samples of Shakespeare's scene painting:

> This is Illyria, lady.

> Well, this is the Forest of Arden.

> This castle hath a pleasant seat; the air
> Nimbly and sweetly recommends itself
> Unto our gentle senses.

On the other hand, it is a mistake to conceive of the Elizabethan stage as bare. Although Shakespeare's Chorus in *Henry V* calls the stage an "unworthy scaffold" and urges the spectators to "eke out our performance with your mind," there was considerable spectacle. The last act of *Macbeth,* for example, has five stage directions calling for "drum and colors," and another sort of appeal to the eye is indicated by the stage direction "Enter Mac-duff, with Macbeth's head." Some scenery and properties may have been substantial; doubtless a throne was used, and in one play of the period we encounter this direction: "Hector takes up a great piece of rock and casts at Ajax, who tears up a young tree by the roots and assails Hector." The matter is of some importance, and will be glanced at again in the next section.

The Texts of Shakespeare

Though eighteen of his plays were published during his lifetime, Shakespeare seems never to have supervised their publication. There is nothing unusual here; when a playwright sold a play to a theatrical company he surrendered his ownership of it. Normally a company would not publish the play, because to publish it meant to allow competitors to acquire the piece. Some plays, however, did get published: apparently treacherous actors sometimes pieced together a play for a publisher, sometimes a company in need of money sold a play, and sometimes a company allowed a play to be published that no longer drew audiences. That Shakespeare did not concern himself with publication, then, is scarcely remarkable; of his contemporaries only Ben Jonson carefully supervised the publication of his own plays. In 1623, seven years after Shakespeare's death, John Heminges and Henry Condell (two senior members of Shakespeare's company, who had performed with him for about twenty years) collected his plays—published and unpublished—into a large volume, commonly called the First Folio. (A folio is a volume consisting of sheets that have been folded once, each sheet thus making two leaves, or four pages. The eighteen plays published during Shakespeare's lifetime had been issued one play per volume in small books called quartos. Each sheet in a quarto has been folded twice, making four leaves, or eight pages.) The First Folio contains thirty-six plays; a thirty-seventh, *Pericles,* though not in the Folio is regarded as canonical. Heminges and Condell suggest in an address "To the great variety of readers" that the republished plays are presented in better form than in the quartos: "Before you were abused with diverse stolen and surreptitious copies, maimed and deformed by the frauds and stealths of injurious impostors that exposed them; even those, are now offered to your view cured and perfect of their limbs, and all the rest absolute in their numbers, as he [i.e., Shakespeare] conceived them."

Whoever was assigned to prepare the texts for publication in the First Folio seems to have taken his job seriously and yet not to have performed it with uniform care. The sources of the texts seem to have been, in general, good unpublished copies or the best published copies. The first play in the collection, *The Tempest,* is divided into acts and scenes, has unusually full stage directions and descriptions of spectacle, and concludes with a list of the characters, but the editor was not able (or willing) to present all of the succeeding texts so fully dressed. Later texts occasionally show signs of carelessness: in one scene of *Much Ado About Nothing* the names of actors, instead of characters, appear as speech prefixes, as they had in the quarto, which the Folio reprints; proofreading throughout the Folio is spotty and apparently was done without reference to the printer's copy; the pagination of *Hamlet* jumps from 156 to 257.

A modern editor of Shakespeare must first select his copy; no problem if the play exists only in the Folio, but a considerable problem if the relationship between a quarto and the Folio—or an early quarto and a later one—is unclear. When an editor has chosen what seems to him to be the most authoritative text or texts for his copy, he has not done with making decisions. First of all, he must reckon with Elizabethan spelling. If he is not producing a facsimile, he probably modernizes it, but ought he to preserve the old form of words that apparently were pronounced quite unlike their modern forms—"lanthorn," "alablaster"? If he preserves these forms, is he really preserving Shakespeare's forms or perhaps those of a compositor in the printing house? What is one to do when one finds "lanthorn" and "lantern" in adjacent lines? (The editors of this series in general, but not invariably, assume that words should be spelled in their modern form.) Elizabethan punctuation, too, presents problems. For example in the First Folio, the only text for the play, Macbeth rejects his wife's idea that he can wash the blood from his hand:

> no: this my Hand will rather
> The multitudinous Seas incarnardine,
> Making the Greene one, Red.

Obviously an editor will remove the superfluous capitals, and he will probably alter the spelling to "incarnadine," but will he leave the comma before "red," letting Macbeth speak of the sea as "the green one," or will he (like most modern editors) remove the comma and thus have Macbeth say that his hand will make the ocean *uniformly* red?

An editor will sometimes have to change more than spelling or punctuation. Macbeth says to his wife:

> I dare do all that may become a man,
> Who dares no more, is none.

For two centuries editors have agreed that the second line is unsatisfactory, and have emended "no" to "do": "Who dares do more is none." But when in the same play Ross says that fearful persons

> floate vpon a wilde and violent Sea
> Each way, and moue,

need "move" be emended to "none," as it often is, on the hunch that the compositor misread the manuscript? The editors of the Signet Classic Shakespeare have restrained themselves from making abundant emendations. In their minds they hear Dr. Johnson on the dangers of emending: "I have adopted the Roman sentiment, that it is more honorable to save a citizen than to kill an enemy." Some departures (in addition to spelling, punctuation, and lineation) from the copy text have of course been made, but the original readings are listed in a note following the play, so that the reader can evaluate them for himself.

The editors of the Signet Classic Shakespeare, following tradition, have added line numbers and in many cases act and scene divisions as well as indications of locale at the beginning of scenes. The Folio divided most of the plays into acts and some into scenes. Early eighteenth-century editors increased the divisions. These divisions, which provide a convenient way of referring to passages in the plays, have been retained, but when not in the text chosen as the basis for the Signet Classic text they are enclosed in square brackets [ ] to indicate that they are editorial additions. Similarly, although no play of Shakespeare's published during his lifetime was equipped with indications of locale at the heads of scene divisions, locales have here been added in square brackets for the convenience of the reader, who lacks the information afforded to spectators by costumes, properties, and gestures. The spectator can tell at a glance he is in the throne room, but without an editorial indication the reader may be puzzled for a while. It should be mentioned, incidentally, that there are a few authentic stage directions —perhaps Shakespeare's, perhaps a prompter's—that suggest locales: for example, "Enter Brutus in his orchard," and "They go up into the Senate house." It is hoped that the bracketed additions provide the reader with the sort of help provided in these two authentic directions, but it is equally hoped that the reader will remember that the stage was not loaded with scenery.

No editor during the course of his work can fail to recollect some words Heminges and Condell prefixed to the Folio:

It had been a thing, we confess, worthy to have been wished, that the author himself had lived to have set forth and overseen his own writings. But since it hath been ordained otherwise, and he by death departed from that right, we pray you do not envy his friends the office of their care and pain to have collected and published them.

Nor can an editor, after he has done his best, forget

Heminges and Condell's final words: "And so we leave you to other of his friends, whom if you need can be your guides. If you need them not, you can lead yourselves, and others. And such readers we wish him."

SYLVAN BARNET
Tufts University

Introduction

At a number of points critics of *The Taming of the Shrew* are in general agreement. No one doubts that Christopher Sly is skillfully characterized—in his coarseness, his liveliness, his unaffectedness, his candor, his partial yielding to illusion, his incongruous mixture of two styles of life, his difficulty in acting the gentleman and attending to even a rather popular brand of theatrical fare. No one doubts that Petruchio and Kate are made, if not altogether well-rounded characters, at least human beings of vitality and imaginativeness, so that they have an interest and plausibility that stereotypes would not have. Each first acts in a way that suggests a rather single-ply, rigid nature, and then reveals a capacity for crucial action of another quality and value. No one doubts that the Bianca plot is of secondary interest, that it turns on a conventional love story, that it has in it more of intrigue than of the romantic intensity that Shakespeare would later develop in his lovers, and that, despite its manifest limitations, Shakespeare has pumped theatrical life into it by the multiplication of candidates for Bianca's hand and by a brisk representation of their schemes and styles. No one doubts that the suitors are effectively distinguished from each other—Gremio, the clownish overage lover; Tranio, the virtuoso quasi-competitor who loves to play the gentleman; Hortensio, who can settle for an unromantic down-to-earth arrangement like a sensible man in Restoration comedy; and Lucentio, the straight man and winner. No one doubts that the lesser characters are, in

brief space, endowed with much individuality and substance—Baptista, the worried and well-meaning father;
Grumio, the spirited servant who finds histrionic pleasure
in opposite roles, whether taking it from Petruchio or
dishing it out to other servants; Biondello, the lively-
talking aide-de-camp in the war of love; the conscientious
and frustrated Tailor; the earnest Pedant, grimly determined to succeed in his role as Lucentio's helpful father;
the actual Vincentio, driven into a temper by successive
experiences of being put upon.

No one doubts, finally, that all these materials from
diverse sources (see A Note on the Sources, p. 157)
have been combined with so much ingenuity that the play
has a convincing air of unity. The play within a play is
an old device: no one feels any hiatus between the audience (Sly and the Lord's household) and the performers
of a play (the actors presenting the two love affairs). The
taming plot and the relatively straight love plot are brought
together mechanically by the fact that the two women are
sisters and that the marriage of one depends on that of
the other; by the fact that Bianca's suitors collaborate in
finding a suitor for Kate and, even more than that, in assisting him in his suit; by the fact that Petruchio first aids
Hortensio and that Hortensio later plays along with Petruchio's game as wife-tamer; and by the fact that the final
wedding celebration is a joint affair. The two actions are
held together organically by the fact that the women
wooed, the wooers, and their methods of wooing are in
contrast, not only aesthetically but, by implication, mor-
ally; and by the still more striking fact that the apparent
contrast, which seems so obvious at first, is reversed in
the final act. When Kate and Bianca undergo a partial
change of roles at the end, we see them, not simply as
ending parallel plots, but as ironically revealing different
aspects of one fundamental situation—the relations of
husbands and wives.

Within the last decade critics have begun to detect a
still subtler form of unity, one that considerably raises the
aesthetic status of the play. This is "the unity of 'supposes.' " When Lucentio is made to use the phrase "coun-

terfeit supposes" (V.i.115), Shakespeare is alluding,* it
is assumed, to his source, Gascoigne's play *Supposes*; in
this title Gascoigne is Englishing the title of his source
play, Ariosto's *I Suppositi*. The idea behind these words
is that of "posing," of assuming identities other than one's
own. From Gascoigne Shakespeare got the Bianca plot,
which is of course full of assumed or "supposed" identities: Hortensio as Litio, Lucentio as Cambio, Tranio as
Lucentio, and the Pedant as Vincentio; and then the true
Vincentio is accused of being someone else posing as
Vincentio. But recent criticism has observed that "supposes" are not limited either to physical identity or to the
Bianca plot. Within the Bianca plot, Bianca and the widow
are both "supposed" to be agreeable women who will be
accommodating wives. That is, the dramatic treatment
encourages us to see that beyond the mere putting on of
a false name and a false social or professional identity
may lie the putting on of a personality or moral identity
(whether as a long-lasting habit or as a short-term device
to secure a given end).

Once given such hints, the reader sees quickly a new
and closer tie between the Bianca plot and the Sly plot
(the Induction): in each, the basic mechanism is the use
of "supposed" identities. The Lord and members of his
household pretend to be Sly's servants and his wife. But
we have hardly noted this when we see, also, that the
mainspring of the Induction is a subtler alteration of identity: Sly is persuaded, or at least half-persuaded, that he
is a Lord. The Lord and his men have voluntarily changed
identity in order to cause Sly involuntarily to change identity (just as Bianca's lovers, so to speak, have voluntarily
changed identity in order to cause Bianca to accept them).
From here it is only a quick step to the remarkable kin-
ship that the main Petruchio-Kate plot has with the other
two: Petruchio voluntarily assumes an identity ("poses"
as a contrary, willful, autocratic, irrational man, a "shrew")
in order to cause Kate involuntarily to change identity, to

---

* There is a similar allusion in Tranio's decision that "supposed
Lucentio / Must get a father, called 'supposed Vincentio' " (II.i.400–01).

give up shrewishness and become a charming, cooperative wife. In three plots a "supposition" or impersonation is the means of inducing a person to act in a certain way: a man accepts a "wife" and two women accept husbands. "Acting" is the means of moving people toward a desired feeling and role; in this sense *The Taming* anticipates the much-quoted line in *As You Like It,* "All the world's a stage. . . ."

But there is a still subtler element in the functional identity of parts which creates the unity of the play. The "supposed" servants of Sly not only tell him he is a Lord but hold before him verbal pictures—of omnipotence, luxury, pleasures—that move him in their own way toward imaginative acceptance of his high role. At least he accepts the external circumstances in which he finds himself; perhaps he even accepts the idea of a lordly personality in himself. The further he goes in this direction, the more fully the Induction anticipates the taming plot. For a part of Petruchio's method (by no means all of it) is to hold before Kate a picture of what she potentially is and may become if she will but cease resisting it—a "most patient, sweet, and virtuous wife" (III.ii.195). It is possible to assume that she imaginatively accepts this picture of herself and, under the stimulus of Petruchio's love, makes it come true. If this interpretation is valid, then the play—not only one of Shakespeare's earliest but a farcical one—has advanced remarkably at least to the edge of a philosophical realm. For it induces us to reflect on the belief in the primacy of the idea, on the creative powers of the imagination, on the view that, in Hamlet's phrase that has become a cliché, "Thinking makes it so." Hence *The Taming,* never thought one of Shakespeare's high achievements, moves up into the company of the truly Shakespearean, in which, however stereotyped the exterior and however obvious the popular appeal, there is a heart of profound meaningfulness and hence enduring excellence. It is possible that a once underrated play may be in danger of being overrated.

So far we have been summarizing the main grounds of agreement among critics, especially the grounds on which

The Taming has been praised. However, the argument for
unity depends somewhat on how we understand the change
in Kate—transformation, acceptance of discipline, discovery of true nature, rejection of an assumed role? This is
not so demonstrable as is the tight interweaving of plots
at the level of overt action. When it is asserted that the
play uncovers Bianca as the real shrew, and reveals that
Kate is not a shrew at all or else was only pretending to
be a shrew to serve her own ends, surely we come into
the realm of the arguable. There is something of the arguable about *The Taming;* indeed there has been, alongside
the areas of unanimity, considerable difference of opinion
about it. We can profitably change our course, then, and
approach the play from the other side—in terms of the
disagreements, or at least the changes of opinion, about it.

One argument grows out of sheer factual uncertainty:
did Shakespeare, or did he not, keep Sly in the play for
occasional comments in the later acts, and for an epilogue
completing the dramatic "frame"? In *The Taming of a
Shrew,* a play related to this one (see A Note on the
Sources, p. 157), Sly stayed on. Hence, what about
The Shrew? There are various opinions: (1) Shakespeare
forgot about Sly; (2) Shakespeare originally wrote a Sly
epilogue, but it dropped out; (3) the loss of Sly, though
not a major blot, is unfortunate; (4) the loss of Sly is
fortunate, and shows Shakespeare's artistry. If Shakespeare
did originally give Sly the closing lines, and if these did
disappear—from an acting script and hence from the
printer's copy—the only compelling reason for this (in
the opinion of the present editor) was not aesthetic but
practical: it simplified production problems such as size
of cast. There is no merit in the argument that the elimi-
nation of Sly prevented an anticlimax, for this begs the
question whether a Sly epilogue would inevitably be anti-
climactic. There is likewise little merit in the argument
that the Sly story comes to its logical end when Sly takes
himself for a Lord and thus in anticipation parallels Kate's
transformation into a lady. For, while Kate can, with effort, retain her new moral identity, Sly cannot, with any
amount of effort, retain his new social identity. Hence it

is possible to visualize a very effective Sly epilogue which would work by contrast, making us note the discrepancy between an imaginable change of being and a temporary change of status, between a hypnotism for the therapy of the subject and the imposition of a dream for the fun of the observers. We can imagine, also, the use of Sly for a cynical irony such as we know in "black comedy": the end of his new lordship might hint the diminution of Kate's new ladyship. Or, in a lighter vein, Sly might entertain, as he does in *A Shrew,* visions of being a wife-tamer, and thus introduce an implicit contrast between those who can pull off such an exploit and those who cannot. Well, the imagining of alternative endings serves only one purpose: showing that the present one is not necessarily ideal. Surely most readers feel spontaneously that, in the treatment of Sly in *The Shrew,* something is left uncomfortably hanging, and many stage directors borrow additional Sly materials from *A Shrew.*

While Petruchio and Kate, as we have noted, are admired as lively and charming creatures, forerunners of Benedick and Beatrice in *Much Ado About Nothing,* there is lack of agreement on their natures and on the nature of the transactions between them. No one doubts, of course, that they come to love each other; the problem is what they bring to that love and how they exercise it. The older view was that Petruchio was a very skillful psychologist, one who really knew how to handle a difficult woman. On the other hand, many commentators, especially in the nineteenth century, tended to feel that Petruchio's methods were not civilized and that, though they may once have been countenanced, they would never do in modern life. That sense of real life, of what it is and should be, which repeatedly infiltrates literary judgments, appears in estimates of Petruchio: there have been editors who get on the bandwagon and declare him out of date and yet rather wistfully intimate that it is too bad he has gone out of date while the world still has need of him. But in repudiating Petruchio's methods, critics have had to find ways of redeeming Petruchio, since the play obviously does not make him an intolerable man. So it has been said that he is not so much "taming" Kate as leading her to a needed discipline; that in no essential does he pass the bounds of gentlemanliness; that he simply offers Kate a picture of male strength that can elicit the respect without which she cannot love; that the heart of his method is a love which begets love. Here we have Petruchio transmuted from the relentless and mechanical taskmaster, required by a monstrous female, into a remarkably gifted gentleman-lover who simply brings out the best in an extraordinary woman—a best that, as it comes out, totally displaces a worst that had once seemed pretty much the whole story. This view is much more in tune with modern views of the right relations between men and women. But this interpretation too, if not utterly replaced, has been given a new twist and all but turned upside down by a still more "modern" view. In this most recent reading of the play, Petruchio, far from "taming" or subtly having a beneficent influence on a woman, is in reality tamed by her. While having the illusion of conquering, he is conquered by her; when she says what he wants to hear, she is being ironic, undermining him with a show of acquiescence and virtually a wink to the audience. In this view, Shakespeare wrote *What Every Woman Knows* over three hundred years before Barrie.

Kate, of course, has been done over in the same way. Once she was naturally and unquestionably taken to be a shrew, that is, a type of woman widely known in life and constantly represented in song and story. Then critics began to contend that Kate differed from the stereotype: that instead of being simply aggressive and contentious, she was ripe for love, wanted love, and really suffered from the fact that, inside the family and out, Bianca more readily attracted affection. Here is the move toward seeing Kate, not as an allegorical abstraction, a figure of shrewishness, but as an actual human being with impulses and motives experienced by all of us. This move goes still further. In one modern view (that of Nevill Coghill and the late Professor Goddard), Kate's disagreeableness of manner is not a primary fact of personality but is caused by lack of affection at home: Baptista, a "family tyrant," has petted and spoiled Bianca, and Kate is the unhappy by-product of parental irresponsibility and stupidity ("gross partiality" toward Bianca). In this view, Kate is very much like a modern problem child. But the distinguished director of Shakespeare, Margaret Webster, offers us a still different Kate. To Miss Webster, Kate is a strong, intelligent, independent woman who is stuck in a stuffy household, "despises" her father and her "horrid little sister," thinks the local boys "beneath contempt," and finds in her fresh and vehement style the only available outlet for the talents and energy of a superior woman. Here we have the feminist's Kate, the modern woman whom it is perilous to hold back from self-expression and leadership—a far cry from the nagging Xanthippe that every now and then, from the beginning of time, would afflict a husband doomed, unless he took strong measures, to be ridiculed for his misfortune. But Goddard and Miss Webster agree in one thing: it is really Kate who takes over Petruchio, takes him over by simulating an obedience that is a paradoxical mastery. Her last long speech, then, is only a prolonged ironic commentary on the subordination of wives, and could be taken literally only by naïve believers in male supremacy.

As might be expected, critics differ on where Shakespeare stood. The most widely held assumption is that Shakespeare believed in the subordination of wives, and that in his age he could hardly do otherwise. While some readers accept this as calmly as most people accept what has happened long ago, others regret that Shakespeare was so little in accord with modern views; as early as 1897, even G. B. Shaw could insist that "the last scene is altogether disgusting to modern sensibility." The reader with a severe case of "modern sensibility" can either join Shaw in slapping Shakespeare's wrist or else go him one better by arguing that Shakespeare was really a modern at heart. The unspoken assumption here is that the "divine Shakespeare" could not possibly disagree with our answers to fundamental problems, especially those we have come to more recently. So various commentators say flatly that Shakespeare did *not* believe in the subordination of wives.

Of Kate's long speech on the duty of wives (V.ii.136–179), Goddard, amazed at three centuries of acceptance, exclaims, "as if Shakespeare could ever have meant it!" But only Miss Webster faced the fact that to make Shakespeare a modern, one had to do something better with the wifely-duty speech than ignore it or just assert that, though the longest speech in the play, it doesn't count. So she went whole hog and treated the speech as Kate's choicest joke of all on Petruchio, who from now on, we judge, will be simply a complacent husband, happy in the laughable illusion that he has an obedient wife.

It is doubtful that we can know "what Shakespeare thought," and in a sense it does not matter; what is important is how the play is to be taken (it is by no means impossible that the play "believes" something other than what Shakespeare as a man may have "believed"). All the aspects of it that have been taken now in one way, now in another, come together pretty well in the issue of what the play is to be called. By many critics it is called a "farce" and is discussed as a farce; yet there are those who deny vigorously that it is a farce. This difference of opinion is caused by a loose use of the term *farce*. Some people take farce as simply hurly-burly theater, with much slapstick, roughhouse (Petruchio with a whip, in the older productions), pratfalls, general confusion, trickery, uproar, gags, and so on. Yet such characteristics, which do appear generally in farce, are surface manifestations. What we need to identify is the "spirit of farce" which lies behind them. We may then be able to get away from insisting either that *The Shrew* is farce or that it is not farce, and to get on to seeing what it does with the genre of farce.

A genre is a conventionalized way of dealing with actuality, and different genres represent different habits of the human mind, or minister to the capacity for finding pleasure in different styles of representation. "Romance," for instance, is the genre that conceives of obstacles, dangers, and threats, especially those of an unusual or spectacular kind, as yielding to human ingenuity, spirit, or just good luck. On the other hand, "naturalism," as a literary mode, conceives of man as overcome by the pressure of outer forces, especially those of a dull, glacier-like, grinding persistence. The essential procedure of farce is to deal with people as if they lack, largely or totally, the physical, emotional, intellectual, and moral sensitivity that we think of as "normal." The enormous popularity of farce for several thousand years indicates that, though "farce" is often a term of disparagement, a great many people, no doubt all of us at times, take pleasure in seeing human beings acting as if they were very limited human beings. Farce offers a spectacle that resembles daily actuality but lets us participate without feeling the responsibilities and liabilities that the situation would normally evoke. Perhaps we feel superior to the diminished men and women in the plot; perhaps we harmlessly work off aggressions (since verbal and physical assaults are frequent in farce). Participation in farce is easy on us; in it we escape the full complexity of our own natures and cut up without physical or moral penalties. Farce is the realm without pain or conscience. Farce offers a holiday from vulnerability, consequences, costs. It is the opposite of all the dramas of disaster in which a man's fate is too much for him. It carries out our desire to simplify life by a selective anesthetizing of the whole person; man retains all his energy yet never gets really hurt. The give-and-take of life becomes a brisk skirmishing in which one needs neither health insurance nor liability insurance; when one is on the receiving end and has to take it, he bounces back up resiliently, and when he dishes it out, his pleasure in conquest is never undercut by the guilt of inflicting injury.

In farce, the human personality is without depth. Hence action is not slowed down by thought or by the friction of competing motives. Everything goes at high speed, with dash, variety, never a pause for stocktaking, and ever an athlete's quick glance ahead at the action coming up next. No sooner do the players come in than the Lord plans a show to help bamboozle Sly. As soon as Baptista appears with his daughters and announces the marriage priority, other lovers plan to find a man for Kate, Lucentio falls in love with Bianca and hits on an approach in disguise, Petruchio plans to go for Kate, Bianca's lovers promise him support, Petruchio begins his suit and introduces Hortensio into the scramble of disguised lovers. Petruchio rushes through the preliminary business with Baptista and the main business with Kate, and we have a marriage. The reader is hurried over to the rivalries of Bianca's lovers, making bids to Baptista and appealing directly to the girl herself, back to Kate's wedding-day scandals and out into the country for the postmarital welter of disturbances; then we shift back and forth regularly from rapid action in the Kate plot to almost equally rapid action in the Bianca plot. And so on. The driving pace made possible, and indeed necessitated by, the absence of depth is brilliantly managed.

In the absence of depth one is not bothered by distractions; in fact, what are logically distractions are not felt as such if they fit into the pattern of carefree farcical hammer and tongs, cut and thrust. At Petruchio's first appearance, the "knocking at the gate" confusion is there for fun, not function (I.ii.5–43). The first hundred lines (in IV.i) between Grumio and Curtis are a lively rattle, full of the verbal and physical blows of farce, but practically without bearing on the action. Kate is virtually forgotten for sixty lines (in IV.iii) as Petruchio and Grumio fall into their virtuoso game of abusing the tailor. Furthermore, action without depth has a mechanical, automatic quality: when two Vincentios appear (V.i), the characters do not reason about the duplication but, frustrated by confusion and bluffing, quickly have recourse to blows and insults, accusations of madness and chicanery, and threats of arrest— standard procedures in farce from Plautus on. Vincentio's "thus strangers may be halèd and abused" is not a bad description of the manners of farce. Mechanical action, in turn, often tends to symmetrical effects (shown most clearly in _The Comedy of Errors,_ in which Shakespeare has two pairs of identical twins): the lovers of Kate and Bianca first bargain with Baptista, then approach the girls; Hortensio and Tranio (as Lucentio) resign their claims to Bianca in almost choral fashion; Bianca and the Widow respond identically to the requests of their husbands. In this final scene we have striking evidence of the manipulation of personality in the interest of symmetrical effect. Shakespeare unmistakably wants a double reversal of roles at the end, a symmetry of converse movements. The new Kate has developed out of a shrew, so the old Bianca must develop into a shrew. The earlier treatment of her hardly justifies her sudden transformation, immediately after marriage, into a cool, offhand, challenging, and even contemptuous near-bitch. Like many another character in farce, she succumbs to the habits of the generic form. Yet by some modern critics she is treated as harshly as if from the start she were a particularly obnoxious female.

All these effects come from a certain arbitrarily limited sense of personality. Those who have this personality are not really hurt, do not think much, are not much troubled by scruples. Farce often turns on practical jokes, in which the sadistic impulse is not restrained by any sense of injury to the victim. It would never occur to anyone that Sly might be pained or humiliated by letting himself act as a Lord and then being let down. No one hesitates to make rough jokes about Kate (even calling her "fiend of hell") in her hearing. No one putting on a disguise to dupe others has any ethical inhibitions; the end always justifies the means. When Kate "breaks the lute to" Hortensio, farce requires that he act terrified; but it does not permit him to be injured or really resentful or grieved by the loss of the lute, as a man in a nonfarcical world might well be. Verbal abuse is almost an art form; it does not hurt, as it would in ordinary life. No one supposes that the victims of Petruchio's manhandling and tantrums—the priest and sexton at the wedding, the servants and tradesmen at his home—really feel the outrageous treatment that they get. When Petruchio and Hortensio call "To her" to Kate and the Widow, it is like starting a dogfight or cockfight. Petruchio's order to Kate to bring out the other wives is like having a trained dog retrieve a stick. The scene is possible because both husbands and all wives are not endowed with full human personalities; if they were, they could not function as trainer, retriever, and sticks.

In identifying the farcical elements in *The Shrew*, we

have gradually shifted from the insensitivity that the characters must have to the mechanicalness of their responses. These people rarely think, hesitate, deliberate, or choose; they act just as quickly and unambiguously as if someone had pressed a control button. Farce simplifies life by making it painless and automatic; indeed the two qualities come together in the concept of man as machine. (The true opposite of farce is Čapek's *R. U. R.*, in which manlike robots actually begin to feel.) There is a sense in which we might legitimately call the age of computers a farcical one, for it lets us feel that basic choices are made without mental struggle or will or anxiety, and as speedily and inevitably as a series of human ninepins falling down one after another on the stage when each is bumped by the one next to it. "Belike you mean," says Kate to Petruchio, "to make a puppet of me" (IV.iii.103). It is what farce does to all characters. Now the least obvious illustration of the farcical view of life lies, not in some of the peripheral goings-on that we have been observing, but in the title action itself: the taming of the shrew. Fundamentally—we will come shortly to the necessary qualifications —Kate is conceived of as responding automatically to a certain kind of calculated treatment, as automatically as an animal to the devices of a skilled trainer. Petruchio not only uses the word *tame* more than once, but openly compares his method to that used in training falcons (IV.i. 184ff.). There is no reason whatever to suppose that this was not meant quite literally. Petruchio is not making a great jest or developing a paradoxical figure but describing a process taken at face value. He tells exactly what he has done and is doing—withholding food and sleep until the absolute need of them brings assent. (We hardly note that up to a point the assumptions are those of the "third degree" and of the more rigorous "cures" of bad habits: making it more unprofitable to assert one's will or one's bad habits than to act differently.) Before he sees Kate, he announces his method: he will assert as true the opposite of whatever she says and does and is, that is to say, will frustrate the manifestations of her will and establish the dominance of his own. Without naming them, he takes other steps that we know to be important in animal training. From the beginning he shows that he will stop at nothing to achieve his end, that he will not hesitate for a second to do anything necessary—to discard all dignity, or carry out any indecorous act or any outrageousness that will serve. He creates an image of utter invincibility, of having no weakness through which he can be appealed to. He does not use a literal whip, such as stage Petruchios were once addicted to, but he unmistakably uses a symbolic whip. Like a good trainer, however, he uses the carrot, too—not only marriage, but a new life, a happier personality for Kate. Above all, he offers love; in the end, the trainer succeeds best who makes the trainee feel the presence of something warmer than technique, rigor, and invincibility. Not that Petruchio fakes love, but that love has its part, ironically, in a process that is farcically conceived and that never wholly loses the markings of farce.

Only in farce could we conceive of the occurrence, almost in a flash, of that transformation of personality which, as known only too well in modern experience, normally requires a long, gradual, painstaking application of psychotherapy. True, conversion is believable and does happen, but even as a secular experience it requires a prior development of readiness, or an extraordinary revelatory shock, or both. (In the romantic form of this psychic event, an old hag, upon marriage to the knight, suddenly turns into a beautiful maiden.) Kate is presented initially as a very troubled woman; aggressiveness and tantrums are her way of feeling a sense of power. Though very modern, the argument that we see in her the results of paternal unkindness is not very impressive. For one thing, recent research on infants—if we may risk applying heavy science to light farce—suggests that basic personality traits precede, and perhaps influence, parental attitudes to children. More important, the text simply does not present Baptista as the overbearing and tyrannical father that he is sometimes said to be. Kate has made him almost as unhappy as she is, and driven him toward Bianca; nevertheless, when he heavily handicaps Bianca in the matrimonial sweepstakes, he is trying to even things up for the daughter that he naturally thinks is a poor runner. Nor is he willing to marry her off to Petruchio simply to get rid of her; "her love," he says, "is all in all." On her wedding day he says, kindly enough, "I cannot blame thee now to weep," and at the risk of losing husbands for both daughters he rebukes Petruchio (III.ii.97ff.). (The Baptista that some commentators describe would surely have said nothing but "What do you expect, you bitch?") We cannot blacken Baptista to save Kate. Shakespeare presents her binding and beating Bianca (II.i.1ff.) to show that he is really committed to a shrew; such episodes make it hard to defend the view that she is an innocent victim or is posing as a shrew out of general disgust. To sum up: in real life her disposition would be difficult to alter permanently, but farce secures its pleasurable effect by assuming a ready and total change in response to the stimuli applied by Petruchio, as if he were going through an established and proved routine. On the other hand, only farce makes it possible for Petruchio to be so skillful a tamer, that is, so unerring, so undeviating, so mechanical an enforcer of the rules for training in falconry. If Petruchio were by nature the disciplinarian that he acts for a while, he would hardly change after receiving compliance; and if he were, in real life, the charming and affectionate gentleman that he becomes in the play, he would find it impossible so rigorously to play the falcon-tamer, to outbully the bully, especially when the bully lies bleeding on the ground, for this role would simply run afoul of too much of his personality. The point here is not that the play is "unrealistic" (this would be a wholly irrelevant criticism) but that we can understand how a given genre works by testing it against the best sense of reality that we can bring to bear. It is the farcical view of life that makes possible the treatment of both Kate and Petruchio.

But this picture, of course, is incomplete; for the sake of clarity we have been stressing the purely generic in *The Shrew,* and gliding over the specific variations. Like any genre, farce is a convention, not a straitjacket; it is a fashion, capable of many variations. Genre provides a perspective, which in the individual work can be used narrowly or inclusively: comedy of manners, for instance, can move toward the character studies of James's novels or toward the superficial entertainments of Terence Rattigan. Shakespeare hardly ever uses a genre constrictively. In both *The Comedy of Errors* and *The Taming of the Shrew,* the resemblances between which are well known, Shakespeare moves away from the limited conception of personality that we find in "basic farce" such as that of Plautus, who influences both these plays. True, he protects both main characters in *The Shrew* against the expectable liabilities that would make one a less perfect reformer, and the other less than a model reformee, but he is unwilling to leave them automatons, textbook types of reformer and reformee. So he equips both with a good deal of intelligence and feeling that they would not have in elementary farce. Take sex, for instance. In basic farce, sex is purely a mechanical response, with no more overtones of feeling than ordinary hunger and thirst; the normal "love affair" is an intrigue with a courtesan. Like virtually all Renaissance lovers, Petruchio tells Kate candidly that he proposes to keep warm "in thy bed" (II.i.260). But there is no doubt that Petruchio, in addition to wanting a good financial bargain and enjoying the challenge of the shrew, develops real warmth of feeling for Kate as an individual —a warmth that makes him strive to bring out the best in her, keep the training in a tone of jesting, well-meant fantasy, provide Kate with face-saving devices (she is "curst . . . for policy" and only "in company"—II.i.285, 298), praise her for her virtues (whether she has them or not) rather than blame her for her vices, never fall into boorishness, repeatedly protest his affection for her, and by asking a kiss at a time she thinks unsuitable show that he really wants it. Here farce expands toward comedy of character by using a fuller range of personality. Likewise with Kate. The fact that she is a shrew does not mean that she cannot have hurt feelings, as it would in a plainer farce; indeed a shrew may be defined—once she develops beyond a mere stereotype—as a person who has an excess of hurt feelings and is taking revenge on the world for them. We do not, because we dislike the revenge, deny the painful feelings that may lie behind. Shakespeare has chosen to show some of those feelings, not making Kate an insentient virago on the one hand, or a pathetic victim on the other. She is jealous of Bianca and her lovers, she accuses Baptista of favoritism (in the opinion of the present editor, without justification); on her wedding day she suffers real anguish rather than simply an automatic, conventionally furious resolve for retaliation. The painful emotions take her way beyond the limitations of the essentially pain-free personality of basic farce. Further, she is witty, though, truth to tell, the first verbal battle between her and Petruchio, like various other such scenes, hardly goes beyond verbal farce, in which words are mechanical jokes or blows rather than an artistic game that delights by its quality, and in which all the speed of the short lines hardly conceals the heavy labors of the dutiful but uninspired punster (the best jokes are the bawdy ones). Kate has imagination. It shows first in a new human sympathy when she defends the servants against Petruchio (IV.i. 150, 162–63). Then it develops into a gay, inspired gamesomeness that rivals Petruchio's own. When he insists, "It shall be what o'clock I say it is" (IV.iii.193) and "[The sun] shall be moon or star or what I list" (IV.v.7), he is at one level saying again that he will stop at nothing, at no irrationality, as tamer; but here he moves the power game into a realm of fancy in which his apparent willfulness becomes the acting of the creative imagination. He is a poet, and he asks her, in effect, less to kiss the rod than to join in the game of playfully transforming ordinary reality. It is the final step in transforming herself. The point here is that, instead of not catching on or simply sulking, Kate has the dash and verve to join in the fun, and to do it with skill and some real touches of originality.

This scene on the road to Padua (IV.v.1–78) is the high point of the play. From here on, it tends to move back closer to the boundaries of ordinary farce. When Petruchio asks a kiss, we do have human beings with feelings, not robots; but the key line in the scene, which is sometimes missed, is Petruchio's "Why, then let's home

again. Come sirrah, let's away" (V.i.146). Here Petruchio is again making the same threat that he made at
IV.v.8–9, that is, not playing an imaginative game but
hinting the symbolic whip, even though the end is a compliance that she is inwardly glad to give. The whole wager
scene, as we have already noted, falls essentially within
the realm of farce: the responses are largely mechanical,
as is their symmetry. Kate's final long speech on the obli-
gations and fitting style of wives (V.ii.136–179) we can
think of as a more or less automatic statement of a generally held doctrine. The easiest way to deal with it is to
say that we no longer believe in it, just as we no longer
believe in the divine right of kings which is an important
dramatic element in many Shakespeare plays. But to some
interpreters, Kate has become such a charming heroine
that they cannot stand her being anything less than a
modern feminist. Hence the claim that she is speaking
ironically. There are two arguments against this interpretation. One is that a careful reading of the lines will show
that most of them have to be taken literally; only the last
seven or eight lines can be read with ironic overtones, but
this means, at most, a return to the imaginative gamesomeness of IV.v, rather than a denial of the doctrine formally
asserted. The second is that forty-five lines of straight
irony would be too much to be borne; it would be incon-
sistent with the straightforwardness of most of the play,
and it would really turn Kate back into a hidden shrew
whose new technique was sarcastic indirection, side-
mouthing at the audience while her not very intelligent
husband, bamboozled, cheered her on. It would be a poor
triumph. If one has to modernize the speech of the obedient wife, a better way to do it is to develop a hint of Professor Goddard's: that behind a passé doctrine lies a
continuing truth. That truth is that there are real differences between the sexes, and that they are to be kept in
mind. That view at least does not strain the spirit of
Kate's speech.

The Katolatry which has developed in recent years reveals the romantic tendency to create heroes and heroines
by denying the existence of flaws in them and by imputing

all sorts of flaws to their families and other associates. We have already seen how the effort to save Kate at the beginning has resulted in an untenable effort to make Baptista into a villainous, punitive father and Bianca into a calculating little devil whose inner shrewishness slowly comes out. But it is hard to see why, if we are to admire Kate's spirit of open defiance at the beginning, and her alleged ironic defiance at the end, we should not likewise admire the spirit of Bianca and Hortensio's widow at the end. It is equally hard to see why we should admire Kate's quiet, ironic, what-every-woman-knows victory, as some would have it, over an attractive man at the end, but should not admire Petruchio's open victory over a very unattractive woman earlier. In fact, it is a little difficult to know just what Kate's supposed victory consists in. The play gives no evidence that from now on she will be twisting her husband around her finger. The evidence is rather that she will win peace and quiet and contentment by giving in to his wishes, and that her willingness will entirely eliminate unreasonable and autocratic wishes in him. But after all, the unreasonable and the autocratic are his strategy, not his nature; he gives up an assumed vice, while Kate gives up a real one. The truth is that Kate's great victory is, with Petruchio's help, over herself; she has come to accept herself as having enough merits so that she can be content without having the last word and scaring everybody off. To see this means to acknowledge that she was originally a shrew, whatever virtues may also have been latent in her personality.

What Shakespeare has done is to take an old, popular farcical situation and turn it into a well-organized, somewhat complex, fast-moving farce of his own. He has worked with the basic conceptions of farce—mainly that of a somewhat limited personality that acts and responds in a mechanical way and hence moves toward a given end with a perfection not likely if all the elements in human nature were really at work. So the tamer never fails in his technique, and the shrew responds just as she should. Now this situation might have tempted the dramatist to let his main characters be flat automatons—he a dull and rough whipwielder, and she a stubborn intransigent until beaten into insensibility (as in the ballad that was perhaps a Shakespearean source). Shakespeare, however, makes a gentleman and lady of his central pair. As tamer, Petruchio is a gay and witty and precocious artist and, beyond that, an affectionate man; and hence, a remarkable therapist. In Kate, Shakespeare has imagined, not merely a harridan who is incurable or a moral stepchild driven into a misconduct by mistreatment, but a difficult woman—a shrew, indeed—who combines willfulness with feelings that elicit sympathy, with imagination, and with a latent cooperativeness that can bring this war of the sexes to an honorable settlement. To have started with farce, to have stuck to the main lines of farce, and yet to have got so much of the supra-farcical into farce—this is the achievement of *The Taming of the Shrew,* and the source of the pleasure that it has always given.

ROBERT B. HEILMAN
University of Washington

The Taming of the Shrew

The Taming of the Shrew

[INDUCTION]

Scene I. [*Outside rural alehouse.*]

Enter Hostess and Beggar, Christophero Sly.

Sly. I'll pheeze°¹ you, in faith.

Hostess. A pair of stocks,° you rogue!

Sly. Y'are a baggage, the Slys are no rogues. Look in the chronicles: we came in with Richard° Conqueror. Therefore, *paucas pallabris;*° let the world   5
slide.° Sessa!°

Hostess. You will not pay for the glasses you have burst?

Sly. No, not a denier.° Go, by St. Jeronimy,° go to thy cold bed and warm thee.   10

Hostess. I know my remedy: I must go fetch the thirdborough.°   [*Exit.*]

Sly. Third or fourth or fifth borough, I'll answer him by law. I'll not budge an inch, boy;° let him come and kindly.°   *Falls asleep.*   15

¹ The degree sign (°) indicates a footnote, which is keyed to the text by line number. Text references are printed in **boldface;** the annotation follows in roman type.
Ind.i.1 **pheeze** do for (cf. *faze*) 2 **stocks** (threatened punishment)
4 **Richard** (he means William) 5 **paucas pallabris** few words (Spanish *pocas palabras*) 6 **slide** go by (proverb; cf. Ind.ii.143) 6 **Sessa** scram (?) shut up (?) 9 **denier** very small coin (cf. "a copper") 9 **Jeronimy** (Sly's oath inaccurately reflects a line in Kyd's *Spanish Tragedy*) 12 **thirdborough** constable 14 **boy** wretch 15 **kindly** by all means

45

Wind° horns. Enter a Lord from hunting,
with his train.

Lord. Huntsman, I charge thee, tender° well my
hounds.
Broach° Merriman—the poor cur is embossed°—
And couple Clowder with the deep-mouthed brach.°
Saw'st thou not, boy, how Silver made it good
20   At the hedge-corner in the coldest fault?°
I would not lose the dog for twenty pound.

First Huntsman. Why, Bellman is as good as he, my
lord;
He cried upon it at the merest loss°
And twice today picked out the dullest scent.
25   Trust me, I take him for the better dog.

Lord. Thou art a fool. If Echo were as fleet,
I would esteem him worth a dozen such.
But sup them well and look unto them all.
Tomorrow I intend to hunt again.

30   *First Huntsman.* I will, my lord.

Lord. What's here? One dead or drunk? See, doth
he breathe?

Second Huntsman. He breathes, my lord. Were he not
warmed with ale,
This were a bed but cold to sleep so soundly.

Lord. O monstrous beast, how like a swine he lies!
35   Grim death, how foul and loathsome is thine image!
Sirs, I will practice on° this drunken man.
What think you, if he were conveyed to bed,
Wrapped in sweet clothes, rings put upon his fin-
gers,
A most delicious banquet by his bed,

15.s.d. **Wind** blow   16 **tender** look after   17 **Broach** bleed, i.e.,
medicate (some editors emend to *Breathe*)   17 **embossed** foaming
at the mouth   18 **brach** hunting bitch   20 **fault** lost ("cold") scent
23 **cried . . . loss** gave cry despite complete loss (of scent)   36 **practice on** play a trick on

And brave° attendants near him when he wakes—   40
Would not the beggar then forget himself?

First Huntsman. Believe me, lord, I think he cannot
    choose.

Second Huntsman. It would seem strange unto him
    when he waked.

Lord. Even as a flatt'ring dream or worthless fancy.
    Then take him up and manage well the jest.   45
    Carry him gently to my fairest chamber
    And hang it round with all my wanton° pictures;
    Balm° his foul head in warm distillèd waters
    And burn sweet wood to make the lodging sweet.
    Procure me music ready when he wakes   50
    To make a dulcet° and a heavenly sound;
    And if he chance to speak, be ready straight°
    And with a low submissive reverence
    Say, "What is it your honor will command?"
    Let one attend him with a silver basin   55
    Full of rose water and bestrewed with flowers;
    Another bear the ewer, the third a diaper,°
    And say, "Will't please your lordship cool your
      hands?"
    Some one be ready with a costly suit
    And ask him what apparel he will wear,   60
    Another tell him of his hounds and horse
    And that his lady mourns at his disease.
    Persuade him that he hath been lunatic,
    And when he says he is,° say that he dreams,
    For he is nothing but a mighty lord.   65
    This do, and do it kindly,° gentle sirs.
    It will be pastime passing excellent
    If it be husbanded with modesty.°

First Huntsman. My lord, I warrant you we will play
    our part

---

40 **brave** well dressed   47 **wanton** gay   48 **Balm** bathe   51 **dulcet**
sweet   52 **straight** without delay   57 **diaper** towel   64 **is** i.e., is
"lunatic" now   66 **kindly** naturally   68 **husbanded with modesty**
carried out with moderation

70   As° he shall think by our true diligence
    He is no less than what we say he is.

Lord. Take him up gently and to bed with him,
    And each one to his office° when he wakes.
            [Sly is carried out.] Sound trumpets.
    Sirrah,° go see what trumpet 'tis that sounds.
                    [Exit Servingman.]

75   Belike° some noble gentleman that means,
    Traveling some journey, to repose him here.

                Enter Servingman.

    How now? Who is it?

Servingman.   An't° please your honor, players
    That offer service to your lordship.

                Enter Players.

Lord. Bid them come near.
            Now, fellows, you are welcome.

80 *Players.* We thank your honor.

Lord. Do you intend to stay with me tonight?

A Player. So please your lordship to accept our duty.°

Lord. With all my heart. This fellow I remember
    Since once he played a farmer's eldest son;
85   'Twas where you wooed the gentlewoman so well.
    I have forgot your name, but sure that part
    Was aptly fitted° and naturally performed.

Second Player. I think 'twas Soto° that your honor
    means.

Lord. 'Tis very true; thou didst it excellent.
90   Well, you are come to me in happy° time,
    The rather for° I have some sport in hand

---

70 **As** so that   73 **office** assignment   74 **Sirrah** (term of address
used to inferiors)   75 **Belike** likely   77 **An't** if it   82 **duty** respect-
ful greeting   87 **aptly fitted** well suited (to you)   88 **Soto** (in John
Fletcher's *Women Pleased,* 1620; reference possibly inserted here
later)   90 **in happy** at the right   91 **The rather for** especially because

Wherein your cunning° can assist me much.
There is a lord will hear you play tonight.
But I am doubtful of your modesties,°
Lest over-eyeing° of his odd behavior—   *95*
For yet his honor never heard a play—
You break into some merry passion°
And so offend him, for I tell you, sirs,
If you should smile he grows impatient.

A Player. Fear not, my lord, we can contain ourselves *100*
Were he the veriest antic° in the world.

Lord. Go, sirrah, take them to the buttery°
And give them friendly welcome every one.
Let them want° nothing that my house affords.
                              Exit one with the Players.
Sirrah, go you to Barthol'mew my page   *105*
And see him dressed in all suits° like a lady.
That done, conduct him to the drunkard's chamber
And call him "madam"; do him obeisance.
Tell him from me—as he will° win my love—
He bear himself with honorable action   *110*
Such as he hath observed in noble ladies
Unto their lords, by them accomplishèd.°
Such duty to the drunkard let him do
With soft low tongue and lowly courtesy,
And say, "What is't your honor will command   *115*
Wherein your lady and your humble wife
May show her duty and make known her love?"
And then, with kind embracements, tempting kisses,
And with declining head into his bosom,
Bid him shed tears, as being overjoyed   *120*
To see her noble lord restored to health
Who for this seven years hath esteemèd him
No better than a poor and loathsome beggar.
And if the boy have not a woman's gift

---

92 **cunning** talent   94 **modesties** self-restraint   95 **over-eyeing** seeing   97 **merry passion** fit of merriment   101 **antic** odd person
102 **buttery** liquor pantry, bar   104 **want** lack   106 **suits** respects
(with pun)   109 **as he will** if he wishes to   112 **by them accomplishèd** i.e., as carried out by the ladies

125   To rain a shower of commanded tears,
       An onion will do well for such a shift,°
       Which in a napkin° being close conveyed°
       Shall in despite° enforce a watery eye.
       See this dispatched with all the haste thou canst;
130   Anon° I'll give thee more instructions.

                              Exit a Servingman.

       I know the boy will well usurp° the grace,
       Voice, gait, and action of a gentlewoman.
       I long to hear him call the drunkard husband,
       And how my men will stay themselves from laughter
135   When they do homage to this simple peasant.
       I'll in to counsel them; haply° my presence
       May well abate the over-merry spleen°
       Which otherwise would grow into extremes.

                                          [Exeunt.]

            [Scene II. *Bedroom in the Lord's house.*]

       Enter aloft° the Drunkard [Sly] with Attendants—
          some with apparel, basin and ewer, and
               other appurtenances—and Lord.

Sly. For God's sake, a pot of small° ale!

First Servingman. Will't please your lordship drink a
     cup of sack?°

Second Servingman. Will't please your honor taste of
     these conserves?°

Third Servingman. What raiment will your honor
     wear today?

126 **shift** purpose   127 **napkin** handkerchief   127 **close conveyed**
secretly carried   128 **Shall in despite** can't fail to   130 **Anon**
then   131 **usurp** take on   136 **haply** perhaps   137 **spleen** spirit
Ind.ii.s.d. **aloft** (on balcony above stage at back)   1 **small** thin,
diluted (inexpensive)   2 **sack** imported sherry (costly)   3 **conserves**
i.e., of fruit

Sly. I am Christophero Sly; call not me "honor" nor   5
"lordship." I ne'er drank sack in my life, and if you
give me any conserves, give me conserves of beef.°
Ne'er ask me what raiment I'll wear, for I have no
more doublets° than backs, no more stockings than
legs nor no more shoes than feet—nay, sometime   10
more feet than shoes or such shoes as my toes look
through the overleather.

Lord. Heaven cease this idle humor° in your honor!
O that a mighty man of such descent,
Of such possessions and so high esteem,   15
Should be infusèd with so foul a spirit!

Sly. What, would you make me mad? Am not I Christopher Sly, old Sly's son of Burton-heath,° by birth
a peddler, by education a cardmaker,° by transmu-
tation a bearherd,° and now by present profession   20
a tinker? Ask Marian Hacket, the fat ale-wife of
Wincot,° if she know me not. If she say I am not
fourteen pence on the score° for sheer ale,° score
me up for the lying'st knave in Christendom. What,
I am not bestraught!° Here's—   25

Third Servingman. O, this it is that makes your lady
mourn.

Second Servingman. O, this is it that makes your servants droop.

Lord. Hence comes it that your kindred shuns your
house
As beaten hence by your strange lunacy.
O noble lord, bethink thee of thy birth,   30
Call home thy ancient thoughts° from banishment

---

7 **conserves of beef** salt beef   9 **doublets** close-fitting jackets
13 **idle humor** unreasonable fantasy   18 **Burton-heath** (probably
Barton-on-the-Heath, south of Stratford)   19 **cardmaker** maker of
cards, or combs, for arranging wool fibers before spinning   20 **bearherd** leader of a tame bear   22 **Wincot** village near Stratford (some
Hackets lived there)   23 **score** charge account   23 **sheer ale** ale
alone (?) undiluted ale (?)   25 **bestraught** distraught, crazy   31
ancient thoughts original sanity

And banish hence these abject lowly dreams.
Look how thy servants do attend on thee,
Each in his office ready at thy beck.
35   Wilt thou have music? Hark, Apollo° plays,   *Music.*
And twenty cagèd nightingales do sing.
Or wilt thou sleep? We'll have thee to a couch
Softer and sweeter than the lustful bed
On purpose trimmed up for Semiramis.°
40   Say thou wilt walk, we will bestrow° the ground.
Or wilt thou ride? Thy horses shall be trapped,°
Their harness studded all with gold and pearl.
Dost thou love hawking? Thou hast hawks will soar
Above the morning lark. Or wilt thou hunt?
45   Thy hounds shall make the welkin° answer them
And fetch shrill echoes from the hollow earth.

First Servingman. Say thou wilt course,° thy grey-
        hounds are as swift
    As breathèd° stags, ay, fleeter than the roe.°

Second Servingman. Dost thou love pictures? We will
        fetch thee straight
50   Adonis° painted by a running brook
    And Cytherea all in sedges° hid,
    Which seem to move and wanton° with her breath
    Even as the waving sedges play with wind.

Lord. We'll show thee Io° as she was a maid
55   And how she was beguilèd and surprised,
    As lively° painted as the deed was done.

Third Servingman. Or Daphne° roaming through a
        thorny wood,

---

35 **Apollo** here, god of music   39 **Semiramis** mythical Assyrian
queen, noted for beauty and sexuality (cf. *Titus Andronicus*, II.i.22,
II.iii.118)   40 **bestrow** cover   41 **trapped** decorated   45 **welkin** sky
47 **course** hunt hares   48 **breathèd** having good wind   48 **roe** small
deer   50 **Adonis** young hunter loved by Venus (Cytherea) and killed
by wild boar   51 **sedges** grasslike plant growing in marshy places
52 **wanton** sway sinuously   54 **Io** mortal loved by Zeus and changed
into a heifer   56 **lively** lifelike   57 **Daphne** nymph loved by Apollo
and changed into laurel to evade him

Scratching her legs that one shall swear she bleeds,
And at that sight shall sad Apollo weep,
So workmanly the blood and tears are drawn.   60

Lord. Thou art a lord and nothing but a lord.
Thou hast a lady far more beautiful
Than any woman in this waning° age.

First Servingman. And till the tears that she hath shed
    for thee
Like envious floods o'errun her lovely face,   65
She was the fairest creature in the world,
And yet° she is inferior to none.

Sly. Am I a lord, and have I such a lady?
Or do I dream? Or have I dreamed till now?
I do not sleep: I see, I hear, I speak,   70
I smell sweet savors and I feel soft things.
Upon my life, I am a lord indeed
And not a tinker nor Christopher Sly.
Well, bring our lady hither to our sight,
And once again a pot o' th' smallest° ale.   75

Second Servingman. Will't please your mightiness to
    wash your hands?
O, how we joy to see your wit° restored!
O, that once more you knew but what you are!
These fifteen years you have been in a dream,
Or when you waked so waked as if you slept.   80

Sly. These fifteen years! By my fay,° a goodly nap.
But did I never speak of° all that time?

First Servingman. O yes, my lord, but very idle words,
For though you lay here in this goodly chamber,
Yet would you say ye were beaten out of door   85
And rail upon the hostess of the house°
And say you would present her at the leet°

---

63 **waning** decadent   67 **yet** now, still   75 **smallest** weakest   77
wit mind   81 **fay** faith   82 **of** in   86 **house** inn   87 **present her at
the leet** accuse her at the court under lord of a manor

Because she brought stone jugs and no sealed°
quarts.
Sometimes you would call out for Cicely Hacket.

90 *Sly.* Ay, the woman's maid of the house.

Third Servingman. Why, sir, you know no house nor
no such maid
Nor no such men as you have reckoned up,
As Stephen Sly° and old John Naps of Greece,°
And Peter Turph and Henry Pimpernell,
95 And twenty more such names and men as these
Which never were nor no man ever saw.

Sly. Now, Lord be thankèd for my good amends!°

All. Amen.

    Enter [the Page, as a] Lady, with Attendants.

Sly. I thank thee; thou shalt not lose by it.

100 *Page.* How fares my noble lord?

Sly. Marry,° I fare well, for here is cheer enough.
Where is my wife?

Page. Here, noble lord. What is thy will with her?

Sly. Are you my wife and will not call me husband?
My men should call me "lord"; I am your good-
105 man.°

Page. My husband and my lord, my lord and husband,
I am your wife in all obedience.

Sly. I know it well. What must I call her?

Lord. Madam.

110 *Sly.* Al'ce madam or Joan madam?

Lord. Madam and nothing else. So lords call ladies.

---

88 **sealed** marked by a seal guaranteeing quantity   93 **Stephen Sly**
Stratford man (Naps, etc., may also be names of real persons)   93
Greece the Green (?) Greet, hamlet not far from Stratford (?)   97
amends recovery   101 **Marry** in truth (originally, [by St.] Mary)
105 **goodman** husband

Sly. Madam wife, they say that I have dreamed
　　And slept above some fifteen year or more.

Page. Ay, and the time seems thirty unto me,
　　Being all this time abandoned° from your bed.　　*115*

Sly. 'Tis much. Servants, leave me and her alone.
　　Madam, undress you and come now to bed.

Page. Thrice noble lord, let me entreat of you
　　To pardon me yet for a night or two
　　Or, if not so, until the sun be set.　　*120*
　　For your physicians have expressly charged,
　　In peril to incur° your former malady,
　　That I should yet absent me from your bed.
　　I hope this reason stands for my excuse.

Sly. Ay, it stands so° that I may hardly tarry so long,　　*125*
　　but I would be loath to fall into my dreams again.
　　I will therefore tarry in despite of the flesh and the
　　blood.

Enter a Messenger.

Messenger. Your Honor's players, hearing your
　　amendment,
　　Are come to play a pleasant comedy.　　*130*
　　For so your doctors hold it very meet,
　　Seeing too much sadness hath congealed your blood,
　　And melancholy is the nurse of frenzy.°
　　Therefore they thought it good you hear a play
　　And frame your mind to mirth and merriment,　　*135*
　　Which bars a thousand harms and lengthens life.

Sly. Marry, I will let them play it. Is not a comontie°
　　a Christmas gambold° or a tumbling trick?

Page. No, my good lord, it is more pleasing stuff.

---

115 **abandoned** excluded　122 **In peril to incur** because of the
danger of a return of　125 **stands so** will do (with phallic pun, playing on "reason," which was pronounced much like "raising")
133 **frenzy** mental illness　137 **comontie** comedy (as pronounced by
Sly　138 **gambold** gambol (game, dance, frolic)

140 *Sly.* What, household stuff?°

Page. It is a kind of history.

Sly. Well, we'll see't. Come, madam wife, sit by my
   side
   And let the world slip.° We shall ne'er be younger.

---

140 **stuff** (with sexual innuendo; see Eric Partridge, *Shakespeare's
Bawdy*)   143 **slip** go by

[ACT I

Scene I. *Padua. A street.*]

Flourish.° Enter Lucentio and his man° Tranio.

Lucentio. Tranio, since for the great desire I had
  To see fair Padua,° nursery of arts,
  I am arrived for fruitful Lombardy,
  The pleasant garden of great Italy,
  And by my father's love and leave am armed   *5*
  With his good will and thy good company,
  My trusty servant well approved° in all,
  Here let us breathe and haply institute
  A course of learning and ingenious° studies.
  Pisa, renownèd for grave citizens,   *10*
  Gave me my being and my father first,°
  A merchant of great traffic° through the world,
  Vincentio, come of the Bentivolii.
  Vincentio's son, brought up in Florence,
  It shall become to serve° all hopes conceived,   *15*
  To deck his fortune with his virtuous deeds;
  And therefore, Tranio, for the time I study,
  Virtue and that part of philosophy
  Will I apply° that treats of happiness
  By virtue specially to be achieved.   *20*
  Tell me thy mind, for I have Pisa left
  And am to Padua come, as he that leaves

I.i.s.d. **Flourish** fanfare of trumpets s.d. **man** servant 2 **Padua** (noted for its university) 7 **approved** proved, found reliable 9 **ingenious** mind-training 11 **first** i.e., before that 12 **traffic** business 15 **serve** work for 19 **apply** apply myself to

    A shallow plash° to plunge him in the deep
    And with satiety seeks to quench his thirst.

25 *Tranio.* Mi perdonato,° gentle master mine,
    I am in all affected° as yourself,
    Glad that you thus continue your resolve
    To suck the sweets of sweet philosophy.
    Only, good master, while we do admire
30   This virtue and this moral discipline,
    Let's be no stoics nor no stocks,° I pray,
    Or so devote° to Aristotle's checks°
    As° Ovid° be an outcast quite abjured.
    Balk logic° with acquaintance that you have
35   And practice rhetoric in your common talk.
    Music and poesy use to quicken° you.
    The mathematics and the metaphysics,
    Fall to them as you find your stomach° serves you.
    No profit grows where is no pleasure ta'en.
40   In brief, sir, study what you most affect.°

Lucentio. Gramercies,° Tranio, well dost thou advise.
    If, Biondello, thou wert come ashore,
    We could at once put us in readiness
    And take a lodging fit to entertain
45   Such friends as time in Padua shall beget.
    But stay awhile, what company is this?

Tranio. Master, some show to welcome us to town.

Enter Baptista with his two daughters, Kate and
Bianca; Gremio, a pantaloon;° [and] Hortensio,
suitor to Bianca. Lucentio [and]
Tranio stand by.°

Baptista. Gentlemen, importune me no farther,
    For how I firmly am resolved you know,

23 **plash** pool   25 **Mi perdonato** pardon me   26 **affected** inclined
31 **stocks** sticks (with pun on Stoics)   32 **devote** devoted   32
checks restraints   33 **As** so that   33 **Ovid** Roman love poet (cf.
III.i.28–29, IV.ii.8)   34 **Balk logic** engage in arguments   36 **quicken**
make alive   38 **stomach** taste, preference   40 **affect** like   41
Gramercies many thanks   47s.d. **pantaloon** laughable old man (a
stock character with baggy pants, in Italian Renaissance comedy)
47s.d. **by** nearby

That is, not to bestow my youngest daughter 50
Before I have a husband for the elder.
If either of you both love Katherina,
Because I know you well and love you well,
Leave shall you have to court her at your pleasure.

Gremio. To cart° her rather. She's too rough for me. 55
There, there, Hortensio, will you any wife?

Kate. I pray you, sir, is it your will
To make a stale° of me amongst these mates?°

Hortensio. Mates, maid? How mean you that? No
mates for you
Unless you were of gentler, milder mold. 60

Kate. I' faith, sir, you shall never need to fear:
Iwis° it° is not halfway to her° heart.
But if it were, doubt not her care should be
To comb your noddle with a three-legged stool
And paint° your face and use you like a fool. 65

Hortensio. From all such devils, good Lord deliver us!

Gremio. And me too, good Lord!

Tranio. [*Aside*] Husht, master, here's some good pas-
time toward.°
That wench is stark mad or wonderful froward.°

Lucentio. [*Aside*] But in the other's silence do I see 70
Maid's mild behavior and sobriety.
Peace, Tranio.

Tranio. [*Aside*] Well said, master. Mum, and gaze
your fill.

Baptista. Gentlemen, that I may soon make good
What I have said: Bianca, get you in,
And let it not displease thee, good Bianca, 75

55 **cart** drive around in an open cart (a punishment for prostitutes)
58 **stale** (1) laughingstock (2) prostitute   58 **mates** low fellows (with
pun on *stalemate* and leading to pun on *mate* = husband)   62 **Iwis**
certainly   62 **it** i.e., getting a mate   62 **her** Kate's   65 **paint** i.e.,
red with blood   68 **toward** coming up   69 **froward** willful

For I will love thee ne'er the less, my girl.

Kate. A pretty peat!° It is best
Put finger in the eye,° and° she knew why.

80 *Bianca.* Sister, content you in my discontent.
Sir, to your pleasure humbly I subscribe.
My books and instruments shall be my company,
On them to look and practice by myself.

Lucentio. [*Aside*] Hark, Tranio, thou mayst hear
Minerva° speak.

85 *Hortensio.* Signior Baptista, will you be so strange?°
Sorry am I that our good will effects
Bianca's grief.

Gremio.   Why will you mew° her up,
Signior Baptista, for this fiend of hell
And make her bear the penance of her tongue?

90 *Baptista.* Gentlemen, content ye. I am resolved.
Go in, Bianca.   [*Exit Bianca.*]
And for° I know she taketh most delight
In music, instruments, and poetry,
Schoolmasters will I keep within my house,
95 Fit to instruct her youth. If you, Hortensio,
Or Signior Gremio, you, know any such,
Prefer° them hither; for to cunning° men
I will be very kind, and liberal
To mine own children in good bringing up.
100 And so, farewell. Katherina, you may stay,
For I have more to commune with° Bianca.   *Exit.*

Kate. Why, and I trust I may go too, may I not?
What, shall I be appointed hours, as though, belike,°
I knew not what to take and what to leave? Ha!
                                        Exit.

---

78 **peat** pet (cf. "teacher's pet") 79 **Put finger in the eye** cry 79
and if 84 **Minerva** goddess of wisdom 85 **strange** rigid 87 **mew**
cage (falconry term) 92 **for** because 97 **Prefer** recommend 97
cunning talented 101 **commune with** communicate to 103 **belike**
it seems likely

Gremio. You may go to the devil's dam;° your gifts 105
are so good, here's none will hold you. Their love is
not so great,° Hortensio, but we may blow our
nails together° and fast it fairly out. Our cake's
dough on both sides.° Farewell. Yet for the love I
bear my sweet Bianca, if I can by any means light 110
on a fit man to teach her that wherein she delights,
I will wish° him to her father.

Hortensio. So will I, Signior Gremio. But a word, I
pray. Though the nature of our quarrel yet never
brooked parle,° know now, upon advice,° it touch- 115
eth° us both—that we may yet again have access
to our fair mistress and be happy rivals in Bianca's
love—to labor and effect one thing specially.

Gremio. What's that, I pray?

Hortensio. Marry, sir, to get a husband for her sister. 120

Gremio. A husband! A devil.

Hortensio. I say, a husband.

Gremio. I say, a devil. Think'st thou, Hortensio,
though her father be very rich, any man is so very°
a fool to° be married to hell? 125

Hortensio. Tush, Gremio, though it pass your patience and mine to endure her loud alarums,° why,
man, there be good fellows in the world, and° a man
could light on them, would take her with all faults,
and money enough. 130

Gremio. I cannot tell, but I had as lief° take her
dowry with this condition, to be whipped at the
high cross° every morning.

---

105 **dam** mother (used of animals)   107 **great** important   107–08
blow our nails together i.e., wait patiently   108–09 **Our cake's dough
on both sides** we've both failed (proverbial)   112 **wish** commend
115 **brooked parle** allowed negotiation   115 **advice** consideration
115–16 **toucheth** concerns   124 **very** thorough   125 **to** as to   127
alarums outcries   128 **and** if   131 **had as lief** would as willingly
133 **high cross** market cross (prominent spot)

Hortensio. Faith, as you say, there's small choice in
135   rotten apples. But come, since this bar in law°
      makes us friends, it shall be so far forth° friendly
      maintained, till by helping Baptista's eldest daugh-
      ter to a husband, we set his youngest free for a hus-
      band, and then have to't° afresh. Sweet Bianca!
140   Happy man be his dole!° He that runs fastest gets
      the ring. How say you, Signior Gremio?

Gremio. I am agreed, and would I had given him the
      best horse in Padua to begin his wooing, that°
      would thoroughly woo her, wed her, and bed her
145   and rid the house of her. Come on.

            Exeunt ambo.° Manet° Tranio and Lucentio.

Tranio. I pray, sir, tell me, is it possible
        That love should of a sudden take such hold?

Lucentio. O Tranio, till I found it to be true
          I never thought it possible or likely.
150   But see, while idly I stood looking on,
          I found the effect of love-in-idleness°
          And now in plainness do confess to thee,
          That art to me as secret° and as dear
          As Anna° to the Queen of Carthage was,
155   Tranio, I burn, I pine, I perish, Tranio,
          If I achieve not this young modest girl.
          Counsel me, Tranio, for I know thou canst.
          Assist me, Tranio, for I know thou wilt.

Tranio. Master, it is no time to chide you now.
160   Affection is not rated° from the heart.

---

135 **bar in law** legal action of preventive sort   136 **so far forth** so
long   139 **have to't** renew our competition   140 **Happy man be his
dole** let being a happy man be his (the winner's) destiny   143 **that**
(antecedent is *his*)   145s.d. **ambo** both   145s.d. **Manet** remain
(though the Latin plural is properly *manent*, the singular with a
plural subject is common in Elizabethan texts)   151 **love-in-idleness**
popular name for pansy (believed to have mysterious power in love;
cf. *Midsummer Night's Dream*, II.i. 165 ff.)   153 **to me as secret** as
much in my confidence   154 **Anna** sister and confidante of Queen
Dido   160 **rated** scolded

If love have touched you, naught remains but so,°
"*Redime te captum, quam queas minimo.*"°

Lucentio. Gramercies,° lad, go forward. This contents.
  The rest will comfort, for thy counsel's sound.

Tranio. Master, you looked so longly° on the maid,   *165*
  Perhaps you marked not what's the pith of all.°

Lucentio. O yes, I saw sweet beauty in her face,
  Such as the daughter of Agenor° had,
  That made great Jove to humble him to her hand
  When with his knees he kissed the Cretan strond.°   *170*

Tranio. Saw you no more? Marked you not how her
    sister
  Began to scold and raise up such a storm
  That mortal ears might hardly endure the din?

Lucentio. Tranio, I saw her coral lips to move
  And with her breath she did perfume the air.   *175*
  Sacred and sweet was all I saw in her.

Tranio. Nay, then, 'tis time to stir him from his trance.
  I pray, awake, sir. If you love the maid,
  Bend thoughts and wits to achieve her. Thus it
    stands:
  Her elder sister is so curst and shrewd°   *180*
  That till the father rid his hands of her,
  Master, your love must live a maid at home;
  And therefore has he closely mewed° her up,
  Because° she will not be annoyed with suitors.

Lucentio. Ah, Tranio, what a cruel father's he!   *185*
  But art thou not advised° he took some care
  To get her cunning° schoolmasters to instruct her?

---

161 **so** to act thus   162 **Redime ... minimo** ransom yourself, a captive, at the smallest possible price (from Terence's play *The Eunuch*, as quoted inaccurately in Lilly's *Latin Grammar*)   163 **Gramercies** many thanks   165 **longly** (1) longingly (2) interminably   166 **pith of all** heart of the matter   168 **daughter of Agenor** Europa, loved by Jupiter, who, in the form of a bull, carried her to Crete   170 **strond** strand, shore   180 **curst and shrewd** sharp-tempered and shrewish   183 **mewed** caged   184 **Because** so that   186 **advised** informed   187 **cunning** knowing

Tranio. Ay, marry, am I, sir—and now 'tis plotted!°

Lucentio. I have it, Tranio!

Tranio.   Master, for° my hand,
190   Both our inventions° meet and jump in one.°

Lucentio. Tell me thine first.

Tranio.   You will be schoolmaster
And undertake the teaching of the maid.
That's your device.

Lucentio.   It is. May it be done?

Tranio. Not possible, for who shall bear° your part
195   And be in Padua here Vincentio's son?
Keep house and ply his book, welcome his friends,
Visit his countrymen and banquet them?

Lucentio. Basta,° content thee, for I have it full.°
We have not yet been seen in any house,
200   Nor can we be distinguished by our faces
For man or master. Then it follows thus:
Thou shalt be master, Tranio, in my stead,
Keep house and port° and servants as I should.
I will some other be—some Florentine,
205   Some Neapolitan, or meaner° man of Pisa.
'Tis hatched and shall be so. Tranio, at once
Uncase° thee, take my colored° hat and cloak.
When Biondello comes he waits on thee,
But I will charm° him first to keep his tongue.

210 *Tranio.* So had you need.
In brief, sir, sith° it your pleasure is
And I am tied° to be obedient—
For so your father charged me at our parting;

---

188 **'tis plotted** I've a scheme   189 **for** I bet   190 **inventions**
schemes   190 **jump in one** are identical   194 **bear** act   198 **Basta**
enough (Italian)   198 **full** fully (worked out)   203 **port** style   205
meaner of lower rank   207 **Uncase** undress   207 **colored** (masters
dressed colorfully; servants wore dark blue)   209 **charm** exercise
power over (he tells him a fanciful tale, lines 225–34)   211 **sith**
since   212 **tied** obligated

"Be serviceable to my son," quoth he,
Although I think 'twas in another sense—   215
I am content to be Lucentio
Because so well I love Lucentio.

Lucentio. Tranio, be so, because Lucentio loves,
    And let me be a slave, t'achieve that maid
    Whose sudden sight hath thralled° my wounded eye.   220

                Enter Biondello

Here comes the rogue. Sirrah, where have you been?

Biondello. Where have I been? Nay, how now, where
        are you?
    Master, has my fellow Tranio stol'n your clothes,
    Or you stol'n his, or both? Pray, what's the news?

Lucentio. Sirrah, come hither. 'Tis no time to jest,   225
    And therefore frame your manners to the time.°
    Your fellow Tranio, here, to save my life,
    Puts my apparel and my count'nance° on,
    And I for my escape have put on his,
    For in a quarrel since I came ashore   230
    I killed a man and fear I was descried.°
    Wait you on him, I charge you, as becomes,
    While I make way from hence to save my life.
    You understand me?

Biondello.   I, sir? Ne'er a whit.

Lucentio. And not a jot of Tranio in your mouth.   235
    Tranio is changed into Lucentio.

Biondello. The better for him. Would I were so too.

Tranio. So could I, faith, boy, to have the next wish
        after,
    That Lucentio indeed had Baptista's youngest
        daughter.

220 **thralled** enslaved   226 **frame your manners to the time** adjust
your conduct to the situation   228 **count'nance** demeanor   231
descried seen, recognized

But, sirrah, not for my sake but your master's, I
240   advise
You use your manners discreetly in all kind of com-
    panies.
When I am alone, why, then I am Tranio,
But in all places else your master, Lucentio.

Lucentio. Tranio, let's go.
245   One thing more rests,° that thyself execute°—
To make one among these wooers. If thou ask me
    why,
Sufficeth my reasons are both good and weighty.
                                                Exeunt.

The Presenters° above speaks.

First Servingman. My lord, you nod; you do not mind°
    the play.

Sly. Yes, by Saint Anne, do I. A good matter, surely.
250   Comes there any more of it?

Page. My lord, 'tis but begun.

Sly. 'Tis a very excellent piece of work, madam lady.
    Would 'twere done!   *They sit and mark.°*

[Scene II. *Padua. The street in front of
         Hortensio's house.*]

Enter Petruchio° and his man Grumio.

Petruchio. Verona, for a while I take my leave
    To see my friends in Padua, but of all
    My best belovèd and approvèd friend,

---

245 **rests** remains   245 **execute** are to perform   247s.d. **Presenters**
commentators, actors thought of collectively, hence the singular verb
248 **mind** pay attention to   253s.d. **mark** observe   I.ii.s.d. **Petruchio**
(correct form *Petrucio,* with *c* pronounced *tch*)

Hortensio, and I trow° this is his house.
Here, sirrah Grumio, knock, I say.   5

Grumio. Knock, sir? Whom should I knock? Is there
any man has rebused° your worship?

Petruchio. Villain, I say, knock me here° soundly.

Grumio. Knock you here, sir? Why, sir, what am I,
sir, that I should knock you here, sir?   10

Petruchio. Villain, I say, knock me at this gate°
And rap me well or I'll knock your knave's pate.°

Grumio. My master is grown quarrelsome. I should
    knock you first,
And then I know after who comes by the worst.

Petruchio. Will it not be?   15
Faith, sirrah, and° you'll not knock, I'll ring° it;
I'll try how you can *sol, fa,°* and sing it.
                               He wrings him by the ears.

Grumio. Help, masters, help! My master is mad.

Petruchio. Now, knock when I bid you, sirrah villain.

                    Enter Hortensio.

Hortensio. How now, what's the matter? My old   20
friend Grumio, and my good friend Petruchio! How
do you all at Verona?

Petruchio. Signior Hortensio, come you to part the
    fray?
Con tutto il cuore ben trovato,° may I say.

Hortensio. Alla nostra casa ben venuto, molto hono-   23
rato signior mio Petruchio.°

---

4 **trow** think 7 **rebused** (Grumio means *abused*) 8 **knock me
here** knock here for me (Grumio plays game of misunderstanding,
taking "me here" as "my ear") 11 **gate** door 12 **pate** head 16
and if 16 **ring** (pun on *wring*) 17 **sol, fa** go up and down the scales
(possibly with puns on meanings now lost) 24 **Con . . . trovato** with
all [my] heart well found (i.e., welcome) 25–26 **Alla . . . Petruchio**
welcome to our house, my much honored Signior Petruchio

Rise, Grumio, rise. We will compound° this quarrel.

Grumio. Nay, 'tis no matter, sir, what he 'leges° in
　　Latin.° If this be not a lawful cause for me to leave
30　his service—look you, sir, he bid me knock him and
　　rap him soundly, sir. Well, was it fit for a servant to
　　use his master so, being perhaps, for aught I see,
　　two-and-thirty, a peep out?°
　　Whom would to God I had well knocked at first,
35　Then had not Grumio come by the worst.

Petruchio. A senseless villain! Good Hortensio,
　　I bade the rascal knock upon your gate
　　And could not get him for my heart° to do it.

Grumio. Knock at the gate? O heavens! Spake you
40　not these words plain, "Sirrah, knock me here, rap
　　me here, knock me well, and knock me soundly"?
　　And come you now with "knocking at the gate"?

Petruchio. Sirrah, be gone or talk not, I advise you.

Hortensio. Petruchio, patience, I am Grumio's pledge.
45　Why, this's a heavy chance° 'twixt him and you,
　　Your ancient, trusty, pleasant servant Grumio.
　　And tell me now, sweet friend, what happy gale
　　Blows you to Padua here from old Verona?

Petruchio. Such wind as scatters young men through
　　　the world
50　To seek their fortunes farther than at home,
　　Where small experience grows. But in a few,°
　　Signior Hortensio, thus it stands with me:
　　Antonio my father is deceased,
　　And I have thrust myself into this maze,°
55　Happily° to wive and thrive as best I may.

---

27 **compound** settle　28 **'leges** alleges　29 **Latin** (as if he were English, Grumio does not recognize Italian)　33 **two-and-thirty, a peep
out** (1) an implication that Petruchio is aged (2) a term from cards,
slang for "drunk" (*peep* is an old form of *pip*, a marking on a card)
38 **heart** life　45 **heavy chance** sad happening　51 **few** i.e., words
54 **maze** traveling; uncertain course　55 **Happily** haply, perchance

Crowns in my purse I have and goods at home
And so am come abroad to see the world.

Hortensio. Petruchio, shall I then come roundly° to
  thee
And wish thee to a shrewd ill-favored° wife?
Thou'ldst thank me but a little for my counsel—
And yet I'll promise thee she shall be rich,   60
And very rich—but thou'rt too much my friend,
And I'll not wish thee to her.

Petruchio. Signior Hortensio, 'twixt such friends as we
Few words suffice; and therefore if thou know   65
One rich enough to be Petruchio's wife—
As wealth is burthen° of my wooing dance—
Be she as foul° as was Florentius'° love,
As old as Sibyl,° and as curst and shrewd
As Socrates' Xanthippe° or a worse,   70
She moves me not, or not removes, at least,
Affection's edge in me, were she as rough
As are the swelling Adriatic seas.
I come to wive it wealthily in Padua;
If wealthily, then happily in Padua.   75

Grumio. Nay, look you, sir, he tells you flatly what
his mind is. Why, give him gold enough and marry
him to a puppet or an aglet-baby° or an old trot°
with ne'er a tooth in her head, though she have as
many diseases as two-and-fifty horses. Why, nothing   80
comes amiss so money comes withal.°

Hortensio. Petruchio, since we are stepped thus far in,
I will continue that° I broached in jest.
I can, Petruchio, help thee to a wife
With wealth enough and young and beauteous,   85

---

58 **come roundly** talk frankly   59 **shrewd ill-favored** shrewish,
poorly qualified   67 **burthen** burden (musical accompaniment)   68
foul homely   68 **Florentius** knight in Gower's *Confessio Amantis*
(cf. Chaucer's Wife of Bath's Tale; knight marries hag who turns
into beautiful girl)   69 **Sibyl** prophetess in Greek and Roman myth
70 **Xanthippe** Socrates' wife, legendarily shrewish   78 **aglet-baby**
small female figure forming metal tip of cord or lace (French
aiguillette, point)   78 **trot** hag   81 **withal** with it   83 **that** what

Brought up as best becomes a gentlewoman.
Her only fault—and that is faults enough—
Is that she is intolerable curst°
And shrewd and froward,° so beyond all measure
90   That were my state° far worser than it is,
I would not wed her for a mine of gold.

Petruchio. Hortensio, peace. Thou know'st not gold's
    effect.
Tell me her father's name, and 'tis enough,
For I will board° her though she chide as loud
95   As thunder when the clouds in autumn crack.°

Hortensio. Her father is Baptista Minola,
An affable and courteous gentleman.
Her name is Katherina Minola,
Renowned in Padua for her scolding tongue.

100 *Petruchio.* I know her father though I know not her,
And he knew my deceasèd father well.
I will not sleep, Hortensio, till I see her,
And therefore let me be thus bold with you,
To give you over° at this first encounter
105 Unless you will accompany me thither.

Grumio. I pray you, sir, let him go while the humor°
lasts. A° my word, and° she knew him as well as I
do, she would think scolding would do little good°
upon him. She may perhaps call him half a score
110 knaves or so—why, that's nothing. And he begin
once, he'll rail in his rope-tricks.° I'll tell you what,
sir, and she stand° him but a little, he will throw a
figure in her face and so disfigure her with it that
she shall have no more eyes to see withal than a
115 cat. You know him not, sir.

---

88 **intolerable curst** intolerably sharp-tempered   89 **froward** willful
90 **state** estate, revenue   94 **board** naval term, with double sense:
(1) accost (2) go on board   95 **crack** make explosive roars   104
give you over leave you   106 **humor** mood   107 **A** on   107 **and if**
(also at lines 110 and 112)   108 **do little good** have little effect   111
rope-tricks (1) Grumio's version of *rhetoric*, going with *figure* just
below (2) rascally conduct, deserving hanging (3) possible sexual
innuendo, as in following lines   112 **stand** withstand

Hortensio. Tarry, Petruchio, I must go with thee,
For in Baptista's keep° my treasure is.
He hath the jewel of my life in hold,°
His youngest daughter, beautiful Bianca,
And her withholds from me and other more,   120
Suitors to her and rivals in my love,
Supposing it a thing impossible,
For° those defects I have before rehearsed,
That ever Katherina will be wooed.
Therefore this order° hath Baptista ta'en,   125
That none shall have access unto Bianca
Till Katherine the curst have got a husband.

Grumio. Katherine the curst!
A title for a maid of all titles the worst.

Hortensio. Now shall my friend Petruchio do me
grace°   130
And offer° me, disguised in sober robes,
To old Baptista as a schoolmaster
Well seen° in music, to instruct Bianca,
That so I may, by this device, at least
Have leave and leisure to make love to her   135
And unsuspected court her by herself.

        Enter Gremio, and Lucentio disguised
        [as a schoolmaster, Cambio].

Grumio. Here's no knavery! See, to beguile the old
folks, how the young folks lay their heads together!
Master, master, look about you. Who goes there,
ha?   140

Hortensio. Peace, Grumio. It is the rival of my love.
Petruchio, stand by awhile.   *[They eavesdrop.]*

Grumio. A proper stripling,° and an amorous!

Gremio. O, very well, I have perused the note.°

117 **keep** heavily fortified inner tower of castle   118 **hold** strong-
hold   123 **For** because of   125 **order** step   130 **grace** a favor   131
offer present, introduce   133 **seen** trained   143 **proper stripling**
handsome youth (sarcastic comment on Gremio)   144 **note** memo-
randum (reading list for Bianca)

145 Hark you, sir, I'll have them very fairly bound—
    All books of love, see that at any hand,°
    And see you read no other lectures° to her.
    You understand me. Over and beside
    Signior Baptista's liberality,
150 I'll mend it with a largess.° Take your paper° too
    And let me have them° very well perfumed,
    For she is sweeter than perfume itself
    To whom they go to. What will you read to her?

Lucentio. Whate'er I read to her, I'll plead for you
155 As for my patron, stand you so assured,
    As firmly as° yourself were still in place°—
    Yea, and perhaps with more successful words
    Than you unless you were a scholar, sir.

Gremio. O this learning, what a thing it is!

160 *Grumio.* [*Aside*] O this woodcock,° what an ass it is!

Petruchio. Peace, sirrah!

Hortensio. Grumio, mum! [*Coming forward*] God save
    you, Signior Gremio.

Gremio. And you are well met, Signior Hortensio.
    Trow° you whither I am going? To Baptista Minola.
165 I promised to inquire carefully
    About a schoolmaster for the fair Bianca,
    And, by good fortune, I have lighted well
    On this young man—for° learning and behavior
    Fit for her turn,° well read in poetry
170 And other books, good ones I warrant ye.

Hortensio. 'Tis well. And I have met a gentleman
    Hath promised me to help me to° another,
    A fine musician to instruct our mistress.

---

146 **at any hand** in any case   147 **read no other lectures** assign no
other readings   150 **mend it with a largess** add a gift of money to it
150 **paper** note (line 144)   151 **them** i.e., the books   156 **as** as if you
156 **in place** present   160 **woodcock** bird easily trapped, so considered silly   164 **Trow** know   168 **for** in   169 **turn** situation (with
unconscious bawdy pun on the sense of "copulation")   172 **help me
to** (1) find (2) become (Hortensio's jest)

So shall I no whit be behind in duty
To fair Bianca, so beloved of me.   175

Gremio. Beloved of me, and that my deeds shall
 prove.

Grumio. [*Aside*] And that his bags° shall prove.

Hortensio. Gremio, 'tis now no time to vent° our love.
Listen to me, and if you speak me fair,
I'll tell you news indifferent° good for either.   180
Here is a gentleman whom by chance I met,
Upon agreement from us to his liking,°
Will undertake° to woo curst Katherine,
Yea, and to marry her if her dowry please.

Gremio. So said, so done, is well.   185
Hortensio, have you told him all her faults?

Petruchio. I know she is an irksome, brawling scold;
If that be all, masters, I hear no harm.

Gremio. No, say'st me so, friend? What countryman?

Petruchio. Born in Verona, old Antonio's son.   190
My father dead, my fortune lives for me,
And I do hope good days and long to see.

Gremio. O, sir, such a life with such a wife were
 strange.
But if you have a stomach,° to't a° God's name;
You shall have me assisting you in all.   195
But will you woo this wildcat?

Petruchio.   Will I live?

Grumio. [*Aside*] Will he woo her? Ay, or I'll hang her.

Petruchio. Why came I hither but to that intent?
Think you a little din can daunt mine ears?
Have I not in my time heard lions roar?   200
Have I not heard the sea, puffed up with winds,
Rage like an angry boar chafèd with sweat?

177 **bags** i.e., of money   178 **vent** express   180 **indifferent** equally
182 **Upon . . . liking** if we agree to his terms (paying costs)   183
undertake promise   194 **stomach** inclination   194 **a** in

Have I not heard great ordnance° in the field
And heaven's artillery thunder in the skies?
205   Have I not in a pitchèd battle heard
Loud 'larums,° neighing steeds, and trumpets'
        clang?
And do you tell me of a woman's tongue,
That gives not half so great a blow to hear
As will a chestnut in a farmer's fire?
Tush, tush, fear° boys with bugs.°

210 *Grumio.* [*Aside*]   For he fears none.

Gremio. Hortensio, hark.
This gentleman is happily arrived,
My mind presumes, for his own good and ours.

Hortensio. I promised we would be contributors
215   And bear his charge of° wooing, whatsoe'er.

Gremio. And so we will, provided that he win her.

Grumio. [*Aside*] I would I were as sure of a good
dinner.

Enter Tranio brave° [*as Lucentio*] *and Biondello.*

Tranio. Gentlemen, God save you. If I may be bold,
Tell me, I beseech you, which is the readiest way
220   To the house of Signior Baptista Minola?

Biondello. He that has the two fair daughters? Is't
he you mean?

Tranio. Even he, Biondello.

Gremio. Hark you, sir. You mean not her to—

Tranio. Perhaps, him and her, sir. What have you
to do?°

Petruchio. Not her that chides, sir, at any hand,° I
225   pray.

---

203 **ordnance** cannon   206 **'larums** calls to arms, sudden attacks
210 **fear** frighten   210 **bugs** bugbears   215 **his charge of** the cost
of his   217s.d. **brave** elegantly attired   224 **to do** i.e., to do with this
225 **at any hand** in any case

Tranio. I love no chiders, sir. Biondello, let's away.

Lucentio. [*Aside*] Well begun, Tranio.

Hortensio.   Sir, a word ere
   you go.
   Are you a suitor to the maid you talk of, yea or no?

Tranio. And if I be, sir, is it any offense?

Gremio. No, if without more words you will get you
   hence.   230

Tranio. Why, sir, I pray, are not the streets as free
   For me as for you?

Gremio.   But so is not she.

Tranio. For what reason, I beseech you?

Gremio. For this reason, if you'll know,
   That she's the choice° love of Signior Gremio.   235

Hortensio. That she's the chosen of Signior Hortensio.

Tranio. Softly, my masters! If you be gentlemen,
   Do me this right: hear me with patience.
   Baptista is a noble gentleman
   To whom my father is not all unknown,   240
   And were his daughter fairer than she is,
   She may more suitors have, and me for one.
   Fair Leda's daughter° had a thousand wooers;
   Then well one more may fair Bianca have.
   And so she shall. Lucentio shall make one,   245
   Though Paris° came° in hope to speed° alone.

Gremio. What, this gentleman will out-talk us all.

Lucentio. Sir, give him head. I know he'll prove a
   jade.°

Petruchio. Hortensio, to what end are all these words?

235 **choice** chosen   243 **Leda's daughter** Helen of Troy   246 **Paris**
lover who took Helen to Troy (legendary cause of Trojan War)
246 **came** should come   246 **speed** succeed   248 **prove a jade** soon
tire (cf. "jaded")

250 *Hortensio.* Sir, let me be so bold as ask you,
Did you yet ever see Baptista's daughter?

Tranio. No, sir, but hear I do that he hath two,
The one as famous for a scolding tongue
As is the other for beauteous modesty.

255 *Petruchio.* Sir, sir, the first's for me; let her go by.

Gremio. Yea, leave that labor to great Hercules,
And let it be more than Alcides'° twelve.

Petruchio. Sir, understand you this of me in sooth:°
The youngest daughter, whom you hearken° for,
260 Her father keeps from all access of suitors
And will not promise her to any man
Until the elder sister first be wed.
The younger then is free, and not before.

Tranio. If it be so, sir, that you are the man
265 Must stead° us all, and me amongst the rest,
And if you break the ice and do this feat,
Achieve° the elder, set the younger free
For our access, whose hap° shall be to have her
Will not so graceless be to be ingrate.°

Hortensio. Sir, you say well, and well you do con-
270 ceive,°
And since you do profess to be a suitor,
You must, as we do, gratify° this gentleman
To whom we all rest° generally beholding.°

Tranio. Sir, I shall not be slack, in sign whereof,
275 Please ye we may contrive° this afternoon
And quaff carouses° to our mistress' health
And do as adversaries° do in law,
Strive mightily but eat and drink as friends.

---

257 **Alcides** Hercules (after Alcaeus, a family ancestor)   258 **sooth**
truth   259 **hearken** long   265 **stead** aid   267 **Achieve** succeed with
268 **whose hap** the man whose luck   269 **to be ingrate** as to be
ungrateful   270 **conceive** put the case   272 **gratify** compensate
273 **rest** remain   273 **beholding** indebted   275 **contrive** pass   276
quaff carouses empty our cups   277 **adversaries** attorneys

Grumio, Biondello. O excellent motion! Fellows, let's
   be gone.

Hortensio. The motion's good indeed, and be it so.   280
   Petruchio, I shall be your *ben venuto.*°   *Exeunt.*

281 **ben venuto** welcome (i.e., host)

[ACT II

Scene I. *In Baptista's house.*]

Enter Kate and Bianca [with her hands tied].

Bianca. Good sister, wrong me not nor wrong your-
self
To make a bondmaid and a slave of me.
That I disdain. But for these other gawds,°
Unbind my hands, I'll pull them off myself,
5   Yea, all my raiment, to my petticoat,
Or what you will command me will I do,
So well I know my duty to my elders.

Kate. Of all thy suitors, here I charge thee, tell
Whom thou lov'st best. See thou dissemble not.

10 *Bianca.* Believe me, sister, of all the men alive
I never yet beheld that special face
Which I could fancy more than any other.

Kate. Minion,° thou liest. Is't not Hortensio?

Bianca. If you affect° him, sister, here I swear
15   I'll plead for you myself but you shall have him.

Kate. O then, belike,° you fancy riches more:
You will have Gremio to keep you fair.°

Bianca. Is it for him you do envy° me so?
Nay, then you jest, and now I well perceive
20   You have but jested with me all this while.
I prithee, sister Kate, untie my hands.

II.i.3 **gawds** adornments   13 **Minion** impudent creature   14 **affect**
like   16 **belike** probably   17 **fair** in fine clothes   18 **envy** hate
78

Kate. If that be jest then all the rest was so.

> *Strikes her.*

Enter Baptista.

Baptista. Why, how now, dame, whence grows this
    insolence?
  Bianca, stand aside. Poor girl, she weeps.
  Go ply thy needle; meddle not with her.
  For shame, thou hilding° of a devilish spirit,   25
  Why dost thou wrong her that did ne'er wrong
    thee?
  When did she cross thee with a bitter word?

Kate. Her silence flouts me and I'll be revenged.

> *Flies after Bianca.*

Baptista. What, in my sight? Bianca, get thee in.   30

> *Exit [Bianca].*

Kate. What, will you not suffer° me? Nay, now I see
  She is your treasure, she must have a husband;
  I must dance barefoot on her wedding day,°
  And, for your love to her, lead apes in hell.°
  Talk not to me; I will go sit and weep   35
  Till I can find occasion of revenge.   *[Exit.]*

Baptista. Was ever gentleman thus grieved as I?
  But who comes here?

*Enter Gremio, Lucentio in the habit of a mean° man
  [Cambio], Petruchio, with [Hortensio as a music
  teacher, Litio, and] Tranio [as Lucentio], with his
  boy [Biondello] bearing a lute and books.*

Gremio. Good morrow, neighbor Baptista.

Baptista. Good morrow, neighbor Gremio. God save   40
  you, gentlemen.

Petruchio. And you, good sir. Pray, have you not a
  daughter

---

26 **hilding** base wretch   31 **suffer** permit (i.e., to deal with you)   33
dance . . . day (expected of older maiden sisters)   34 **lead apes in
hell** (proverbial occupation of old maids; cf. *Much Ado About Nothing*, II.i.41)   38s.d. **mean** lower class

Called Katherina, fair and virtuous?

Baptista. I have a daughter, sir, called Katherina.

45 *Gremio.* [*Aside*] You are too blunt; go to it orderly.°

Petruchio. [*Aside*] You wrong me, Signior Gremio,
    give me leave.
  [*To Baptista*] I am a gentleman of Verona, sir,
  That, hearing of her beauty and her wit,
  Her affability and bashful modesty,
50   Her wondrous qualities and mild behavior,
  Am bold to show myself a forward° guest
  Within your house, to make mine eye the witness
  Of that report which I so oft have heard.
  And, for an entrance to° my entertainment,°
55   I do present you with a man of mine,
                    [*presenting Hortensio*]
  Cunning in music and the mathematics,
  To instruct her fully in those sciences,
  Whereof I know she is not ignorant.
  Accept of him, or else you do me wrong.
60   His name is Litio, born in Mantua.

Baptista. Y'are welcome, sir, and he for your good
    sake.
  But for my daughter Katherine, this I know,
  She is not for your turn,° the more my grief.

Petruchio. I see you do not mean to part with her,
65   Or else you like not of my company.

Baptista. Mistake me not; I speak but as I find.
  Whence are you, sir? What may I call your name?

Petruchio. Petruchio is my name, Antonio's son,
  A man well known throughout all Italy.

Baptista. I know him well. You are welcome for his
70   sake.

Gremio. Saving° your tale, Petruchio, I pray,

---

45 **orderly** gradually   51 **forward** eager   54 **entrance to** price of
admission for   54 **entertainment** reception   63 **turn** purpose (again,
with bawdy pun)   71 **Saving** with all respect for

Let us, that are poor petitioners, speak too.
Backare,° you are marvelous° forward.

Petruchio. O pardon me, Signior Gremio, I would
    fain° be doing.°

Gremio. I doubt it not, sir, but you will curse your
    wooing.
    Neighbor, this is a gift very grateful,° I am sure of   75
    it. To express the like kindness myself, that° have
    been more kindly beholding to you than any, freely
    give unto you this young scholar [*presenting Lu-*
    centio] that hath been long studying at Rheims—as   80
    cunning in Greek, Latin, and other languages, as
    the other in music and mathematics. His name is
    Cambio.° Pray accept his service.

Baptista. A thousand thanks, Signior Gremio. Wel-
    come, good Cambio. [*To Tranio*] But, gentle sir,   85
    methinks you walk like° a stranger. May I be so
    bold to know the cause of your coming?

Tranio. Pardon me, sir, the boldness is mine own,
    That,° being a stranger in this city here,
    Do make myself a suitor to your daughter,   90
    Unto Bianca, fair and virtuous.
    Nor is your firm resolve unknown to me
    In the preferment of° the eldest sister.
    This liberty is all that I request,
    That, upon knowledge of my parentage,   95
    I may have welcome 'mongst the rest that woo
    And free access and favor° as the rest.
    And, toward the education of your daughters
    I here bestow a simple instrument,°
    And this small packet of Greek and Latin books.   100
    If you accept them, then their worth is great.

---

73 **Backare** back (proverbial quasi-Latin)   73 **marvelous** very   74
would fain am eager to   74 **doing** (with a sexual jest)   76 **grateful**
worthy of gratitude   77 **myself, that** I myself, who   83 **Cambio**
(Italian for "exchange")   86 **walk like** have the bearing of   89 **That**
who   93 **preferment of** giving priority to   97 **favor** countenance,
acceptance   99 **instrument** i.e., the lute

Baptista. [*Looking at books*] Lucentio is your name.
  Of whence, I pray?

Tranio. Of Pisa, sir, son to Vincentio.

Baptista. A mighty man of Pisa; by report
105 I know him° well. You are very welcome, sir.
     [*To Hortensio*] Take you the lute, [*to Lucentio*]
       and you the set of books;
     You shall go see your pupils presently.°
     Holla, within!

                    Enter a Servant.

                    Sirrah, lead these gentlemen
     To my daughters and tell them both
110 These are their tutors; bid them use them well.
                    [*Exit Servant, with Lucentio,
                    Hortensio, and Biondello following.*]
     We will go walk a little in the orchard°
     And then to dinner. You are passing° welcome,
     And so I pray you all to think yourselves.

Petruchio. Signior Baptista, my business asketh haste,
115 And every day I cannot come to woo.
     You knew my father well, and in him me,
     Left solely heir to all his lands and goods,
     Which I have bettered rather than decreased.
     Then tell me, if I get your daughter's love
120 What dowry shall I have with her to wife?

Baptista. After my death the one half of my lands,
     And in possession° twenty thousand crowns.

Petruchio. And, for that dowry, I'll assure her of
     Her widowhood,° be it that she survive me,
125 In all my lands and leases whatsoever.
     Let specialties° be therefore drawn between us
     That covenants may be kept on either hand.

---

105 **him** his name   107 **presently** at once   111 **orchard** garden
112 **passing** very   122 **possession** i.e., at the time of marriage   124
widowhood estate settled on a widow (Johnson)   126 **specialties**
special contracts

Baptista. Ay, when the special thing is well obtained,
That is, her love, for that is all in all.

Petruchio. Why, that is nothing, for I tell you, father, *130*
I am as peremptory° as she proud-minded.
And where two raging fires meet together
They do consume the thing that feeds their fury.
Though little fire grows great with little wind,
Yet extreme gusts will blow out fire and all. *135*
So I to her, and so she yields to me,
For I am rough and woo not like a babe.

Baptista. Well mayst thou woo, and happy be thy
speed!°
But be thou armed for some unhappy words.

Petruchio. Ay, to the proof,° as mountains are for
winds *140*
That shakes not, though they blow perpetually.

Enter Hortensio with his head broke.

Baptista. How now, my friend, why dost thou look
so pale?

Hortensio. For fear, I promise you, if I look pale.

Baptista. What, will my daughter prove a good musician?

Hortensio. I think she'll sooner prove a soldier. *145*
Iron may hold with her,° but never lutes.

Baptista. Why, then thou canst not break° her to
the lute?

Hortensio. Why, no, for she hath broke the lute to me.
I did but tell her she mistook her frets°
And bowed° her hand to teach her fingering, *150*
When, with a most impatient devilish spirit,
"Frets, call you these?" quoth she; "I'll fume with
them."

131 **peremptory** resolved　138 **speed** progress　140 **to the proof** in
tested steel armor　146 **hold with her** stand her treatment　147
break train　149 **frets** ridges where strings are pressed　150 **bowed**
bent

And with that word she stroke° me on the head,
And through the instrument my pate made way.
155 And there I stood amazèd for a while
As on a pillory,° looking through the lute,
While she did call me rascal, fiddler,
And twangling Jack,° with twenty such vile terms
/ As° had she studied° to misuse me so.

160 *Petruchio.* Now, by the world, it is a lusty° wench!
I love her ten times more than e'er I did.
O how I long to have some chat with her!

Baptista. [*To Hortensio*] Well, go with me, and be
not so discomfited.
Proceed in practice° with my younger daughter;
165 She's apt° to learn and thankful for good turns.
Signior Petruchio, will you go with us
Or shall I send my daughter Kate to you?
                    Exit [*Baptista, with Gremio, Tranio, and
                    Hortensio*]. *Manet Petruchio.*°

Petruchio. I pray you do. I'll attend° her here
And woo her with some spirit when she comes.
170 Say that she rail,° why then I'll tell her plain
She sings as sweetly as a nightingale.
Say that she frown, I'll say she looks as clear
As morning roses newly washed with dew.
Say she be mute and will not speak a word,
175 Then I'll commend her volubility
And say she uttereth piercing eloquence.
If she do bid me pack,° I'll give her thanks
As though she bid me stay by her a week.
If she deny° to wed, I'll crave the day
180 When I shall ask the banns° and when be marrièd.
But here she comes, and now, Petruchio, speak.

---

153 **stroke** struck   156 **pillory** i.e., with a wooden collar (old structure for public punishment)   158 **Jack** (term of contempt)   159 **As**
as if   159 **studied** prepared   160 **lusty** spirited   164 **practice** instruction   165 **apt** disposed   167s.d. (is in the F position, which
need not be changed; Petruchio speaks to the departing Baptista)
168 **attend** wait for   170 **rail** scold, scoff   177 **pack** go away   179
deny refuse   180 **banns** public announcement in church of intent to
marry

Enter Kate.

Good morrow, Kate, for that's your name, I hear.

Kate. Well have you heard,° but something hard of
   hearing.
They call me Katherine that do talk of me.

Petruchio. You lie, in faith, for you are called plain
   Kate,   *185*
And bonny° Kate, and sometimes Kate the curst.
But, Kate, the prettiest Kate in Christendom,
Kate of Kate Hall,° my super-dainty Kate,
For dainties° are all Kates,° and therefore, Kate,
Take this of me, Kate of my consolation.   *190*
Hearing thy mildness praised in every town,
Thy virtues spoke of, and thy beauty sounded°—
Yet not so deeply as to thee belongs—
Myself am moved to woo thee for my wife.

Kate. Moved! In good time,° let him that moved you
   hither   *195*
Remove you hence. I knew you at the first
You were a movable.°

Petruchio.   Why, what's a movable?

Kate. A joint stool.°

Petruchio   Thou hast hit it; come sit on me.

Kate. Asses are made to bear° and so are you.

Petruchio. Women are made to bear° and so are you. *200*

Kate. No such jade° as you, if me you mean.

---

183 **heard** (pun: pronounced like *hard*)   186 **bonny** big, fine (perhaps with pun on *bony*, the F spelling)   188 **Kate Hall** (possible
topical reference; several places have been proposed)   189 **dainties**
delicacies   189 **Kates** i.e., *cates*, delicacies   192 **sounded** (1) meas-
ured (effect of *deeply*) (2) spoken of (pun)   195 **In good time** indeed
197 **movable** article of furniture (with pun)   198 **joint stool** stool
made by a joiner (standard term of disparagement)   199 **bear** carry
200 **bear** i.e., bear children (with second sexual meaning in Petruchio's "I will not burden thee")   201 **jade** worn-out horse (Kate has
now called him both "ass" and "sorry horse")

Petruchio. Alas, good Kate, I will not burden thee,
　For, knowing thee to be but young and light—

Kate. Too light for such a swain° as you to catch
205　And yet as heavy as my weight should be.

Petruchio. Should be!° Should—buzz!

Kate.　　　　　　　　　　Well ta'en, and like a buzzard.°

Petruchio. O slow-winged turtle,° shall a buzzard
　take° thee?

Kate. Ay, for a turtle, as he takes a buzzard.°

Petruchio. Come, come, you wasp, i' faith you are
　too angry.

210　*Kate.* If I be waspish, best beware my sting.

Petruchio. My remedy is then to pluck it out.

Kate. Ay, if the fool could find it where it lies.

Petruchio. Who knows not where a wasp does wear
　his sting?
　In his tail.

Kate.　　　　In his tongue.

Petruchio.　　　　　　　　Whose tongue?

215　*Kate.* Yours, if you talk of tales,° and so farewell.

Petruchio. What, with my tongue in your tail? Nay,
　come again.
　Good Kate, I am a gentleman—

Kate.　　　　　　　　　　That I'll try.
　　　　　　　　　　　　　She strikes him.

Petruchio. I swear I'll cuff you if you strike again.

---

204 **swain** country boy　206 **be** (pun on *bee*; hence *buzz*, scandal,
i.e., about "light" woman)　206 **buzzard** hawk unteachable in falconry (hence idiot)　207 **turtle** turtledove, noted for affectionate-
ness　207 **take** capture (with pun, "mistake for," in next line)　208
buzzard buzzing insect (hence "wasp")　215 **of tales** idle tales (leading to bawdy pun on *tail* = pudend)

Kate. So may you lose your arms:°
　If you strike me you are no gentleman, 　　　220
　And if no gentleman, why then no arms.

Petruchio. A herald,° Kate? O, put me in thy books.°

Kate. What is your crest?° A coxcomb?°

Petruchio. A combless° cock, so° Kate will be my hen.

Kate. No cock of mine; you crow too like a craven.° 　225

Petruchio. Nay, come, Kate, come, you must not look
　so sour.

Kate. It is my fashion when I see a crab.°

Petruchio. Why, here's no crab, and therefore look
　not sour.

Kate. There is, there is.

Petruchio. Then show it me.

Kate. 　　　　　　　　　Had I a glass° I would. 　　230

Petruchio. What, you mean my face?

Kate. 　　　　　　　　　Well aimed of°
　such a young one.

Petruchio. Now, by Saint George, I am too young
　for you.

Kate. Yet you are withered.

Petruchio. 　　　　　　　'Tis with cares.

Kate. 　　　　　　　　　　　I care not.

Petruchio. Nay, hear you, Kate, in sooth° you scape°
　not so.

Kate. I chafe° you if I tarry. Let me go. 　　　235

219 arms (pun on "coat of arms")　　222 herald one skilled in heraldry
222 books registers of heraldry (with pun on "in your good books")
223 crest heraldic device　　223 coxcomb identifying feature of court
Fool's cap; the cap itself　224 combless i.e., unwarlike　224 so if
225 craven defeated cock　227 crab crab apple　230 glass mirror
231 well aimed of a good shot (in the dark)　234 sooth truth　234
scape escape　235 chafe (1) annoy (2) warm up

Petruchio. No, not a whit. I find you passing gentle.
    'Twas told me you were rough and coy° and sullen,
    And now I find report a very liar,
    For thou art pleasant, gamesome, passing courteous,
240   But slow in speech, yet sweet as springtime flowers.
    Thou canst not frown, thou canst not look askance,
    Nor bite the lip as angry wenches will,
    Nor hast thou pleasure to be cross in talk,
    But thou with mildness entertain'st thy wooers,
245   With gentle conference,° soft and affable.
    Why does the world report that Kate doth limp?
    O sland'rous world! Kate like the hazel-twig
    Is straight and slender, and as brown in hue
    As hazelnuts and sweeter than the kernels.
250   O, let me see thee walk. Thou dost not halt.°

Kate. Go, fool, and whom thou keep'st° command.

Petruchio. Did ever Dian° so become a grove
    As Kate this chamber with her princely gait?
    O, be thou Dian and let her be Kate,
255   And then let Kate be chaste and Dian sportful!°

Kate. Where did you study all this goodly speech?

Petruchio. It is extempore, from my mother-wit.°

Kate. A witty mother! Witless else° her son.

Petruchio. Am I not wise?

Kate.   Yes,° keep you warm.

Petruchio. Marry, so I mean, sweet Katherine, in thy
260   bed.
    And therefore, setting all this chat aside,
    Thus in plain terms: your father hath consented
    That you shall be my wife, your dowry 'greed on,
    And will you, nill° you, I will marry you.

---

237 **coy** offish   245 **conference** conversation   250 **halt** limp   251
whom thou keep'st i.e., your servants   252 **Dian** Diana, goddess of
hunting and virginity   255 **sportful** (i.e., in the game of love)   257
mother-wit natural intelligence   258 **else** otherwise would be   259
Yes yes, just enough to (refers to a proverbial saying)   264 **nill**
won't

Now, Kate, I am a husband for your turn,° 265
For, by this light, whereby I see thy beauty—
Thy beauty that doth make me like thee well—
Thou must be married to no man but me.

Enter Baptista, Gremio, Tranio.

For I am he am born to tame you, Kate,
And bring you from a wild Kate° to a Kate 270
Conformable° as other household Kates.
Here comes your father. Never make denial;
I must and will have Katherine to my wife.

Baptista. Now, Signior Petruchio, how speed° you
with my daughter?

Petruchio. How but well, sir? How but well? 275
It were impossible I should speed amiss.

Baptista. Why, how now, daughter Katherine, in your
dumps?°

Kate. Call you me daughter? Now, I promise° you
You have showed a tender fatherly regard
To wish me wed to one half lunatic, 280
A madcap ruffian and a swearing Jack
That thinks with oaths to face° the matter out.

Petruchio. Father, 'tis thus: yourself and all the world
That talked of her have talked amiss of her.
If she be curst it is for policy,° 285
For she's not froward but modest as the dove.
She is not hot° but temperate as the morn;
For patience she will prove a second Grissel°
And Roman Lucrece° for her chastity.
And to conclude, we have 'greed so well together 290
That upon Sunday is the wedding day.

Kate. I'll see thee hanged on Sunday first.

---

265 **turn** advantage (with bawdy second meaning)   270 **wild Kate**
(pun on "wildcat")   271 **Conformable** submissive   274 **speed** get
on   277 **dumps** low spirits   278 **promise** tell   282 **face** brazen
285 **policy** tactics   287 **hot** intemperate   288 **Grissel** Griselda (patient wife in Chaucer's Clerk's Tale)   289 **Lucrece** (killed herself
after Tarquin raped her)

Gremio. Hark, Petruchio, she says she'll see thee
    hanged first.

Tranio. Is this your speeding?° Nay, then good night
    our part!

Petruchio. Be patient, gentlemen, I choose her for
295   myself.
    If she and I be pleased, what's that to you?
    'Tis bargained 'twixt us twain, being alone,
    That she shall still be curst in company.
    I tell you, 'tis incredible to believe
300   How much she loves me. O, the kindest Kate,
    She hung about my neck, and kiss on kiss
    She vied° so fast, protesting oath on oath,
    That in a twink° she won me to her love.
    O, you are novices. 'Tis a world° to see
305   How tame, when men and women are alone,
    A meacock° wretch can make the curstest shrew.
    Give me thy hand, Kate. I will unto Venice
    To buy apparel 'gainst° the wedding day.
    Provide the feast, father, and bid the guests;
310   I will be sure my Katherine shall be fine.°

Baptista. I know not what to say, but give me your
    hands.
    God send you joy, Petruchio! 'Tis a match.

Gremio, Tranio. Amen, say we. We will be witnesses.

Petruchio. Father, and wife, and gentlemen, adieu.
315   I will to Venice; Sunday comes apace.
    We will have rings and things and fine array,
    And, kiss me, Kate, "We will be married a Sun-
    day."°

                     Exit Petruchio and Kate.

Gremio. Was ever match clapped° up so suddenly?

---

294 **speeding** success   302 **vied** made higher bids (card-playing
terms), i.e., kissed more frequently   303 **twink** twinkling   304
world wonder   306 **meacock** timid   308 **'gainst** in preparation for
310 **fine** well dressed   317 **"We . . . Sunday"** (line from a ballad)
318 **clapped** fixed

Baptista. Faith, gentlemen, now I play a merchant's
part
And venture madly on a desperate mart.° 320

Tranio. 'Twas a commodity° lay fretting° by you;
'Twill bring you gain or perish on the seas.

Baptista. The gain I seek is quiet in the match.

Gremio. No doubt but he hath got a quiet catch.
But now, Baptista, to your younger daughter; 325
Now is the day we long have lookèd for.
I am your neighbor and was suitor first.

Tranio. And I am one that love Bianca more
Than words can witness or your thoughts can guess.

Gremio. Youngling, thou canst not love so dear as I. 330

Tranio. Graybeard, thy love doth freeze.

Gremio.   But thine doth fry.
Skipper,° stand back, 'tis age that nourisheth.

Tranio. But youth in ladies' eyes that flourisheth.

Baptista. Content you, gentlemen; I will compound°
this strife.
'Tis deeds must win the prize, and he of both° 335
That can assure my daughter greatest dower°
Shall have my Bianca's love.
Say, Signior Gremio, what can you assure her?

Gremio. First, as you know, my house within the city
Is richly furnishèd with plate and gold, 340
Basins and ewers to lave° her dainty hands;
My hangings all of Tyrian° tapestry;
In ivory coffers I have stuffed my crowns,
In cypress chests my arras counterpoints,°

---

320 **mart** "deal"   321 **commodity** (here a coarse term for women;
see Partridge, *Shakespeare's Bawdy*)   321 **fretting** decaying in stor-
age (with pun)   332 **Skipper** skipping (irresponsible) fellow   334
compound settle   335 **he of both** the one of you two   336 **dower**
man's gift to bride   341 **lave** wash   342 **Tyrian** purple   344 **arras
counterpoints** counterpanes woven in Arras

345 Costly apparel, tents,° and canopies,
Fine linen, Turkey cushions bossed° with pearl,
Valance° of Venice gold in needlework,
Pewter and brass, and all things that belongs
To house or housekeeping. Then, at my farm
350 I have a hundred milch-kine to the pail,°
Six score fat oxen standing in my stalls
And all things answerable to this portion.°
Myself am struck° in years, I must confess,
And if I die tomorrow, this is hers,
355 If whilst I live she will be only mine.

Tranio. That "only" came well in. Sir, list to me.
I am my father's heir and only son.
If I may have your daughter to my wife,
I'll leave her houses three or four as good,
360 Within rich Pisa walls, as any one
Old Signior Gremio has in Padua,
Besides two thousand ducats° by the year
Of° fruitful land, all which shall be her jointure.°
What, have I pinched° you, Signior Gremio?

Gremio. [*Aside*] Two thousand ducats by the year of
365 land!
My land amounts not to so much in all.
[*To others*] That she shall have besides an argosy°
That now is lying in Marcellus' road.°
What, have I choked you with an argosy?

370 *Tranio.* Gremio, 'tis known my father hath no less
Than three great argosies, besides two galliasses°
And twelve tight° galleys. These I will assure her
And twice as much, whate'er thou off'rest next.

345 **tents** bed tester (hanging cover)   346 **bossed** embroidered   347
Valance bed fringes and drapes   350 **milch-kine to the pail** cows
producing milk for human use   352 **answerable to this portion** corresponding to this settlement (?)   353 **struck** advanced   362 **ducats**
Venetian gold coins   363 **Of** from   363 **jointure** settlement   364
pinched put the screws on   367 **argosy** largest type of merchant
ship   368 **Marcellus' road** Marseilles' harbor   371 **galliasses** large
galleys   372 **tight** watertight

Gremio. Nay, I have off'red all. I have no more,
  And she can have no more than all I have.   375
  If you like me, she shall have me and mine.

Tranio. Why, then the maid is mine from all the world
  By your firm promise. Gremio is outvied.°

Baptista. I must confess your offer is the best,
  And let your father make her the assurance,°   380
  She is your own; else you must pardon me.
  If you should die before him, where's her dower?

Tranio. That's but a cavil.° He is old, I young.

Gremio. And may not young men die as well as old?

Baptista. Well, gentlemen,   385
  I am thus resolved. On Sunday next, you know,
  My daughter Katherine is to be married.
  Now on the Sunday following shall Bianca
  Be bride to you if you make this assurance;
  If not, to Signior Gremio.   390
  And so I take my leave and thank you both.   *Exit.*

Gremio. Adieu, good neighbor. Now I fear thee not.
  Sirrah° young gamester,° your father were° a fool
  To give thee all and in his waning age
  Set foot under thy table.° Tut, a toy!°   395
  An old Italian fox is not so kind, my boy.   *Exit.*

Tranio. A vengeance on your crafty withered hide!
  Yet I have faced it with a card of ten.°
  'Tis in my head to do my master good.
  I see no reason but supposed Lucentio   400
  Must get° a father, called "supposed Vincentio,"
  And that's a wonder. Fathers commonly
  Do get their children, but in this case of wooing
  A child shall get a sire if I fail not of my cunning.
                                        Exit.

---

378 **outvied** outbid   380 **assurance** guarantee   383 **cavil** small point
393 **Sirrah** (used contemptuously)   393 **gamester** gambler   393
were would be   395 **Set foot under thy table** be dependent on you
395 **a toy** a joke   398 **faced it with a card of ten** bluffed with a ten-
spot   401 **get** beget

ACT III

[Scene I. *Padua. In Baptista's house.*]

*Enter Lucentio [as Cambio], Hortensio [as Litio],
and Bianca.*

Lucentio. Fiddler, forbear. You grow too forward, sir.
Have you so soon forgot the entertainment°
Her sister Katherine welcomed you withal?

Hortensio. But, wrangling pedant, this is
5   The patroness of heavenly harmony.
Then give me leave to have prerogative,°
And when in music we have spent an hour,
Your lecture° shall have leisure for as much.

Lucentio. Preposterous° ass, that never read so far
10   To know the cause why music was ordained!
Was it not to refresh the mind of man
After his studies or his usual pain?°
Then give me leave to read° philosophy,
And while I pause, serve in your harmony.

Hortensio. Sirrah, I will not bear these braves° of
15   thine.

Bianca. Why, gentlemen, you do me double wrong
To strive for that which resteth in my choice.

III.i.2 **entertainment** i.e., "pillorying" him with the lute   6 **preroga-tive** priority   8 **lecture** instruction   9 **Preposterous** putting later things (*post-*) first (*pre-*)   12 **pain** labor   13 **read** give a lesson in 15 **braves** defiances

I am no breeching° scholar° in the schools.
I'll not be tied to hours nor 'pointed times,
But learn my lessons as I please myself.   20
And, to cut off all strife, here sit we down.
[*To Hortensio*] Take you your instrument, play you
  the whiles;°
His lecture will be done ere you have tuned.

Hortensio. You'll leave his lecture when I am in tune?

Lucentio. That will be never. Tune your instrument.   25

Bianca. Where left we last?

Lucentio. Here, madam:
  Hic ibat Simois, hic est Sigeia tellus,
    Hic steterat Priami regia celsa senis.°

Bianca. Conster° them.   30

Lucentio. Hic ibat, as I told you before, *Simois,* I am
  Lucentio, *hic est,* son unto Vincentio of Pisa, *Sigeia
  tellus,* disguised thus to get your love, *Hic steterat,*
  and that Lucentio that comes a wooing, *Priami,* is
  my man Tranio, *regia,* bearing my port,° *celsa senis,* 33
  that we might beguile the old pantaloon.°

Hortensio. [*Breaks in*] Madam, my instrument's in
  tune.

Bianca. Let's hear. O fie, the treble jars.°

Lucentio. Spit in the hole, man, and tune again.

Bianca. Now let me see if I can conster it. *Hic ibat*   40
  Simois, I know you not, *hic est Sigeia tellus,* I trust
  you not, *Hic steterat Priami,* take heed he hear us
  not, *regia,* presume not, *celsa senis,* despair not.

Hortensio. [*Breaks in again*] Madam, 'tis now in tune.

---

18 **breeching** (1) in breeches (young) (2) whippable   18 **scholar**
schoolboy   22 **the whiles** meanwhile   28–29 **Hic . . . senis** here
flowed the Simois, here is the Sigeian (Trojan) land, here had stood
old Priam's high palace (Ovid)   30 **Conster** construe   35 **bearing**
my port taking on my style   36 **pantaloon** Gremio (see I.i.47.s.d.
note)   38 **treble jars** highest tone is off

Lucentio.   All but the bass.

Hortensio. The bass is right; 'tis the base knave that
45   jars.
    [*Aside*] How fiery and forward our pedant is!
    Now, for my life, the knave doth court my love.
    Pedascule,° I'll watch you better yet.

Bianca. In time I may believe, yet I mistrust.

50   *Lucentio.* Mistrust it not, for sure Aeacides
    Was Ajax,° called so from his grandfather.

Bianca. I must believe my master; else, I promise you,
    I should be arguing still upon that doubt.
    But let it rest. Now, Litio, to you.
55   Good master, take it not unkindly, pray,
    That I have been thus pleasant° with you both.

Hortensio. [*To Lucentio*] You may go walk and give
    me leave° a while.
    My lessons make no music in three parts.°

Lucentio. Are you so formal, sir? [*Aside*] Well, I
    must wait
60   And watch withal,° for but° I be deceived,
    Our fine musician groweth amorous.

Hortensio. Madam, before you touch the instrument,
    To learn the order of my fingering,
    I must begin with rudiments of art
65   To teach you gamut° in a briefer sort,
    More pleasant, pithy, and effectual,
    Than hath been taught by any of my trade;
    And there it is in writing, fairly drawn.

Bianca. Why, I am past my gamut long ago.

70   *Hortensio.* Yet read the gamut of Hortensio.

---

48 **Pedascule** little pedant (disparaging quasi-Latin)   50–51 **Aea-
cides/Was Ajax** Ajax, Greek warrior at Troy, was grandson of
Aeacus (Lucentio comments on next passage in Ovid)   56 **pleasant**
merry   57 **give me leave** leave me alone   58 **in three parts** for three
voices   60 **withal** besides   60 **but** unless   65 **gamut** the scale

Bianca. [*Reads*]

   Gamut I am, the ground° of all accord.°
     A re, to plead Hortensio's passion:
   B mi, Bianca, take him for thy lord,
     C fa ut, that loves with all affection;
   D sol re, one clef, two notes have I: 75
     E la mi, show pity or I die.

   Call you this gamut? Tut, I like it not.
   Old fashions please me best; I am not so nice°
   To change true rules for odd inventions.

Enter a Messenger.

Messenger. Mistress, your father prays you leave your
     books   80
   And help to dress your sister's chamber up.
   You know tomorrow is the wedding day.

Bianca. Farewell, sweet masters both, I must be gone.
               [Exeunt Bianca and Messenger.]

Lucentio. Faith, mistress, then I have no cause to stay.
               [Exit.]

Hortensio. But I have cause to pry into this pedant.   85
   Methinks he looks as though he were in love.
   Yet if thy thoughts, Bianca, be so humble
   To cast thy wand'ring eyes on every stale,°
   Seize thee that list.° If once I find thee ranging,°
   Hortensio will be quit with thee by changing.° *Exit.* 90

---

71 **ground** beginning, first note   71 **accord** harmony   78 **nice**
whimsical   88 **stale** lure (as in hunting)   89 **Seize thee that list** let
him who likes capture you   89 **ranging** going astray   90 **changing**
i.e., sweethearts

[Scene II. *Padua. The street in front of
Baptista's house.*]

*Enter Baptista, Gremio, Tranio [as Lucentio], Kate,
Bianca, [Lucentio as Cambio]
and others, Attendants.*

Baptista. [*To Tranio*] Signior Lucentio, this is the
'pointed day
That Katherine and Petruchio should be marrièd,
And yet we hear not of our son-in-law.
What will be said? What mockery will it be
5   To want° the bridegroom when the priest attends
To speak the ceremonial rites of marriage!
What says Lucentio to this shame of ours?

Kate. No shame but mine. I must, forsooth, be forced
To give my hand opposed against my heart
10   Unto a mad-brain rudesby,° full of spleen,°
Who wooed in haste and means to wed at leisure.
I told you, I, he was a frantic fool,
Hiding his bitter jests in blunt behavior.
And to be noted for° a merry man,
15   He'll woo a thousand, 'point the day of marriage,
Make friends, invite,° and proclaim the banns,
Yet never means to wed where he hath wooed.
Now must the world point at poor Katherine
And say, "Lo, there is mad Petruchio's wife,
20   If it would please him come and marry her."

Tranio. Patience, good Katherine, and Baptista too.
Upon my life, Petruchio means but well,
Whatever fortune stays° him from his word.

III.ii.5 **want** be without   10 **rudesby** uncouth fellow   10 **spleen**
caprice   14 **noted for** reputed   16 **Make friends, invite** (some editors emend to "Make feast, invite friends")   23 **stays** keeps

Though he be blunt, I know him passing° wise;
Though he be merry, yet withal he's honest.   25

Kate. Would Katherine had never seen him though!
  Exit weeping [followed by Bianca and others].

Baptista. Go, girl, I cannot blame thee now to weep.
For such an injury would vex a very saint,
Much more a shrew of thy impatient humor.°

    Enter Biondello.

Biondello. Master, master, news! And such old° news   30
as you never heard of!

Baptista. Is it new and old too? How may that be?

Biondello. Why, is it not news to hear of Petruchio's
coming?

Baptista. Is he come?   35

Biondello. Why, no, sir.

Baptista. What then?

Biondello. He is coming.

Baptista. When will he be here?

Biondello. When he stands where I am and sees you   40
there.

Tranio. But, say, what to thine old news?

Biondello. Why, Petruchio is coming in a new hat and
an old jerkin;° a pair of old breeches thrice turned;°
a pair of boots that have been candle-cases,° one   45
buckled, another laced; an old rusty sword ta'en
out of the town armory, with a broken hilt and
chapeless;° with two broken points;° his horse
hipped° (with an old mothy saddle and stirrups of

---

24 **passing** very   29 **humor** temper   30 **old** strange   44 **jerkin** short
outer coat   44 **turned** i.e., inside out (to conceal wear and tear)   45
candle-cases worn-out boots used to keep candle ends in   48 **chapeless** lacking the metal mounting at end of scabbard   48 **points** laces
to fasten hose to garment above   49 **hipped** with dislocated hip

50   no kindred),° besides, possessed with the glanders°
      and like to mose in the chine;° troubled with the
      lampass,° infected with the fashions,° full of wind-
      galls,° sped with spavins,° rayed° with the yellows,°
      past cure of the fives,° stark spoiled with the stag-
55   gers,° begnawn with the bots,° swayed° in the
      back, and shoulder-shotten;° near-legged before,°
      and with a half-cheeked° bit and a head-stall° of
      sheep's leather,° which, being restrained° to keep
      him from stumbling, hath been often burst and
60   now repaired with knots; one girth° six times
      pieced,° and a woman's crupper° of velure,° which
      hath two letters for her name fairly set down in
      studs,° and here and there pieced with packthread.°

Baptista. Who comes with him?

65 *Biondello.* O sir, his lackey, for all the world capari-
      soned° like the horse: with a linen stock° on one
      leg and a kersey boot-hose° on the other, gart'red
      with a red and blue list;° an old hat, and the humor
      of forty fancies° pricked° in't for a feather—a mon-
70   ster, a very monster in apparel, and not like a Chris-
      tian footboy° or a gentleman's lackey.

49–50 **of no kindred** not matching   50 **glanders** bacterial disease
affecting mouth and nose   51 **mose in the chine** (1) glanders (2)
nasal discharge   52 **lampass** swollen mouth   52 **fashions** tumors
(related to glanders)   52–53 **windgalls** swellings on lower leg   53
spavins swellings on upper hind leg   53 **rayed** soiled   53 **yellows**
jaundice   54 **fives** vives: swelling of submaxillary glands   54–55
staggers nervous disorder causing loss of balance   55 **begnawn with
the bots** gnawed by parasitic worms (larvae of the botfly)   55
swayed sagging   56 **shoulder-shotten** with dislocated shoulder   56
near-legged before with forefeet knocking together   57 **half-cheeked**
wrongly adjusted to bridle and affording less control   57 **head-stall**
part of bridle which surrounds head   58 **sheep's leather** (weaker
than pigskin)   58 **restrained** pulled back   60 **girth** saddle strap
under belly   61 **pieced** patched   61 **crupper** leather loop under
horse's tail to help steady saddle   61 **velure** velvet   63 **studs** large-
headed nails of brass or silver   63 **pieced with packthread** tied together with coarse thread   65–66 **caparisoned** outfitted   66 **stock**
stocking   67 **kersey boot-hose** coarse stocking worn with riding boot
68 **list** strip of discarded border-cloth   68–69 **humor of forty fan-
cies** fanciful decoration (in place of feather)   69 **pricked** pinned
71 **footboy** page in livery

Tranio. 'Tis some odd humor° pricks° him to this
    fashion,
  Yet oftentimes he goes but mean-appareled.

Baptista. I am glad he's come, howsoe'er he comes.

Biondello. Why, sir, he comes not.   73

Baptista. Didst thou not say he comes?

Biondello. Who? That Petruchio came?

Baptista. Ay, that Petruchio came.

Biondello. No, sir, I say his horse comes, with him
  on his back.   80

Baptista. Why, that's all one.°

Biondello. [*Sings*]

        Nay, by Saint Jamy,
        I hold° you a penny,
        A horse and a man
        Is more than one
        And yet not many.   85

     Enter Petruchio and Grumio.

Petruchio. Come, where be these gallants?° Who's at
  home?

Baptista. You are welcome, sir.

Petruchio.   And yet I come not well.

Baptista. And yet you halt° not.

Tranio.   Not so well appareled
  As I wish you were.   90

Petruchio. Were it better,° I should rush in thus.
  But where is Kate? Where is my lovely bride?
  How does my father? Gentles,° methinks you frown.

---

72 **humor** mood, fancy   72 **pricks** incites   81 **all one** the same thing
83 **hold** bet   87 **gallants** men of fashion   89 **halt** limp (pun on
come meaning "walk")   91 **Were it better** even if I were better   93
Gentles sirs

And wherefore gaze this goodly company
95   As if they saw some wondrous monument,°
Some comet or unusual prodigy?°

Baptista. Why, sir, you know this is your wedding day.
First were we sad, fearing you would not come,
Now sadder that you come so unprovided.°
100   Fie, doff this habit,° shame to your estate,°
An eyesore to our solemn festival.

Tranio. And tell us what occasion of import°
Hath all so long detained you from your wife
And sent you hither so unlike yourself.

105   *Petruchio.* Tedious it were to tell and harsh to hear.
Sufficeth, I am come to keep my word
Though in some part enforcèd to digress,°
Which, at more leisure, I will so excuse
As you shall well be satisfied with all.
110   But where is Kate? I stay too long from her.
The morning wears, 'tis time we were at church.

Tranio. See not your bride in these unreverent robes.
Go to my chamber; put on clothes of mine.

Petruchio. Not I, believe me; thus I'll visit her.

115   *Baptista.* But thus, I trust, you will not marry her.

Petruchio. Good sooth,° even thus; therefore ha' done
with words.
To me she's married, not unto my clothes.
Could I repair what she will wear° in me
As I can change these poor accoutrements,
120   'Twere well for Kate and better for myself.
But what a fool am I to chat with you
When I should bid good morrow to my bride
And seal the title° with a lovely° kiss.

Exit [with Grumio].

---

95 **monument** warning sign   96 **prodigy** marvel   99 **unprovided** ill-
outfitted   100 **habit** costume   100 **estate** status   102 **of import** important   107 **enforcèd to digress** forced to depart (perhaps from
his plan to "buy apparel 'gainst the wedding day," II.i.308)   116
Good sooth yes indeed   118 **wear** wear out   123 **title** i.e., as of
ownership   123 **lovely** loving

Tranio. He hath some meaning in his mad attire.
   We will persuade him, be it possible,   *125*
   To put on better ere he go to church.

Baptista. I'll after him and see the event° of this.
           Exit [*with Gremio and Attendants*].

Tranio. But to her love concerneth us to add
   Her father's liking, which to bring to pass,
   As I before imparted to your worship,   *130*
   I am to get a man—whate'er he be
   It skills° not much, we'll fit him to our turn°—
   And he shall be Vincentio of Pisa,
   And make assurance° here in Padua
   Of greater sums than I have promisèd.   *135*
   So shall you quietly enjoy your hope
   And marry sweet Bianca with consent.

Lucentio. Were it not that my fellow schoolmaster
   Doth watch Bianca's steps so narrowly,
   'Twere good, methinks, to steal our marriage,°   *140*
   Which once performed, let all the world say no,
   I'll keep mine own despite of all the world.

Tranio. That by degrees we mean to look into
   And watch our vantage° in this business.
   We'll overreach° the graybeard, Gremio,   *145*
   The narrow-prying father, Minola,
   The quaint° musician, amorous Litio—
   All for my master's sake, Lucentio.

              Enter Gremio.

Signior Gremio, came you from the church?

Gremio. As willingly as e'er I came from school.   *150*

Tranio. And is the bride and bridegroom coming
   home?

Gremio. A bridegroom say you? 'Tis a groom° indeed,

127 **event** upshot, outcome   132 **skills** matters   132 **turn** purpose
134 **assurance** guarantee   140 **steal our marriage** elope   144 **vantage** advantage   145 **overreach** get the better of   147 **quaint** artful
152 **groom** menial (i.e., coarse fellow)

A grumbling groom, and that the girl shall find.

Tranio. Curster than she? Why, 'tis impossible.

155 *Gremio.* Why, he's a devil, a devil, a very fiend.

Tranio. Why, she's a devil, a devil, the devil's dam.°

Gremio. Tut, she's a lamb, a dove, a fool to° him.
    I'll tell you, Sir Lucentio, when the priest
    Should ask, if Katherine should be his wife,
    "Ay, by goggs woones!"° quoth he and swore so
160   loud
    That, all amazed, the priest let fall the book,
    And as he stooped again to take it up,
    This mad-brained bridegroom took° him such a cuff
    That down fell priest and book and book and priest.
165   "Now, take them up," quoth he, "if any list."°

Tranio. What said the wench when he rose again?

Gremio. Trembled and shook, for why° he stamped
     and swore
    As if the vicar meant to cozen° him.
    But after many ceremonies done
170   He calls for wine. "A health!" quoth he as if
    He had been aboard, carousing° to his mates
    After a storm; quaffed off the muscadel°
    And threw the sops° all in the sexton's face,
    Having no other reason
175   But that his beard grew thin and hungerly,°
    And seemed to ask him sops as he was drinking.
    This done, he took the bride about the neck
    And kissed her lips with such a clamorous smack
    That at the parting all the church did echo,
180   And I, seeing this, came thence for very shame.

---

156 **dam** mother   157 **fool to** harmless person compared with   160
goggs woones by God's wounds (a common oath)   163 **took** gave
165 **list** pleases to   167 **for why** because   168 **cozen** cheat   171
carousing calling "Bottoms up"   172 **muscadel** sweet wine, conventionally drunk after marriage service   173 **sops** pieces of cake
soaked in wine; dregs   175 **hungerly** as if poorly nourished

And after me, I know, the rout° is coming.
Such a mad marriage never was before.
Hark, hark, I hear the minstrels play.   *Music plays.*

Enter Petruchio, Kate, Bianca, Hortensio [as Litio],
Baptista [with Grumio and others].

Petruchio. Gentlemen and friends, I thank you for
    your pains.
I know you think to dine with me today   185
And have prepared great store of wedding cheer,°
But so it is, my haste doth call me hence
And therefore here I mean to take my leave.

Baptista. Is't possible you will away tonight?

Petruchio. I must away today, before night come.   190
Make it no wonder;° if you knew my business,
You would entreat me rather go than stay.
And, honest company, I thank you all
That have beheld me give away myself
To this most patient, sweet, and virtuous wife.   195
Dine with my father, drink a health to me,
For I must hence, and farewell to you all.

Tranio. Let us entreat you stay till after dinner.

Petruchio. It may not be.

Gremio.   Let me entreat you.

Petruchio. It cannot be.

Kate.   Let me entreat you.   200

Petruchio. I am content.

Kate.   Are you content to stay?

Petruchio. I am content you shall entreat me stay,
    But yet not stay, entreat me how you can.

Kate. Now if you love me, stay.

Petruchio.   Grumio, my horse!°

181 **rout** crowd   186 **cheer** food and drink   191 **Make it no wonder**
don't be surprised   204 **horse** horses

205 *Grumio.* Ay, sir, they be ready; the oats have eaten
    the horses.°

  Kate. Nay then,
    Do what thou canst, I will not go today,
    No, nor tomorrow, not till I please myself.
210   The door is open, sir, there lies your way.
    You may be jogging whiles your boots are green;°
    For me, I'll not be gone till I please myself.
    'Tis like you'll prove a jolly° surly groom,
    That take it on you° at the first so roundly.°

  Petruchio. O Kate, content thee; prithee,° be not
215   angry.

  Kate. I will be angry. What hast thou to do?°
    Father, be quiet; he shall stay my leisure.°

  Gremio. Ay, marry, sir, now it begins to work.

  Kate. Gentlemen, forward to the bridal dinner.
220   I see a woman may be made a fool
    If she had not a spirit to resist.

  Petruchio. They shall go forward, Kate, at thy com-
    mand.
    Obey the bride, you that attend on her.
    Go to the feast, revel and domineer,°
225   Carouse full measure to her maidenhead,
    Be mad and merry, or go hang yourselves.
    But for my bonny Kate, she must with me.
    Nay, look not big,° nor stamp, nor stare,° nor fret;
    I will be master of what is mine own.
230   She is my goods, my chattels; she is my house,
    My household stuff, my field, my barn,
    My horse, my ox, my ass, my anything,°

205–06 **oats have eaten the horses** (1) a slip of the tongue or (2) an
ironic jest 211 **You . . . green** (proverbial way of suggesting departure to a guest, *green* = new, cleaned) 213 **jolly** domineering
214 **take it on you** do as you please 214 **roundly** roughly 215
prithee I pray thee 216 **What hast thou to do** what do you have to
do with it 217 **stay my leisure** await my willingness 224 **domineer**
cut up in a lordly fashion 228 **big** challenging 228 **stare** swagger
232 **My horse . . . anything** (echoing Tenth Commandment)

And here she stands. Touch her whoever dare,
I'll bring mine action° on the proudest he
That stops my way in Padua. Grumio,   235
Draw forth thy weapon, we are beset with thieves.
Rescue thy mistress, if thou be a man.
Fear not, sweet wench; they shall not touch thee,
   Kate.
I'll buckler° thee against a million.
            Exeunt Petruchio, Kate [and Grumio].

Baptista. Nay, let them go, a couple of quiet ones.   240

Gremio. Went they not quickly, I should die with
   laughing.

Tranio. Of all mad matches never was the like.

Lucentio. Mistress, what's your opinion of your sister?

Bianca. That being mad herself, she's madly mated.

Gremio. I warrant him, Petruchio is Kated.   245

Baptista. Neighbors and friends, though bride and
   bridegroom wants°
For to supply the places at the table,
You know there wants no junkets° at the feast.
[*To Tranio*] Lucentio, you shall supply the bride-
   groom's place,
And let Bianca take her sister's room.   250

Tranio. Shall sweet Bianca practice how to bride it?

Baptista. She shall, Lucentio. Come, gentlemen, let's
   go.   *Exeunt.*

---

234 action lawsuit   **239 buckler** shield   **246 wants** are lacking   **248
junkets** sweetmeats, confections

[ACT IV

Scene I. *Petruchio's country house.*]

Enter Grumio.

Grumio. Fie, fie, on all tired jades,° on all mad masters, and all foul ways!° Was ever man so beaten?
Was ever man so rayed?° Was ever man so weary?
I am sent before to make a fire, and they are coming
after to warm them. Now were not I a little pot and
soon hot,° my very lips might freeze to my teeth,
my tongue to the roof of my mouth, my heart in my
belly, ere I should come by a fire to thaw me. But I
with blowing the fire shall warm myself, for considering the weather, a taller° man than I will take
cold. Holla, ho, Curtis!

Enter Curtis [a Servant].

Curtis. Who is that calls so coldly?

Grumio. A piece of ice. If thou doubt it, thou mayst
slide from my shoulder to my heel with no greater
a run° but my head and my neck. A fire, good
Curtis.

Curtis. Is my master and his wife coming, Grumio?

IV.i.1 **jades** worthless horses   2 **foul ways** bad roads   3 **rayed** be-
fouled   5–6 **little pot and soon hot** (proverbial for small person of
short temper)   10 **taller** sturdier (with allusion to "little pot")   15
run running start

108

Grumio. O ay, Curtis, ay, and therefore fire, fire;
cast on no water.°

Curtis. Is she so hot a shrew as she's reported?   20

Grumio. She was, good Curtis, before this frost, but
thou know'st winter tames man, woman, and beast;
for it hath tamed my old master, and my new mistress, and myself, fellow Curtis.

Curtis. Away, you three-inch° fool! I am no beast.   23

Grumio. Am I but three inches? Why, thy horn° is a
foot, and so long am I at the least. But wilt thou
make a fire, or shall I complain on thee to our mistress, whose hand—she being now at hand—thou
shalt soon feel, to thy cold comfort, for being slow   30
in thy hot office?°

Curtis. I prithee, good Grumio, tell me, how goes
the world?

Grumio. A cold world, Curtis, in every office but
thine, and therefore, fire. Do thy duty and have thy   35
duty,° for my master and mistress are almost frozen
to death.

Curtis. There's fire ready, and therefore, good Grumio,
the news.

Grumio. Why, "Jack boy, ho boy!"° and as much   40
news as wilt thou.

Curtis. Come, you are so full of cony-catching.°

Grumio. Why therefore fire, for I have caught extreme
cold. Where's the cook? Is supper ready, the house
trimmed, rushes strewed,° cobwebs swept, the serv-   43

---

19 **cast on no water** (alters "Cast on more water" in a well-known
round)   25 **three-inch** (1) another allusion to Grumio's small stat-
ure (2) a phallic jest, the first of several   26 **horn** (symbol of cuck-
old)   31 **hot office** job of making a fire   35–36 **thy duty** what is
due thee   40 **"Jack boy, ho boy!"** (from another round or catch)
42 **cony-catching** rabbit-catching (i.e., tricking simpletons; with pun
on *catch*, the song)   45 **strewed** i.e., on floor (for special occasion)

ingmen in their new fustian,° the white stockings,
and every officer° his wedding garment on? Be the
jacks° fair within, the jills° fair without, the car-
pets° laid and everything in order?

50 *Curtis.* All ready, and therefore, I pray thee, news.

Grumio. First, know my horse is tired, my master and
mistress fall'n out.

Curtis. How?

Grumio. Out of their saddles into the dirt—and
55 thereby hangs a tale.

Curtis. Let's ha't, good Grumio.

Grumio. Lend thine ear.

Curtis. Here.

Grumio. There.   [*Strikes him.*]

60 *Curtis.* This 'tis to feel a tale, not to hear a tale.

Grumio. And therefore 'tis called a sensible° tale, and
this cuff was but to knock at your ear and beseech
list'ning. Now I begin. *Imprimis,*° we came down
a foul° hill, my master riding behind my mistress—

65 *Curtis.* Both of° one horse?

Grumio. What's that to thee?

Curtis. Why, a horse.

Grumio. Tell thou the tale. But hadst thou not
crossed° me thou shouldst have heard how her
70 horse fell and she under her horse. Thou shouldst
have heard in how miry a place, how she was bemoiled,° how he left her with the horse upon her,
how he beat me because her horse stumbled, how

46 **fustian** coarse cloth (cotton and flax)   47 **officer** servant   48
jacks (1) menservants (2) half-pint leather drinking cups   48 **jills**
(1) maids (2) gill-size metal drinking cups   48–49 **carpets** table
covers   61 **sensible** (1) rational (2) "feel"-able   63 **Imprimis** first
64 **foul** muddy   65 **of** on   69 **crossed** interrupted   72 **bemoiled**
muddied

she waded through the dirt to pluck him off me;
how he swore, how she prayed that never prayed   73
before; how I cried, how the horses ran away, how
her bridle was burst, how I lost my crupper, with
many things of worthy memory which now shall
die in oblivion, and thou return unexperienced° to
thy grave.   80

Curtis. By this reck'ning° he is more shrew than she.

Grumio. Ay, and that thou and the proudest of you
all shall find when he comes home. But what° talk
I of this? Call forth Nathaniel, Joseph, Nicholas,
Philip, Walter, Sugarsop, and the rest. Let their   85
heads be slickly° combed, their blue° coats brushed,
and their garters of an indifferent° knit. Let them
curtsy with their left legs and not presume to touch
a hair of my master's horsetail till they kiss their
hands. Are they all ready?   90

Curtis. They are.

Grumio. Call them forth.

Curtis. Do you hear, ho? You must meet my master
to countenance° my mistress.

Grumio. Why, she hath a face of her own.   95

Curtis. Who knows not that?

Grumio. Thou, it seems, that calls for company to
countenance her.

Curtis. I call them forth to credit° her.

Grumio. Why, she comes to borrow nothing of them.   100

Enter four or five Servingmen.

Nathaniel. Welcome home, Grumio!

---

79 **unexperienced** uninformed   81 **reck'ning** account   83 **what** why
86 **slickly** smoothly   86 **blue** (usual color of servants' clothing)   87
indifferent matching (?) appropriate (?)   94 **countenance** show respect to (with puns following)   99 **credit** honor

Philip. How now, Grumio?

Joseph. What, Grumio!

Nicholas. Fellow Grumio!

105 *Nathaniel.* How now, old lad!

Grumio. Welcome, you; how now, you; what, you;
fellow, you; and thus much for greeting. Now, my
spruce companions, is all ready and all things neat?

Nathaniel. All things is ready. How near is our
110   master?

Grumio. E'en at hand, alighted by this,° and therefore be not—Cock's° passion, silence! I hear my
master.

Enter Petruchio and Kate.

Petruchio. Where be these knaves? What, no man at
door
115   To hold my stirrup nor to take my horse?
Where is Nathaniel, Gregory, Philip?

All Servingmen. Here, here, sir, here, sir.

Petruchio. Here, sir, here, sir, here, sir, here, sir!
You loggerheaded° and unpolished grooms!
120   What, no attendance? No regard? No duty?
Where is the foolish knave I sent before?

Grumio. Here, sir, as foolish as I was before.

Petruchio. You peasant swain!° You whoreson° malt-
horse drudge!°
Did I not bid thee meet me in the park°
125   And bring along these rascal knaves with thee?

Grumio. Nathaniel's coat, sir, was not fully made
And Gabrel's pumps were all unpinked° i' th' heel.

---

111 **this** now   112 **Cock's** God's (i.e., Christ's)   119 **loggerheaded**
blockheaded   123 **swain** bumpkin   123 **whoreson** bastardly   123
malt-horse drudge slow horse on brewery treadmill   124 **park** coun-
try-house grounds   127 **unpinked** lacking embellishment made by
pinking (making small holes in leather)

There was no link° to color Peter's hat,
And Walter's dagger was not come from sheathing.°
There were none fine but Adam, Rafe, and Gregory; 130
The rest were ragged, old, and beggarly.
Yet, as they are, here are they come to meet you.

Petruchio. Go, rascals, go, and fetch my supper in.

                              Exeunt Servants.

[*Sings*] "Where is the life that late I led?"°

Where are those°—Sit down, Kate, and welcome. 135
   Soud,° soud, soud, soud!

                Enter Servants with supper.

Why, when,° I say?—Nay, good sweet Kate, be
   merry.—
Off with my boots, you rogues, you villains! When?
[*Sings*] "It was the friar of orders gray,
As he forth walkèd on his way"°—   140
Out, you rogue, you pluck my foot awry!
Take that, and mend° the plucking of the other.

                              [*Strikes him.*]

Be merry, Kate. Some water here! What ho!

                Enter one with water.

Where's my spaniel Troilus? Sirrah, get you hence
And bid my cousin Ferdinand come hither—   145

                              [*Exit Servant.*]

One, Kate, that you must kiss and be acquainted with.
Where are my slippers? Shall I have some water?
Come, Kate, and wash, and welcome heartily.
You whoreson villain, will you let it fall?

                              [*Strikes him.*]

Kate. Patience, I pray you. 'Twas a fault unwilling. 150

Petruchio. A whoreson, beetle-headed,° flap-eared
   knave!

128 **link** torch, providing blacking   129 **sheathing** repairing scabbard   134 **"Where . . . led?"** (from an old ballad)   135 **those**
servants   136 **Soud** (exclamation variously explained; some editors
emend to *Food*)   137 **when** (exclamation of annoyance, as in next
line)   139–40 **"It was . . . his way"** (from another old song)   142
mend improve   151 **beetle-headed** mallet-headed

Come, Kate, sit down; I know you have a stomach.°
Will you give thanks,° sweet Kate, or else shall I?
What's this? Mutton?

First Servingman.   Ay.

Petruchio.   Who brought it?

Peter.   I.

155 *Petruchio.* 'Tis burnt, and so is all the meat.
What dogs are these! Where is the rascal cook?
How durst you, villains, bring it from the dresser,°
And serve it thus to me that love it not?
There, take it to you, trenchers,° cups, and all,
          [*Throws food and dishes at them.*]
160 You heedless joltheads° and unmannered slaves!
What, do you grumble? I'll be with° you straight.°

Kate. I pray you, husband, be not so disquiet.
The meat was well if you were so contented.°

Petruchio. I tell thee, Kate, 'twas burnt and dried away,
165 And I expressly am forbid to touch it,
For it engenders choler,° planteth anger,
And better 'twere that both of us did fast—
Since of ourselves, ourselves are choleric°—
Than feed it° with such overroasted flesh.
170 Be patient. Tomorrow't shall be mended,°
And for this night we'll fast for company.°
Come, I will bring thee to thy bridal chamber.
                                        Exeunt.

Enter Servants severally.

Nathaniel. Peter, didst ever see the like?

Peter. He kills her in her own humor.°

152 **stomach** (1) hunger (2) irascibility   153 **give thanks** say grace
157 **dresser** sideboard   159 **trenchers** wooden platters   160 **jolt-
heads** boneheads (*jolt* is related to *jaw* or *jowl*)   161 **with** even with
161 **straight** directly   163 **so contented** willing to see it as it was
166 **choler** bile, the "humor" (fluid) supposed to produce anger
168 **choleric** bilious, i.e., hot-tempered   169 **it** i.e., their choler   170
't shall be mended things will be better   171 **for company** together
174 **kills her in her own humor** conquers her by using her own disposition

Enter Curtis, a Servant.

Grumio. Where is he?   175

Curtis. In her chamber, making a sermon of continency
    to her,
    And rails and swears and rates,° that she, poor soul,
    Knows not which way to stand, to look, to speak,
    And sits as one new-risen from a dream.   180
    Away, away, for he is coming hither.   [*Exeunt.*]

Enter Petruchio.

Petruchio. Thus have I politicly° begun my reign,
    And 'tis my hope to end successfully.
    My falcon° now is sharp° and passing empty,
    And till she stoop° she must not be full gorged,°   185
    For then she never looks upon her lure.°
    Another way I have to man° my haggard,°
    To make her come and know her keeper's call,
    That is, to watch° her as we watch these kites°
    That bate and beat° and will not be obedient.   190
    She eat° no meat today, nor none shall eat.
    Last night she slept not, nor tonight she shall not.
    As with the meat, some undeservèd fault
    I'll find about the making of the bed,
    And here I'll fling the pillow, there the bolster,°   195
    This way the coverlet, another way the sheets.
    Ay, and amid this hurly° I intend°
    That all is done in reverent care of her,
    And in conclusion she shall watch° all night.
    And if she chance to nod I'll rail and brawl   200
    And with the clamor keep her still awake.

---

178 **rates** scolds   182 **politicly** with a calculated plan   184 **falcon**
hawk trained for hunting (falconry figures continue for seven lines)
184 **sharp** pinched with hunger   185 **stoop** (1) obey (2) swoop to
the lure   185 **full gorged** fully fed   186 **lure** device used in training
a hawk to return from flight   187 **man** (1) tame (2) be a man to
187 **haggard** hawk captured after reaching maturity   189 **watch**
keep from sleep   189 **kites** type of small hawk   190 **bate and beat**
flap and flutter (i.e., in jittery resistance to training)   191 **eat** ate
(pronounced *et*, as still in Britain)   195 **bolster** cushion extending
width of bed as under-support for pillows   197 **hurly** disturbance
197 **intend** profess   199 **watch** stay awake

This is a way to kill a wife with kindness,°
And thus I'll curb her mad and headstrong humor.
He that knows better how to tame a shrew,°
205   Now let him speak—'tis charity to show.   *Exit.*

[Scene II. *Padua. The street in front of
Baptista's house.*]

Enter Tranio [as Lucentio] and Hortensio [as Litio].

Tranio. Is't possible, friend Litio, that Mistress Bianca
Doth fancy° any other but Lucentio?
I tell you, sir, she bears me fair in hand.°

Hortensio. Sir, to satisfy you in what I have said,
5   Stand by and mark the manner of his teaching.
                              [*They eavesdrop.*]

Enter Bianca [and Lucentio as Cambio].

Lucentio. Now mistress, profit you in what you read?

Bianca. What, master, read you? First resolve° me that.

Lucentio. I read that° I profess,° the Art to Love.°

Bianca. And may you prove, sir, master of your art.

Lucentio. While you, sweet dear, prove mistress of my
10   heart.   [*They court.*]

Hortensio. Quick proceeders,° marry!° Now, tell me,
        I pray,
You that durst swear that your mistress Bianca
Loved none in the world so well as Lucentio.

202 **kill a wife with kindness** (ironic allusion to proverb on ruining a
wife by pampering)   204 **shrew** (rhymes with "show")   IV.ii.2 **fancy**
like   3 **bears me fair in hand** leads me on   7 **resolve** answer   8 **that**
what   8 **profess** avow, practice   8 **Art to Love** (i.e., Ovid's *Ars
Amandi*)   11 **proceeders** (pun on idiom "proceed Master of Arts";
cf. line 9)   11 **marry** by Mary (mild exclamation)

Tranio. O despiteful° love! Unconstant womankind!
　I tell thee, Litio, this is wonderful.°   15

Hortensio. Mistake no more. I am not Litio,
　Nor a musician, as I seem to be,
　But one that scorn to live in this disguise,
　For such a one as leaves a gentleman
　And makes a god of such a cullion.°   20
　Know, sir, that I am called Hortensio.

Tranio. Signior Hortensio, I have often heard
　Of your entire affection to Bianca,
　And since mine eyes are witness of her lightness,°
　I will with you, if you be so contented,   25
　Forswear° Bianca and her love forever.

Hortensio. See, how they kiss and court! Signior
　Lucentio,
　Here is my hand and here I firmly vow
　Never to woo her more, but do forswear her,
　As one unworthy all the former favors°   30
　That I have fondly° flattered her withal.

Tranio. And here I take the like unfeignèd oath,
　Never to marry with her though she would entreat.
　Fie on her! See how beastly° she doth court him.

Hortensio. Would all the world but he had quite for-
　sworn.°   35
　For me, that I may surely keep mine oath,
　I will be married to a wealthy widow
　Ere three days pass, which° hath as long loved me
　As I have loved this proud disdainful haggard.°
　And so farewell, Signior Lucentio.   40
　Kindness in women, not their beauteous looks,
　Shall win my love, and so I take my leave
　In resolution as I swore before.   [*Exit.*]

---

14 **despiteful** spiteful   15 **wonderful** causing wonder   20 **cullion**
low fellow (literally, testicle)   24 **lightness** (cf. "light woman")   26
Forswear "swear off"   30 **favors** marks of esteem   31 **fondly** fool-
ishly   34 **beastly** unashamedly   35 **Would . . . forsworn** i.e., would
she had only one lover   38 **which** who   39 **haggard** (cf. IV.i.187)

Tranio. Mistress Bianca, bless you with such grace
45   As 'longeth to a lover's blessèd case.
      Nay, I have ta'en you napping,° gentle love,
      And have forsworn you with Hortensio.

Bianca. Tranio, you jest. But have you both forsworn
      me?

Tranio. Mistress, we have.

Lucentio.   Then we are rid of Litio.

50 *Tranio.* I' faith, he'll have a lusty° widow now,
      That shall be wooed and wedded in a day.

Bianca. God give him joy!

Tranio. Ay, and he'll tame her.

Bianca.   He says so, Tranio.

Tranio. Faith, he is gone unto the taming school.

Bianca. The taming school! What, is there such a
55   place?

Tranio. Ay, mistress, and Petruchio is the master,
      That teacheth tricks eleven and twenty long°
      To tame a shrew and charm her chattering tongue.

Enter Biondello.

Biondello. O master, master, I have watched so long
60   That I am dog-weary, but at last I spied
      An ancient angel° coming down the hill
      Will serve the turn.°

Tranio.   What° is he, Biondello?

Biondello. Master, a mercatante° or a pedant,°
      I know not what, but formal in apparel,

---

46 ta'en you napping seen you "kiss and court" (line 27)   50 lusty
lively   57 tricks eleven and twenty long (1) many tricks (2) possibly
an allusion to card game "thirty-one" (cf.I.ii.33)   61 ancient angel
man of good old stamp (*angel* = coin; cf. "gentleman of the old
school")   62 Will serve the turn who will do for our purposes   62
What what kind of man   63 mercatante merchant   63 pedant
schoolmaster

    In gait and countenance° surely like a father.   65

Lucentio. And what of him, Tranio?

Tranio. If he be credulous and trust my tale,
    I'll make him glad to seem Vincentio,
    And give assurance to Baptista Minola
    As if he were the right Vincentio.   70
    Take in your love and then let me alone.
                              [*Exeunt Lucentio and Bianca.*]

                    Enter a Pedant.

Pedant. God save you, sir.

Tranio.   And you, sir. You are welcome.
    Travel you far on, or are you at the farthest?

Pedant. Sir, at the farthest for a week or two,
    But then up farther and as far as Rome,   75
    And so to Tripoli if God lend me life.

Tranio. What countryman,° I pray?

Pedant.   Of Mantua.

Tranio. Of Mantua, sir? Marry, God forbid!
    And come to Padua, careless of your life?

Pedant. My life, sir? How, I pray? For that goes
    hard.°   80

Tranio. 'Tis death for anyone in Mantua
    To come to Padua. Know you not the cause?
    Your ships are stayed° at Venice and the Duke,
    For private quarrel 'twixt your duke and him,
    Hath published and proclaimed it openly.   85
    'Tis marvel, but that you are but newly come,
    You might have heard it else proclaimed about.

Pedant. Alas, sir, it is worse for me than so,°
    For I have bills for money by exchange
    From Florence and must here deliver them.   90

---

65 **gait and countenance** bearing and style   77 **What countryman** a
man of what country   80 **goes hard** (cf. "is rough")   83 **stayed** held
88 **than so** than it appears so far

Tranio. Well, sir, to do you courtesy,
    This will I do and this I will advise° you.
    First tell me, have you ever been at Pisa?

Pedant. Ay, sir, in Pisa have I often been—
95   Pisa, renownèd for grave citizens.

Tranio. Among them, know you one Vincentio?

Pedant. I know him not but I have heard of him—
    A merchant of incomparable wealth.

Tranio. He is my father, sir, and, sooth to say,
100   In count'nance somewhat doth resemble you.

Biondello. [*Aside*] As much as an apple doth an oyster, and all one.°

Tranio. To save your life in this extremity,
    This favor will I do you for his sake,
105   And think it not the worst of all your fortunes
    That you are like to Sir Vincentio.
    His name and credit° shall you undertake,°
    And in my house you shall be friendly lodged.
    Look that you take upon you° as you should.
110   You understand me, sir? So shall you stay
    Till you have done your business in the city.
    If this be court'sy, sir, accept of it.

Pedant. O sir, I do, and will repute° you ever
    The patron of my life and liberty.

115 *Tranio.* Then go with me to make the matter good.
    This, by the way,° I let you understand:
    My father is here looked for every day
    To pass assurance° of a dower in marriage
    'Twixt me and one Baptista's daughter here.
120   In all these circumstances I'll instruct you.
    Go with me to clothe you as becomes you. *Exeunt.*

---

92 **advise** explain to   102 **all one** no difference   107 **credit** standing
107 **undertake** adopt   109 **take upon you** assume your role   113 **repute** esteem   116 **by the way** as we walk along   118 **pass assurance** give a guarantee

[Scene III. *In Petruchio's house.*]

Enter Kate and Grumio.

Grumio. No, no, forsooth, I dare not for my life.

Kate. The more my wrong,° the more his spite appears.
What, did he marry me to famish me?
Beggars that come unto my father's door,
Upon entreaty have a present° alms;   3
If not, elsewhere they meet with charity.
But I, who never knew how to entreat
Nor never needed that I should entreat,
Am starved for meat,° giddy for lack of sleep,
With oaths kept waking and with brawling fed.   10
And that which spites me more than all these wants,
He does it únder name of perfect love,
As who should say,° if I should sleep or eat
'Twere deadly sickness or else present death.
I prithee go and get me some repast,   13
I care not what, so° it be wholesome food.

Grumio. What say you to a neat's° foot?

Kate. 'Tis passing good; I prithee let me have it.

Grumio. I fear it is too choleric° a meat.
How say you to a fat tripe finely broiled?   20

Kate. I like it well. Good Grumio, fetch it me.

Grumio. I cannot tell, I fear 'tis choleric.
What say you to a piece of beef and mustard?

IV.iii.2 **The more my wrong** the greater the wrong done me   5
present prompt   9 **meat** food   13 **As who should say** as if to say
16 **so** as long as   17 **neat's** ox's or calf's   19 **choleric** temper-producing

Kate. A dish that I do love to feed upon.

25   *Grumio.* Ay, but the mustard is too hot a little.

Kate. Why then, the beef, and let the mustard rest.

Grumio. Nay then, I will not. You shall have the mustard
Or else you get no beef of Grumio.

Kate. Then both or one, or anything thou wilt.

30   *Grumio.* Why then, the mustard without the beef.

Kate. Go, get thee gone, thou false deluding slave,
                         Beats him.
That feed'st me with the very name° of meat.
Sorrow on thee and all the pack of you
That triumph thus upon my misery.
35   Go, get thee gone, I say.

Enter Petruchio and Hortensio with meat.

Petruchio. How fares my Kate? What, sweeting, all
amort?°

Hortensio. Mistress, what cheer?°

Kate.   Faith, as cold° as can be.

Petruchio. Pluck up thy spirits; look cheerfully upon
me.
Here, love, thou seest how diligent I am
40   To dress thy meat° myself and bring it thee.
I am sure, sweet Kate, this kindness merits thanks.
What, not a word? Nay then, thou lov'st it not,
And all my pains is sorted to no proof.°
Here, take away this dish.

Kate.   I pray you, let it stand.

45   *Petruchio.* The poorest service is repaid with thanks,
And so shall mine before you touch the meat.

---

32 **very name** name only   36 **all amort** depressed, lifeless (cf. "mor-
tified")   37 **what cheer** how are things   37 **cold** (cf. "not so hot";
"cold comfort," IV.i.30)   40 **To dress thy meat** in fixing your food
43 **sorted to no proof** have come to nothing

Kate. I thank you, sir.

Hortensio. Signior Petruchio, fie, you are to blame.
Come, Mistress Kate, I'll bear you company.

Petruchio. [*Aside*] Eat it up all, Hortensio, if thou
    lovest me;   *50*
Much good do it unto thy gentle heart.
Kate, eat apace. And now, my honey love,
Will we return unto thy father's house
And revel it as bravely° as the best,
With silken coats and caps and golden rings,   *55*
With ruffs° and cuffs and fardingales° and things,
With scarfs and fans and double change of brav'ry,°
With amber bracelets, beads, and all this knav'ry.°
What, hast thou dined? The tailor stays thy leisure°
To deck thy body with his ruffling° treasure.   *60*

Enter Tailor.

Come, tailor, let us see these ornaments.

Enter Haberdasher.

Lay forth the gown. What news with you, sir?

Haberdasher. Here is the cap your Worship did be-
    speak.°

Petruchio. Why, this was molded on a porringer°—
A velvet dish. Fie, fie, 'tis lewd° and filthy.   *65*
Why, 'tis a cockle° or a walnut shell,
A knack,° a toy, a trick,° a baby's cap.
Away with it! Come, let me have a bigger.

Kate. I'll have no bigger. This doth fit the time,°
And gentlewomen wear such caps as these.   *70*

---

54 **bravely** handsomely dressed   56 **ruffs** stiffly starched, wheel-
shaped collars   56 **fardingales** farthingales, hooped skirts of petti-
coats . 57 **brav'ry** handsome clothes   58 **knav'ry** girlish things   59
stays thy leisure awaits your permission   60 **ruffling** gaily ruffled
63 **bespeak** order   64 **porringer** soup bowl   65 **lewd** vile   66 **cockle**
shell of a mollusk   67 **knack** knickknack   67 **trick** plaything   69
doth fit the time is in fashion

Petruchio. When you are gentle you shall have one
     too,
     And not till then.

Hortensio. [*Aside*] That will not be in haste.

Kate. Why, sir, I trust I may have leave to speak,
     And speak I will. I am no child, no babe.
75   Your betters have endured me say my mind,
     And if you cannot, best you stop your ears.
     My tongue will tell the anger of my heart,
     Or else my heart, concealing it, will break,
     And rather than it shall I will be free
80   Even to the uttermost, as I please, in words.

Petruchio. Why, thou sayst true. It is a paltry cap,
     A custard-coffin,° a bauble, a silken pie.°
     I love thee well in that thou lik'st it not.

Kate. Love me or love me not, I like the cap,
85   And it I will have or I will have none.
                              [*Exit Haberdasher.*]

Petruchio. Thy gown? Why, ay. Come, tailor, let us
     see't.
     O mercy, God! What masquing° stuff is here?
     What's this? A sleeve? 'Tis like a demi-cannon.°
     What, up and down,° carved like an apple tart?
90   Here's snip and nip and cut and slish and slash,
     Like to a censer° in a barber's shop.
     Why, what, a° devil's name, tailor, call'st thou this?

Hortensio. [*Aside*] I see she's like to have neither cap
     nor gown.

Tailor. You bid me make it orderly and well,
95   According to the fashion and the time.

Petruchio. Marry, and did, but if you be rememb'red,

---

82 **custard-coffin** custard crust   82 **pie** meat pie   87 **masquing** for
masquerades or actors' costumes   88 **demi-cannon** big cannon   89
up and down entirely   91 **censer** incense burner with perforated top
92 **a** in the

I did not bid you mar it to the time.°
Go, hop me over every kennel° home,
For you shall hop without my custom, sir.
I'll none of it. Hence, make your best of it.   100

Kate. I never saw a better-fashioned gown,
More quaint,° more pleasing, nor more commend-
able.
Belike° you mean to make a puppet of me.

Petruchio. Why, true, he means to make a puppet of
thee.

Tailor. She says your worship means to make a puppet of her.   105

Petruchio. O monstrous arrogance!
Thou liest, thou thread, thou thimble,
Thou yard, three-quarters, half-yard, quarter, nail!°
Thou flea, thou nit,° thou winter cricket thou!
Braved° in mine own house with° a skein of thread!   110
Away, thou rag, thou quantity,° thou remnant,
Or I shall so bemete° thee with thy yard
As thou shalt think on prating° whilst thou liv'st.
I tell thee, I, that thou hast marred her gown.

Tailor. Your worship is deceived. The gown is made   115
Just as my master had direction.°
Grumio gave order how it should be done.

Grumio. I gave him no order; I gave him the stuff.

Tailor. But how did you desire it should be made?

Grumio. Marry, sir, with needle and thread.   120

Tailor. But did you not request to have it cut?

Grumio. Thou hast faced° many things.

---

97 **to the time** for all time (cf. line 95, in which "the time" is "the contemporary style")   98 **kennel** gutter (canal)   102 **quaint** skillfully made   103 **Belike** no doubt   108 **nail** 1/16 of a yard   109 **nit** louse's egg   110 **Braved** defied   110 **with** by   111 **quantity** fragment   112 **bemete** (1) measure (2) beat   113 **think on prating** remember your silly talk   116 **had direction** received orders   122 **faced** trimmed

Tailor. I have.

Grumio. Face° not me. Thou hast braved° many men;
125   brave° not me. I will neither be faced nor braved. I
say unto thee, I bid thy master cut out the gown,
but I did not bid him cut it to pieces. *Ergo,°* thou
liest.

Tailor. Why, here is the note° of the fashion to testify.

130 *Petruchio.* Read it.

Grumio. The note lies in's throat° if he° say I said so.

Tailor. "Imprimis,°* a loose-bodied gown."°

Grumio. Master, if ever I said loose-bodied gown, sew
me in the skirts of it and beat me to death with a
135   bottom° of brown thread. I said, a gown.

Petruchio. Proceed.

Tailor. "With a small compassed° cape."

Grumio. I confess the cape.

Tailor. "With a trunk° sleeve."

140 *Grumio.* I confess two sleeves.

Tailor. "The sleeves curiously° cut."

Petruchio. Ay, there's the villainy.

Grumio. Error i' th' bill,° sir, error i' th' bill. I commanded the sleeves should be cut out and sewed
145   up again, and that I'll prove upon° thee, though thy
little finger be armed in a thimble.

Tailor. This is true that I say. And° I had thee in
place where,° thou shouldst know it.

124 **Face** challenge   124 **braved** equipped with finery   125 **brave**
defy   127 **Ergo** therefore   129 **note** written notation   131 **in's**
throat from the heart, with premeditation   131 **he** it   132 **Imprimis**
first   132 **loose-bodied gown** (worn by prostitutes, with *loose* in pun)
135 **bottom** spool   137 **compassed** with circular edge   139 **trunk**
full (cf. line 88)   141 **curiously** painstakingly   143 **bill** i.e., the
"note"   145 **prove upon** test by dueling with   147 **And** if   148
place where the right place

Grumio. I am for° thee straight.° Take thou the bill,°
  give me thy mete-yard,° and spare not me.   150

Hortensio. God-a-mercy, Grumio, then he shall have
  no odds.

Petruchio. Well, sir, in brief, the gown is not for me.

Grumio. You are i' th' right, sir; 'tis for my mistress.

Petruchio. Go, take it up unto° thy master's use.°   155

Grumio. Villain, not for thy life! Take up my mistress'
  gown for thy master's use!

Petruchio. Why sir, what's your conceit° in that?

Grumio. O sir, the conceit is deeper than you think
  for.
  Take up my mistress' gown to his master's use!   160
  O, fie, fie, fie!

Petruchio. [*Aside*] Hortensio, say thou wilt see the
  tailor paid.
  [*To Tailor*] Go take it hence; be gone and say no
  more.

Hortensio. Tailor, I'll pay thee for thy gown tomor-
  row;
  Take no unkindness of his hasty words.   165
  Away, I say, commend me to thy master.

                                        Exit Tailor.

Petruchio. Well, come, my Kate, we will unto your
  father's,
  Even in these honest mean habiliments.°
  Our purses shall be proud, our garments poor,
  For 'tis the mind that makes the body rich,   170
  And as the sun breaks through the darkest clouds
  So honor peereth° in the meanest habit.°

---

149 **for** ready for   149 **straight** right now   149 **bill** (1) written order
(2)long-handled weapon   150 **mete-yard** yardstick   155 **up unto**
away for   155 **use** i.e., in whatever way he can; Grumio uses these
words for a sex joke   158 **conceit** idea   168 **habiliments** clothes
172 **peereth** is recognized   172 **habit** clothes

What, is the jay more precious than the lark
Because his feathers are more beautiful?
175 Or is the adder better than the eel
Because his painted skin contents the eye?
O no, good Kate, neither art thou the worse
For this poor furniture° and mean array.
If thou account'st it shame, lay° it on me,
180 And therefore frolic. We will hence forthwith
To feast and sport us at thy father's house.
[*To Grumio*] Go call my men, and let us straight
       to him;
And bring our horses unto Long-lane end.
There will we mount, and thither walk on foot.
185 Let's see, I think 'tis now some seven o'clock,
And well we may come there by dinnertime.°

Kate. I dare assure you, sir, 'tis almost two,
And 'twill be suppertime ere you come there.

Petruchio. It shall be seven ere I go to horse.
190 Look what° I speak or do or think to do,
You are still crossing° it. Sirs, let't alone:
I will not go today, and ere I do,
It shall be what o'clock I say it is.

Hortensio. [*Aside*] Why, so this gallant will command
       the sun.   [*Exeunt.*]

---

178 **furniture** outfit   179 **lay** blame   186 **dinnertime** midday   190
Look what whatever   191 **crossing** obstructing, going counter to

[Scene IV. *Padua. The street in front
of Baptista's house.*]

*Enter Tranio [as Lucentio] and the Pedant
dressed like Vincentio.*

Tranio. Sir, this is the house. Please it you that I call?

Pedant. Ay, what else? And but° I be deceived,
   Signior Baptista may remember me
   Near twenty years ago in Genoa,
   Where we were lodgers at the Pegasus.°   *3*

Tranio. 'Tis well, and hold your own° in any case
   With such austerity as 'longeth to a father.

Pedant. I warrant° you. But sir, here comes your boy;
   'Twere good he were schooled.°

             Enter Biondello.

Tranio. Fear you not him. Sirrah Biondello,   *10*
   Now do your duty throughly,° I advise you.
   Imagine 'twere the right Vincentio.

Biondello. Tut, fear not me.

Tranio. But hast thou done thy errand to Baptista?

Biondello. I told him that your father was at Venice   *15*
   And that you looked for him this day in Padua.

Tranio. Th' art a tall° fellow. Hold thee that° to drink.
   Here comes Baptista. Set your countenance, sir.

IV.iv.2 **but** unless   3–5 **Signior Baptista . . . Pegasus** (the Pedant is
practicing as Vincentio) 5 **Pegasus** common English inn name
(after mythical winged horse symbolizing poetic inspiration) **6 hold
your own** act your role 8 **warrant** guarantee 9 **schooled** informed
(about his role) 11 **throughly** thoroughly 17 **tall** excellent 17
Hold thee that i.e., take this tip

Enter Baptista and Lucentio [as Cambio].
Pedant booted and bareheaded.°

Signior Baptista, you are happily met.
[*To the Pedant*] Sir, this is the gentleman I told
20 you of.
I pray you, stand good father to me now,
Give me Bianca for my patrimony.

Pedant. Soft,° son.
Sir, by your leave. Having come to Padua
25 To gather in some debts, my son Lucentio
Made me acquainted with a weighty cause°
Of love between your daughter and himself.
And—for the good report I hear of you,
And for the love he beareth to your daughter,
30 And she to him—to stay° him not too long,
I am content, in a good father's care,
To have him matched. And if you please to like°
No worse than I, upon some agreement
Me shall you find ready and willing
35 With one consent to have her so bestowed,
For curious° I cannot be with you,
Signior Baptista, of whom I hear so well.

Baptista. Sir, pardon me in what I have to say.
Your plainness and your shortness° please me well.
40 Right true it is, your son Lucentio here
Doth love my daughter and she loveth him—
Or both dissemble deeply their affections—
And therefore, if you say no more than this,
That like a father you will deal with him
45 And pass° my daughter a sufficient dower,
The match is made, and all is done.
Your son shall have my daughter with consent.

---

18 s.d. **booted and bareheaded** i.e., arriving from a journey and cour-
teously greeting Baptista   23 **Soft** take it easy   26 **weighty cause**
important matter   30 **stay** delay   32 **like** i.e., the match   36 **curious** overinsistent on fine points   39 **shortness** conciseness   45 **pass**
legally settle upon

Tranio. I thank you, sir. Where, then, do you know°
  best
  We be affied° and such assurance ta'en
  As shall with either part's° agreement stand?   *50*

Baptista. Not in my house, Lucentio, for you know
  Pitchers have ears, and I have many servants.
  Besides, old Gremio is heark'ning still,°
  And happily° we might be interrupted.

Tranio. Then at my lodging and it like° you.   *55*
  There doth my father lie,° and there this night
  We'll pass° the business privately and well.
  Send for your daughter by your servant here;
  My boy shall fetch the scrivener° presently.
  The worst is this, that at so slender warning°   *60*
  You are like to have a thin and slender pittance.°

Baptista. It likes° me well. Cambio, hie you home
  And bid Bianca make her ready straight,
  And, if you will, tell what hath happenèd:
  Lucentio's father is arrived in Padua,
  And how she's like to be Lucentio's wife.   *65*

                          [*Exit Lucentio.*]

Biondello. I pray the gods she may with all my heart!
                          Exit.

Tranio. Dally not with the gods, but get thee gone.
  Signior Baptista, shall I lead the way?
  Welcome, one mess° is like to be your cheer.°   *70*
  Come, sir, we will better it in Pisa.

Baptista. I follow you.   *Exeunt.*

      Enter Lucentio [*as Cambio*] *and Biondello.*

Biondello. Cambio!

Lucentio. What sayst thou, Biondello?

---

48 know think   49 affied formally engaged   50 part's party's   53
heark'ning still listening constantly   54 happily perchance   55 and
it like if it please   56 lie stay   57 pass settle   59 scrivener notary
60 slender warning short notice   61 pittance meal   62 likes pleases
70 mess dish   70 cheer entertainment

75 *Biondello.* You saw my master° wink and laugh upon
        you?

    Lucentio. Biondello, what of that?

    Biondello. Faith, nothing, but has° left me here be-
        hind to expound the meaning or moral of his signs
80   and tokens.

    Lucentio. I pray thee, moralize° them.

    Biondello. Then thus. Baptista is safe, talking with
        the deceiving father of a deceitful son.

    Lucentio. And what of him?

85 *Biondello.* His daughter is to be brought by you to
        the supper.

    Lucentio. And then?

    Biondello. The old priest at Saint Luke's church is at
        your command at all hours.

90 *Lucentio.* And what of all this?

    Biondello. I cannot tell, except they are busied about
        a counterfeit assurance.° Take you assurance° of
        her, *"cum previlegio ad impremendum solem."*° To
        th' church! Take the priest, clerk, and some suffi-
95   cient honest witnesses.
        If this be not that you look for, I have no more
            to say,
        But bid Bianca farewell forever and a day.

    Lucentio. Hear'st thou, Biondello?

    Biondello. I cannot tarry. I knew a wench married
100   in an afternoon as she went to the garden for pars-
        ley to stuff a rabbit. And so may you, sir. And so
        adieu, sir. My master hath appointed me to go to

---

75 **my master** i.e., Tranio; cf. line 59   78 **has** he has   81 **moralize**
"expound"   92 **assurance** betrothal document   92 **Take you assurance** make sure   93 **cum . . . solem** (Biondello's version of *cum
previlegio ad imprimendum solum,* "with right of sole printing," a
licensing phrase, with sexual pun in *imprimendum,* literally "pressing
upon")

Saint Luke's, to bid the priest be ready to come
against you come° with your appendix.°   *Exit.*

Lucentio. I may, and will, if she be so contented.   105
She will be pleased; then wherefore should I doubt?
Hap what hap may, I'll roundly° go about° her.
It shall go hard if Cambio go without her.   *Exit.*

[Scene V. *The road to Padua.*]

Enter Petruchio, Kate, Hortensio
[*with Servants.*]

Petruchio. Come on, a° God's name, once more toward our father's.
Good Lord, how bright and goodly shines the moon.

Kate. The moon? The sun. It is not moonlight now.

Petruchio. I say it is the moon that shines so bright.

Kate. I know it is the sun that shines so bright.   5

Petruchio. Now, by my mother's son, and that's my-
self,
It shall be moon or star or what I list,°
Or ere° I journey to your father's house.
[*To Servants*] Go on and fetch our horses back
again.
Evermore crossed and crossed, nothing but crossed!°   10

Hortensio. [*To Kate*] Say as he says or we shall never
go.

Kate. Forward, I pray, since we have come so far,
And be it moon or sun or what you please.

104 **against you come** in preparing for your coming   104 **appendix**
(1) servant (2) wife (another metaphor from printing)   107 **roundly**
directly   107 **about** after   IV.v.1 **a** in   7 **list** please   8 **Or ere** before   10 **crossed** opposed, challenged

And if you please to call it a rush-candle,°
15 Henceforth I vow it shall be so for me.

Petruchio. I say it is the moon.

Kate.   I know it is the moon.

Petruchio. Nay, then you lie. It is the blessèd sun.

Kate. Then God be blessed, it is the blessèd sun.
    But sun it is not when you say it is not,
20 And the moon changes even as your mind.
    What you will have it named, even that it is,
    And so it shall be so for Katherine.

Hortensio. [*Aside*] Petruchio, go thy ways. The field
    is won.

Petruchio. Well, forward, forward! Thus the bowl°
    should run
25 And not unluckily against the bias.°
    But soft,° company° is coming here.

Enter Vincentio.

[*To Vincentio*] Good morrow, gentle mistress;
    where away?
    Tell me, sweet Kate, and tell me truly too,
    Hast thou beheld a fresher° gentlewoman?
30 Such war of white and red within her cheeks!
    What stars do spangle heaven with such beauty
    As those two eyes become that heavenly face?
    Fair lovely maid, once more good day to thee.
    Sweet Kate, embrace her for her beauty's sake.

35 *Hortensio.* [*Aside*]. 'A° will make the man mad, to
    make a woman of him.

Kate. Young budding virgin, fair and fresh and sweet,
    Whither away, or where is thy abode?

14 **rush-candle** rush dipped in grease and used as candle   24 **bowl**
bowling ball   25 **against the bias** not in the planned curving route,
made possible by a lead insertion (bias) weighting one side of the
ball   26 **soft** hush   26 **company** someone   29 **fresher** more radiant
35 **'A** he

Happy the parents of so fair a child!
Happier the man whom favorable stars   40
Allots thee for his lovely bedfellow!

Petruchio. Why, how now, Kate, I hope thou are not
    mad.
This is a man, old, wrinkled, faded, withered,
And not a maiden, as thou sayst he is.

Kate. Pardon, old father, my mistaking eyes   45
That have been so bedazzled with the sun
That everything I look on seemeth green.°
Now I perceive thou art a reverend father;
Pardon, I pray thee, for my mad mistaking.

Petruchio. Do, good old grandsire, and withal make
    known   50
Which way thou travelest. If along with us,
We shall be joyful of thy company.

Vincentio. Fair sir, and you my merry mistress,
That with your strange encounter° much amazed
    me,
My name is called Vincentio, my dwelling Pisa,   55
And bound I am to Padua, there to visit
A son of mine which long I have not seen.

Petruchio. What is his name?

Vincentio.   Lucentio, gentle sir.

Petruchio. Happily met, the happier for thy son.
And now by law as well as reverend age,   60
I may entitle thee my loving father.
The sister to my wife, this gentlewoman,
Thy son by this° hath married. Wonder not
Nor be not grieved. She is of good esteem,
Her dowry wealthy, and of worthy birth;   65
Beside, so qualified° as may beseem°
The spouse of any noble gentleman.
Let me embrace with old Vincentio

47 **green** young   54 **encounter** mode of address   63 **this** now   66 **so**
qualified having qualities   66 **beseem** befit

And wander we to see thy honest son,
70   Who will of thy arrival be full joyous.

Vincentio. But is this true, or is it else your pleasure,
Like pleasant° travelers, to break a jest
Upon the company you overtake?

Hortensio. I do assure thee, father, so it is.

75   *Petruchio.* Come, go along, and see the truth hereof,
For our first merriment hath made thee jealous.°
                                    Exeunt [all but Hortensio].

Hortensio. Well, Petruchio, this has put me in heart.
Have to° my widow, and if she be froward,°
Then hast thou taught Hortensio to be untoward.°
                                                    Exit.

[ACT V

Scene I. *Padua. The street in front of Lucentio's house.*]

Enter Biondello, Lucentio [as Cambio], and Bianca; Gremio is out before.°

Biondello. Softly and swiftly, sir, for the priest is ready.

Lucentio. I fly, Biondello. But they may chance to need thee at home; therefore leave us.

                      Exit [with Bianca].

Biondello. Nay, faith, I'll see the church a your back,°   *5* and then come back to my master's as soon as I can.   *[Exit.]*

Gremio. I marvel Cambio comes not all this while.

Enter Petruchio, Kate, Vincentio, [and] Grumio, with Attendants.

Petruchio. Sir, here's the door, this is Lucentio's house.
My father's bears° more toward the marketplace;   *10*
Thither must I, and here I leave you, sir.

Vincentio. You shall not choose but drink before you go.
I think I shall command your welcome here,
And by all likelihood some cheer is toward.° *Knock.*

V.i.s.d. **out before** precedes, and does not see, the others   5 **a your back** on your back (see you enter the church? or, married?)   10 **bears** lies   14 **toward** at hand

15 *Gremio.* They're busy within. You were best knock
    louder.

        *Pedant [as Vincentio] looks out of
            the window [above].*

    Pedant. What's° he that knocks as he would beat
    down the gate?

    Vincentio. Is Signior Lucentio within, sir?

20 *Pedant.* He's within, sir, but not to be spoken withal.°

    Vincentio. What if a man bring him a hundred pound
    or two, to make merry withal?

    Pedant. Keep your hundred pounds to yourself; he
    shall need none so long as I live.

25 *Petruchio.* Nay, I told you your son was well beloved
    in Padua. Do you hear, sir? To leave frivolous cir-
    cumstances,° I pray you tell Signior Lucentio that
    his father is come from Pisa and is here at the door
    to speak with him.

30 *Pedant.* Thou liest. His father is come from Padua°
    and here looking out at the window.

    Vincentio. Art thou his father?

    Pedant. Ay sir, so his mother says, if I may believe
    her.

35 *Petruchio.* [*To Vincentio*] Why how now, gentleman?
    Why this is flat° knavery, to take upon you another
    man's name.

    Pedant. Lay hands on the villain. I believe 'a° means
    to cozen° somebody in this city under my counte-
40 nance.°

        Enter Biondello.

---

17 **What's** who is   20 **withal** with   26–27 **frivolous circumstances**
trivial matters   30 **Padua** (perhaps Shakespeare's slip of the pen for
Pisa, home of the real Vincentio, or *Mantua*, where the Pedant
comes from; cf. IV.ii.77)   36 **flat** unvarnished   38 **'a** he   39 **cozen**
defraud   39–40 **countenance** identity

Biondello. I have seen them in the church together;
God send 'em good shipping!° But who is here?
Mine old master, Vincentio! Now we are undone°
and brought to nothing.°

Vincentio. Come hither, crack-hemp.°   45

Biondello. I hope I may choose,° sir.

Vincentio. Come hither, you rogue. What, have you
forgot me?

Biondello. Forgot you? No, sir. I could not forget you,
for I never saw you before in all my life.   50

Vincentio. What, you notorious° villain, didst thou
never see thy master's father, Vincentio?

Biondello. What, my old worshipful old master? Yes,
marry, sir, see where he looks out of the window.

Vincentio. Is't so, indeed?   *He beats Biondello.*   55

Biondello. Help, help, help! Here's a madman will
murder me.   [*Exit.*]

Pedant. Help, son! Help, Signior Baptista!
                                    [*Exit from above.*]

Petruchio. Prithee, Kate, let's stand aside and see the
end of this controversy.   60
                                    [*They stand aside.*]

   Enter Pedant [*below*] *with Servants, Baptista,*
         [*and*] *Tranio* [*as Lucentio*].

Tranio. Sir, what are you that offer° to beat my
servant?

Vincentio. What am I, sir? Nay, what are you, sir?
O immortal gods! O fine° villain! A silken doublet,

---

42 **shipping** journey   43 **undone** defeated   44 **brought to nothing**
(cf. "annihilated")   45 **crack-hemp** rope-stretcher (i.e., subject for
hanging)   46 **choose** have some choice (in the matter)   51 **notori-
ous** extraordinary   61 **offer** attempt   64 **fine** well dressed

65   a velvet hose, a scarlet cloak, and a copatain° hat!
O, I am undone, I am undone! While I play the
good husband° at home, my son and my servant
spend all at the university.

Tranio. How now, what's the matter?

70 *Baptista.* What, is the man lunatic?

Tranio. Sir, you seem a sober ancient gentleman by
your habit,° but your words show you a madman.
Why sir, what 'cerns° it you if I wear pearl and
gold? I thank my good father, I am able to main-
73   tain it.

Vincentio. Thy father! O villain, he is a sailmaker in
Bergamo.

Baptista. You mistake, sir, you mistake, sir. Pray,
what do you think is his name?

80 *Vincentio.* His name! As if I knew not his name! I
have brought him up ever since he was three years
old, and his name is Tranio.

Pedant. Away, away, mad ass! His name is Lucentio,
and he is mine only son and heir to the lands of me,
85   Signior Vincentio.

Vincentio. Lucentio! O he hath murd'red his master.
Lay hold on him, I charge you in the Duke's name.
O my son, my son! Tell me, thou villain, where is
my son Lucentio?

90 *Tranio.* Call forth an officer.

[*Enter an Officer.*]

Carry this mad knave to the jail. Father Baptista,
I charge you see that he be forthcoming.°

Vincentio. Carry me to the jail!

Gremio. Stay, officer. He shall not go to prison.

---

65 copatain high conical   67 husband manager   72 habit manner
73 'cerns concerns   92 forthcoming available (for trial)

Baptista. Talk not, Signior Gremio. I say he shall go   95
    to prison.

Gremio. Take heed, Signior Baptista, lest you be cony-
    catched° in this business. I dare swear this is the
    right Vincentio.

Pedant. Swear, if thou dar'st.   100

Gremio. Nay, I dare not swear it.

Tranio. Then thou wert best° say that I am not
    Lucentio.

Gremio. Yes, I know thee to be Signior Lucentio.

Baptista. Away with the dotard,° to the jail with him!   105

Vincentio. Thus strangers may be haled° and abused.
    O monstrous villain!

        Enter Biondello, Lucentio, and Bianca.

Biondello. O we are spoiled°—and yonder he is. Deny
    him, forswear him, or else we are all undone.
            *Exit Biondello, Tranio, and Pedant as fast
                                as may be.*

Lucentio. Pardon, sweet father.   *Kneel.*

Vincentio.   Lives my sweet son?   110

Bianca. Pardon, dear father.

Baptista.   How hast thou offended?
    Where is Lucentio?

Lucentio.   Here's Lucentio,
    Right son to the right Vincentio,
    That have by marriage made thy daughter mine
    While counterfeit supposes° bleared thine eyne.°   115

97–98 **cony-catched** fooled   102 **thou wert best** maybe you'll dare
105 **dotard** old fool   106 **haled** pulled about   108 **spoiled** ruined
115 **supposes** pretendings (evidently an allusion to Gascoigne's play
Supposes, one of Shakespeare's sources)   115 **eyne** eyes

Gremio. Here's packing,° with a witness,° to deceive
　　us all!

Vincentio. Where is that damnèd villain Tranio
　　That faced and braved° me in this matter so?

120 *Baptista.* Why, tell me, is not this my Cambio?

Bianca. Cambio is changed into Lucentio.

Lucentio. Love wrought these miracles. Bianca's love
　　Made me exchange my state with Tranio
　　While he did bear my countenance° in the town,
125 And happily I have arrived at the last
　　Unto the wishèd haven of my bliss.
　　What Tranio did, myself enforced him to.
　　Then pardon him, sweet father, for my sake.

Vincentio. I'll slit the villain's nose that would have
130 sent me to the jail.

Baptista. [*To Lucentio*] But do you hear, sir? Have
　　you married my daughter without asking my good
　　will?

Vincentio. Fear not, Baptista; we will content you, go
135 to.° But I will in, to be revenged for this villainy.
　　　　　　　　　　　　　　　　　　　　　　Exit.

Baptista. And I, to sound the depth° of this knavery.
　　　　　　　　　　　　　　　　　　　　　　Exit.

Lucentio. Look not pale, Bianca. Thy father will not
　　frown.　　　　　　　　*Exeunt [Lucentio and Bianca].*

Gremio. My cake is dough,° but I'll in among the rest
140 Out of hope of all but my share of the feast. [*Exit.*]

Kate. Husband, let's follow, to see the end of this ado.

Petruchio. First kiss me, Kate, and we will.

116 **packing** plotting　116 **with a witness** outright, unabashed　119
faced and braved impudently challenged and defied　124 **bear my
countenance** take on my identity　134–35 **go to** (mild remonstrance;
cf. "go on," "come, come," "don't worry")　136 **sound the depth**
get to the bottom of　139 **cake is dough** project hasn't worked out
(proverbial; cf. I.i.108–09)

Kate. What, in the midst of the street?

Petruchio. What, art thou ashamed of me?

Kate. No sir, God forbid, but ashamed to kiss.   145

Petruchio. Why, then let's home again. [*To Grumio*]
    Come sirrah, let's away.

Kate. Nay, I will give thee a kiss. Now pray thee, love,
    stay.

Petruchio. Is not this well? Come, my sweet Kate.
    Better once° than never, for never too late.° *Exeunt.*

[Scene II. *Padua. In Lucentio's house.*]

Enter Baptista, Vincentio, Gremio, the Pedant,
Lucentio, and Bianca, [Petruchio, Kate, Hortensio,]
Tranio, Biondello, Grumio, and Widow; the
Servingmen with Tranio bringing in a banquet.°

Lucentio. At last, though long,° our jarring notes agree,
    And time it is, when raging war is done,
    To smile at 'scapes and perils overblown.°
    My fair Bianca, bid my father welcome
    While I with self-same kindness welcome thine.   *3*
    Brother Petruchio, sister Katherina,
    And thou, Hortensio, with thy loving widow,
    Feast with the best and welcome to my house.
    My banquet is to close our stomachs° up
    After our great good cheer.° Pray you, sit down,   *10*
    For now we sit to chat as well as eat.

Petruchio. Nothing but sit and sit, and eat and eat.

149 once at some time   149 Better . . . late better late than never
V.ii.s.d. banquet dessert   1 At last, though long at long last   3 over-
blown that have blown over   9 stomachs (with pun on "irascibility";
cf. IV.i.152)   10 cheer (reception at Baptista's)

Baptista. Padua affords this kindness, son Petruchio.

Petruchio. Padua affords nothing but what is kind.

15 *Hortensio.* For both our sakes I would that word were true.

Petruchio. Now, for my life, Hortensio fears° his widow.

Widow. Then never trust me if I be afeard.°

Petruchio. You are very sensible and yet you miss my sense:
I mean Hortensio is afeard of you.

20 *Widow.* He that is giddy thinks the world turns round.

Petruchio. Roundly° replied.

Kate.   Mistress, how mean you that?

Widow. Thus I conceive by° him.

Petruchio. Conceives by° me! How likes Hortensio that?

Hortensio. My widow says, thus she conceives her tale.°

25 *Petruchio.* Very well mended. Kiss him for that, good widow.

Kate. "He that is giddy thinks the world turns round."
I pray you, tell me what you meant by that.

Widow. Your husband, being troubled with a shrew,
Measures° my husband's sorrow by his° woe,
30 And now you know my meaning.

Kate. A very mean° meaning.

---

16 **fears** is afraid of (the Widow puns on the meaning "frightens")
17 **afeard** (1) frightened (2) suspected   21 **Roundly** outspokenly
22 **conceive by** understand   23 **Conceives by** is made pregnant by
24 **conceives her tale** understands her statement (with another pun)
29 **Measures** estimates   29 **his** his own   31 **mean** paltry

Widow.   Right, I mean you.

Kate. And I am mean° indeed, respecting you.

Petruchio. To her, Kate!

Hortensio. To her, widow!

Petruchio. A hundred marks, my Kate does put her
    down.°   35

Hortensio. That's my office.°

Petruchio. Spoke like an officer. Ha'° to thee, lad.
                         Drinks to Hortensio.

Baptista. How likes Gremio these quick-witted folks?

Gremio. Believe me, sir, they butt° together well.

Bianca. Head and butt!° An hasty-witted body   40
    Would say your head and butt were head and horn.°

Vincentio. Ay, mistress bride, hath that awakened
    you?

Bianca. Ay, but not frighted me; therefore I'll sleep
    again.

Petruchio. Nay, that you shall not. Since you have
    begun,
    Have at you° for a bitter° jest or two.   45

Bianca. Am I your bird?° I mean to shift my bush,
    And then pursue me as you draw your bow.
    You are welcome all.
                         Exit Bianca [with Kate and Widow].

Petruchio. She hath prevented me.° Here, Signior
    Tranio,

32 am mean (1) am moderate (2) have a low opinion   35 put her
down defeat her (with sexual pun by Hortensio)   36 office job
37 Ha' here's, hail   39 butt (perhaps also "but," i.e., argue or
differ)   40 butt (with pun on "bottom")   41 horn (1) butting instrument (2) symbol of cuckoldry (3) phallus   45 Have at you let's
have   45 bitter biting (but good-natured)   46 bird prey   49 prevented me beaten me to it

50 This bird you aimed at, though you hit her not;
Therefore a health to all that shot and missed.

Tranio. O sir, Lucentio slipped° me, like his grey-
hound,
Which runs himself and catches for his master.

Petruchio. A good swift° simile but something currish.

55 *Tranio.* 'Tis well, sir, that you hunted for yourself;
'Tis thought your deer° does hold you at a bay.°

Baptista. O, O, Petruchio, Tranio hits you now.

Lucentio. I thank thee for that gird,° good Tranio.

Hortensio. Confess, confess, hath he not hit you here?

60 *Petruchio.* 'A has a little galled° me, I confess,
And as the jest did glance away from me,
'Tis ten to one it maimed you two outright.

Baptista. Now, in good sadness,° son Petruchio,
I think thou hast the veriest° shrew of all.

Petruchio. Well, I say no. And therefore, for assur-
65 ance,°
Let's each one send unto his wife,
And he whose wife is most obedient
To come at first when he doth send for her
Shall win the wager which we will propose.

Hortensio. Content. What's the wager?

70 *Lucentio.*   Twenty crowns.

Petruchio. Twenty crowns!
I'll venture so much of° my hawk or hound,
But twenty times so much upon my wife.

Lucentio. A hundred then.

Hortensio.   Content.°

---

52 **slipped** unleashed   54 **swift** quick-witted   56 **deer** (1) doe (2)
dear   56 **at a bay** at bay (i.e., backed up at a safe distance)   58 **gird**
gibe   60 **galled** chafed   63 **sadness** seriousness   64 **veriest** most
genuine   65 **assurance** proof   72 **of** on   74 **Content** agreed

Petruchio.   A match,° 'tis done.

Hortensio. Who shall begin?

Lucentio.   That will I.   73
Go Biondello, bid your mistress come to me.

Biondello. I go.   *Exit.*

Baptista. Son, I'll be your half,° Bianca comes.

Lucentio. I'll have no halves; I'll bear it all myself.

Enter Biondello.

How now,° what news?

Biondello.   Sir, my mistress sends you
   word   80
That she is busy and she cannot come.

Petruchio. How?° She's busy and she cannot come?
Is that an answer?

Gremio.   Ay, and a kind one too.
Pray God, sir, your wife send you not a worse.

Petruchio. I hope, better.   83

Hortensio. Sirrah Biondello, go and entreat my wife
To come to me forthwith.°   *Exit Biondello.*

Petruchio.   O ho, entreat her!
Nay, then she must needs come.

Hortensio.   I am afraid, sir,
Do what you can, yours will not be entreated.

Enter Biondello.

Now where's my wife?   90

Biondello. She says you have some goodly jest in hand.
She will not come. She bids you come to her.

74 A match (it's) a bet   78 be your half assume half your bet   80
How now (mild exclamation; cf. "well")   82 How what   87 forthwith right away

Petruchio. Worse and worse. She will not come. O vile,
   Intolerable, not to be endured!
95 Sirrah Grumio, go to your mistress; say
   I command her come to me.   *Exit* [*Grumio*].

Hortensio. I know her answer.

Petruchio.   What?

Hortensio.   She will not.

Petruchio. The fouler fortune mine, and there an end.

                    Enter Kate.

Baptista. Now, by my holidame,° here comes Katherina.

100 *Kate.* What is your will, sir, that you send for me?

Petruchio. Where is your sister and Hortensio's wife?

Kate. They sit conferring° by the parlor fire.

Petruchio. Go fetch them hither. If they deny° to come,
   Swinge° me them soundly° forth unto their husbands.
105   Away, I say, and bring them hither straight.
                        [*Exit Kate.*]

Lucentio. Here is a wonder, if you talk of a wonder.

Hortensio. And so it is. I wonder what it bodes.

Petruchio. Marry, peace it bodes, and love, and quiet life,
   An awful° rule and right supremacy;
110   And, to be short, what not° that's sweet and happy.

Baptista. Now fair befall° thee, good Petruchio.

---

99 **holidame** holy dame (some editors emend to *halidom,* sacred place or relic)   102 **conferring** conversing   103 **deny** refuse   104 **Swinge** thrash   104 **soundly** thoroughly (cf. "sound beating")   109 **awful** inspiring respect   110 **what not** i.e., everything   111 **fair befall** good luck to

The wager thou hast won, and I will add
Unto their losses twenty thousand crowns,
Another dowry to another daughter,
For she is changed as she had never been.   *115*

Petruchio. Nay, I will win my wager better yet
And show more sign of her obedience,
Her new-built virtue and obedience.

Enter Kate, Bianca, and Widow.

See where she comes and brings your froward°
    wives
As prisoners to her womanly persuasion.   *120*
Katherine, that cap of yours becomes you not.
Off with that bauble, throw it under foot.

                                 [She throws it.]

Widow. Lord, let me never have a cause to sigh
Till I be brought to such a silly pass.°

Bianca. Fie, what a foolish—duty call you this?   *125*

Lucentio. I would your duty were as foolish too.
The wisdom of your duty, fair Bianca,
Hath cost me five hundred° crowns since supper-
    time.

Bianca. The more fool you for laying° on my duty.

Petruchio. Katherine, I charge thee, tell these head-
    strong women   *130*
What duty they do owe their lords and husbands.

Widow. Come, come, you're mocking. We will have
    no telling.

Petruchio. Come on, I say, and first begin with her.

Widow. She shall not.

---

119 **froward** uncooperative   124 **pass** situation   128 **five hundred**
(1) Lucentio makes it look worse than it is, or (2) he made several
bets, or (3) the text errs (some editors emend to "a hundred," assuming that the manuscript's "a" was misread as the Roman numeral v)
129 **laying** betting

135 *Petruchio.* I say she shall—and first begin with her.

Kate. Fie, fie, unknit that threatening unkind° brow
    And dart not scornful glances from those eyes
    To wound thy lord, thy king, thy governor.
    It blots thy beauty as frosts do bite the meads,
    Confounds thy fame° as whirlwinds shake° fair
140   buds,
    And in no sense is meet or amiable.
    A woman moved° is like a fountain troubled,
    Muddy, ill-seeming, thick, bereft of beauty,
    And while it is so, none so dry or thirsty
145 Will deign to sip or touch one drop of it.
    Thy husband is thy lord, thy life, thy keeper,
    Thy head, thy sovereign—one that cares for thee,
    And for thy maintenance commits his body
    To painful labor both by sea and land,
150 To watch° the night in storms, the day in cold,
    Whilst thou li'st warm at home, secure and safe;
    And craves no other tribute at thy hands
    But love, fair looks, and true obedience:
    Too little payment for so great a debt.
155 Such duty as the subject owes the prince,
    Even such a woman oweth to her husband,
    And when she is froward, peevish, sullen, sour,
    And not obedient to his honest° will,
    What is she but a foul contending rebel
160 And graceless traitor to her loving lord?
    I am ashamed that women are so simple°
    To offer war where they should kneel for peace,
    Or seek for rule, supremacy, and sway,
    When they are bound to serve, love, and obey.
165 Why are our bodies soft and weak and smooth,
    Unapt to° toil and trouble in the world,
    But that our soft conditions° and our hearts

---

136 **unkind** hostile   140 **Confounds thy fame** spoils people's opinion
of you   140 **shake** shake off   142 **moved** i.e., by ill temper   150
watch stay awake, be alert during   158 **honest** honorable   161 **simple** silly   166 **Unapt to** unfitted for   167 **conditions** qualities

Should well agree with our external parts?
Come, come, you froward and unable worms,°
My mind hath been as big° as one of yours,   170
My heart as great, my reason haply more,
To bandy word for word and frown for frown.
But now I see our lances are but straws,
Our strength as weak, our weakness past compare,
That seeming to be most which we indeed least are.   175
Then vail your stomachs,° for it is no boot,°
And place your hands below your husband's foot,
In token of which duty, if he please,
My hand is ready, may it° do him ease.

Petruchio. Why, there's a wench! Come on and kiss
    me, Kate.   180

Lucentio. Well, go thy ways, old lad, for thou shalt
    ha't.

Vincentio. 'Tis a good hearing° when children are
    toward.°

Lucentio. But a harsh hearing when women are fro-
    ward.

Petruchio. Come, Kate, we'll to bed.
We three are married, but you two are sped.°   185
'Twas I won the wager, [*to Lucentio*] though you
    hit the white,°
And, being a winner, God give you good night.
                        Exit Petruchio [with Kate].

Hortensio. Now, go thy ways; thou hast tamed a curst
    shrow.

Lucentio. 'Tis a wonder, by your leave, she will be
    tamèd so.   [*Exeunt.*]

FINIS

169 **unable worms** weak, lowly creatures   170 **big** inflated (cf. "think
big")   176 **vail your stomachs** fell your pride   176 **no boot** useless,
profitless   179 **may it** (1) I hope it may (2) if it may   182 **hearing**
thing to hear; report   182 **toward** tractable   185 **sped** done for
186 **white** (1) bull's eye (2) *Bianca* means white

Textual Note

The authority for the present text is the Folio of 1623 (F). Based on it were the Quarto of 1631 and three later folios. These introduce a number of errors of their own but also make some corrections and some changes accepted by most subsequent editors. The present text adheres as closely as possible to F, accepting standard emendations only when F seems clearly erroneous. These emendations come mainly from such early editors as Rowe, Theobald, and Capell.

F's incomplete division into acts is almost universally altered by modern editors, and the present text conforms to standard practice. F has *"Actus primus. Scoena [sic] Prima"* at the beginning, whereas in modern practice approximately the first 275 lines are placed in an "Induction" with two scenes. F lacks a designation for Act II. F's *"Actus Tertia [sic],"* beginning with Lucentio's "Fiddler, forbear, etc.," is universally accepted. F's *"Actus Quartus. Scena Prima"* generally becomes modern IV.iii, and F's *"Actus Quintus,"* modern V.ii.

F makes a number of erroneous or unclear speech assignments (at one time naming an actor, Sincklo, instead of the character). These are at Ind.i.88; III.i.46ff.; IV.ii.4ff. They are specifically listed below. Names of speakers, nearly always abbreviated in F, are regularly spelled out in the present edition. Speakers in F designated *Beggar*, *Lady*, and *Man* are given as *Sly*, *Page*, and *Servingman*, respectively.

F is not consistent in the spelling of some proper

names. In the stage directions, the shrew, for instance, appears as *Katerina, Katherina, Katherine* (sometimes with *a* in the second syllable), and *Kate;* she is spoken to and of as *Katherine* and *Kate;* her speeches are headed *Ka, Kat,* and *Kate*. Since *Kate* is the most frequent form, this edition uses it throughout and does not include the change in the following list. In F, the name adopted by Hortensio when he pretends to be a music teacher appears three times as *Litio,* which we use here, and four times as *Lisio*. Many editors follow F2 and Rowe in emending to *Licio*.

Editors vary in the treatment of F's short lines, sometimes letting a short line stand independently, and sometimes joining several short lines into a quasi-pentameter. The latter practice is generally followed in the present edition. Modern editors are quite consistent in identifying as verse a few passages set as prose in F, and vice versa.

Errors in foreign languages in F are allowed to stand if they are conceivably errors made by the speaker, e.g., errors in Latin and Spanish. Spellings of English words are corrected and modernized. The punctuation is modern. Obvious typographical errors, of which there are a great many, are corrected silently. The following materials, lacking in F, are given in square brackets in this edition: cast of characters, missing act and scene designations, indications of place of action, certain stage directions (F has an unusually copious supply of stage directions, some of which make interesting references to properties).

The following list includes all significant variations from F. The reading in the present text is in italics, followed by the F reading in roman.

Ind.i.s.d. *Hostess and Beggar* Begger and Hostes   12 *thirdborough* Head-borough   17 *Broach* Brach   82 *A Player* 2. Player   88 2. *Player* Sincklo

Ind.ii.2 *lordship* Lord   18 *Sly's* Sies   137 *play it. Is* play, it is

I.i.13 *Vincentio* Vincentio's   25 *Mi perdonato* Me Pardonato   47 s.d. *suitor* sister   73 *master* Mr   162 *captum* captam   207 *colored* Conlord   243 *your* you
I.ii.13 *master* Mr   17s.d. *wrings* rings   18 *masters* mistris   24 *Con*

. . . *trovato* Contutti le core bene trobatto 25 *ben* bene 25
molto multo 45 *this's* this 69, 89 *shrewd* shrow'd 70 *Xanthippe*
Zentippe 72 *she* she is 120 *me and other* me. Other 172 *help
me* helpe one 190 *Antonio's* Butonios 213 *ours* yours 266 *feat*
seeke

II.i.3 *gawds* goods 8 *charge thee* charge 73 *Backare* Bacare
75–76 *wooing. Neighbor,* wooing neighbors: 79 *unto you this*
vnto this 104 *Pisa; by report* Pisa by report 158 *vile* vilde 186
bonny bony 241 *askance* a sconce 323 *in* me

III.i.28 *Sigeia* Sigeria (also in 32, 41) 46 *[Aside]* Luc. 49 *Bianca*
[F omits] 50 *Lucentio* Bian. 52 *Bianca* Hort. 73 *B mi* Beeme
79 *change* charge 79 *odd* old 80 *Messenger* Nicke

III.ii.29 *of thy* of 30 *such old* such 33 *hear* heard 55 *swayed*
Waid 57 *half-cheeked* halfe-chekt 128 *to her love* sir, Loue
130 *As I* As

IV.i.25 *Curtis* Grumio 100s.d. *Enter . . . Servingmen* [F places
after 99] 174s.d. [in F, after 175] 198 *reverent* reuerend

IV.ii.4 *Hortensio* Luc. 6 *Lucentio* Hor. 8 *Lucentio* Hor. 13
none me 31 *her* them 63 *mercatante* Marcantant 71 *Take in*
Par. Take me.

IV.iii.63 *Haberdasher* Fel. 81 *is a* is 88 *like a* like 179 *account-
'st* accountedst

IV.iv:1 *Sir* Sirs 5 [in F, Tranio's speech begins here] 9s.d. [F
places after 7] 19 *Signior* Tra. Signior 68 [F adds s.d., Enter
Peter] 91 *except* expect

IV.v.18 *is* in 36 *make a* make the 38 *Whither* Whether 38
where whether 41 *Allots* A lots 48 *reverend* reuerent (also in
60) 78 *she be* she

V.i.6 *master's* mistris 52 *master's* Mistris 107s.d. [F places after
105] 145 *No* Mo

V.ii.2 *done* come 37 *thee, lad* the lad 45 *bitter* better 65 *for* sir

A Note on the Sources of
The Taming of the Shrew

Some time ago it was a rather generally held opinion that *The Taming of the Shrew* was Shakespeare's reworking of an anonymous play, *The Taming of* a *Shrew* (the conventional shorter form of a much longer title), published in 1594. There were at least two variations of the basic theory—one, that *A Shrew* itself was based on an earlier play; the other (and more widely held), that there was an intermediate play between *A Shrew* and Shakespeare's *The Shrew*. Such speculations were ways of explaining the similarities and dissimilarities between the two plays, and to some extent, also, the apparent inconsistencies within the plays. The latter led likewise, it may be added, to much theorizing about authorship: *A Shrew* was attributed to various contemporary dramatists whose styles were supposedly recognizable in it, and *The Shrew* was believed to reveal the hand, not only of Shakespeare, but of a less gifted collaborator.

Another theory of the relationship between *The Shrew* and *A Shrew* was that they were siblings—different offspring of a single parent-play (either by Shakespeare or by someone else). Another theory of authorship was that Shakespeare himself had helped write *A Shrew*. Long before the putting forward of these hypotheses, Alexander Pope (1725) attributed *A Shrew* entirely to Shakespeare, and in his *History of English Poetry* (1895–1910) W. J. Courthope expressed the same conviction, though it ran counter to orthodox views at the time. The justification for mentioning these points of view here is that, in different ways and in different measure, they anticipate what is apparently the prevailing view at the present time—namely, that Shakespeare's *The Shrew* is the prior play and that *A Shrew* in some way derives from it. (For the first expression of this view, see the bibliography entry under "Hickson.") One theory is that *A Shrew* is a "memorial reconstruction" of *The Shrew,* that is, an acting company's effort to put together from memory a script perhaps sold to another company. This explains parts of *A Shrew* that sound like badly remembered parts of *The Shrew,* but it hardly explains the larger extent of the Christopher Sly framework plot in *A Shrew,* the addition of a third daughter for Baptista, or the changing of the names of all the characters. To deal with these problems there is the hypothesis that, though *A Shrew* is based on *The Shrew,* it is a conscious revision, for whatever reasons, rather than a reassembling from memory. Obviously, much is still left unexplained. But that is true of all these theories, most of which are based on assumptions and likelihoods rather than on very hard evidence. In the end, we do not really know what the relation between the two plays is.

Scholars who believed that *The Shrew* was the later play tended to date it after 1595. Those who accept it as the prior play date it 1592 or 1593.

If *The Shrew* is the prior play, the problem of sources is simplified, for we need not consider the differences between the two plays. *The Shrew* is usually admired for its ingenious merging of three different bodies of material—the Christopher Sly business in the Induction, the taming plot, and the straight love story involving rival lovers (Bianca, Lucentio, etc.)—that are all, so to speak, old stories.

The story of the trick played upon the sleeper when he awakes is at least as old as the *Arabian Nights* (collected ca. 1450), in which Harun al-Rashid victimizes Abu Hassan. One scholar theorizes that ambassadors from the East may have told this story to Philip the Good (1396–1467), Duke of Burgundy, who is said to have played the trick upon a drunken man in Brussels. An officer of the

Duke told it to the theologian and educator, Juan Luis Vives (1492–1540), who reported it in a letter (*Epistolarum . . . Farrago,* Antwerp, 1556). From him it passed to Heuterus, whose version in *De rebus burgundicis* (1584) is the most probable immediate source for Shakespeare (from Heuterus the story went via France into other English works later than *The Shrew*). Shakespeare may also have known the story in Richard Edwards'. 1570 version, one of a collection of prose tales now lost.

In the taming plot Shakespeare utilized another old story of which there were versions in many countries. A possible immediate source is a long ballad (over 1100 lines) published in mid-sixteenth century, *A Merry Jest of a Shrewd and Curst Wife Lapped in Morel's Skin for Her Good Behavior,* but this is a cruder story of a rough and unsubtle husband ("Morel's Skin" is the salt hide of an old horse that the husband kills). Shakespeare, as Professor Hosley has shown, follows the humanist tradition embodied in, and perhaps derives some details from, Erasmus' colloquy, *A Merry Dialogue Declaring the Properties of Shrewd Shrews and Honest Wives* (1557). Several features of the Shakespeare story had appeared in Don Juan Manuel's *El Conde Lucanor,* a fourteenth-century collection of tales of which there was a sixteenth-century edition. Sisters somewhat like Baptista's daughters are contrasted in a tale in Giovanni Straparola's *Piacevoli notti* (1553).

Of the three main elements in *The Shrew,* the Bianca story is the only one whose source may be securely identified. That source is George Gascoigne's *Supposes* (acted 1566, published 1573; alluded to in *The Shrew,* V.i.115). Gascoigne's play, in turn, is a translation of an Italian play, Ariosto's *I Suppositi* (first acted at Ferrara in 1509). Ariosto, in turn, makes use of comic conventions that derive from the Romans Plautus and Terence and the Athenian Menander. The names *Tranio* and *Grumio* both come from Plautus. The Latin lesson may derive from a scene in R. W.'s *Three Lords and Three Ladies of London* (ca. 1590).

The farcical elements in *The Shrew* seem to have inspired revisers to outdo the farce of the original; Shakespeare's play is high comedy in contrast with versions of it that held the stage from mid-seventeenth to mid-nineteenth century. In 1667 Pepys saw an adaptation by John Lacy called *Sauny the Scot*: this magnifies Grumio's part (in *A Shrew,* the Grumio character was named Sander) and gives Grumio (i.e., Sauny) a Scots accent. Garrick's *Catherine and Petruchio* (1756), which cut out the Sly and Bianca parts, was popular for over a century; indeed, toward the end of the nineteenth century Shaw was attacking Garrick for this commercialistic version that was still competing with Shakespeare's play. In the 1920's Fritz Lieber mounted a production in which Grumio was a Negro comic in a bellhop's uniform, and Grumio and Petruchio rode motorcycles. In 1948 Cole Porter wrote the musical *Kiss Me, Kate,* which is only nominally related to the original. However, modern productions tend, with variations, to produce *The Taming of the Shrew* in the 1623 version; the return to this began in 1844, with J. R. Planché's production at the Haymarket in London (under the sponsorship of Ben Webster, an ancestor of Margaret Webster, the modern director of Shakespeare). For more details of the stage history, see the entry under "Harold Child" in the bibliography.

Commentaries

NEVILL COGHILL

The Basis of Shakespearian Comedy

I

Compared with the comedies of Shakespeare, those of Ben Jonson are no laughing matter. A harsh ethic in them yokes punishment with derision; foibles are persecuted and vices flayed; the very simpletons are savaged for being what they are. The population he chooses for his comedies in part accounts for this: it is a congeries of cits, parvenus, mountebanks, cozeners, dupes, braggarts, bullies, and bitches. No one loves anyone. If we are shown virtue in distress, it is the distress, not the virtue that matters. All this is done with an incredible, stupendous force of style.

In Shakespeare things are different. Princes and dukes, lords and ladies jostle with merchants, weavers, joiners, country sluts, friendly rogues, schoolmasters, and village policemen, hardly one of whom is incapable of a generous impulse; even a bawd may be found nursing a bastard at her own expense.

"The Basis of Shakespearian Comedy" appeared originally in *Essays and Studies*, III (1950). It was reprinted, in revised form, in *Shakespeare Criticism 1935-60*, selected with an Introduction by Anne Ridler, Oxford World's Classics (London: Oxford University Press, 1963), pp. 201-227, from which it is reprinted with the permission of the Oxford University Press and the author.

In all this it is possible to discern the promptings of two opposed temperaments; but, more objectively, we should see the operations of two different theories of comic form: for Shakespeare was not simply following the chances of temperament in designing his comedies, any more than Jonson was; each was following earlier traditions, that evolved during the Middle Ages and at the Renaissance, from the same parent stock of thought which is to be found in the writings of the Latin grammarians of the fourth century, particularly in Evanthius, Diomedes, and Donatus.

It must be confessed their observations are sketchy: from their barely coordinated jottings I have taken the following for this discussion, omitting nothing that is relevant to the form and content of a comedy.

From *Evanthius*: ". . . As between Tragedy and Comedy, while there are many distinguishing marks, the first is this: in Comedy the characters are men of middle fortune, the dangers they run are neither serious nor pressing, their actions lead to happy conclusions; but in Tragedy things are just the opposite. Then again be it noted that in Tragedy is expressed the idea that life is to be fled from; in Comedy, that it is to be grasped."

From *Diomedes*: "Comedy differs from Tragedy in that, in Tragedy, heroes, generals and kings are introduced; in Comedy, humble and private people. In the former, grief, exile and slaughter. In the latter, love affairs and the abduction of girls (*virginum raptus*). Then in the former there are often and almost invariably sad endings to happy circumstances and a discovery (*agnitio*) of former fortune and family taking an ill turn . . . for sad things are the property of Tragedy. . . . The first comic poets . . . offered plots of the old kind, with less skill than charm . . . in the second age were Aristophanes, Eupolis and Cratinus, who, pursuing the vices of the principal characters, composed very bitter comedies. The third age was that of Menander, Diphilus and Philemon, who palliated all the bitterness (*acerbitatem mitigaverunt*) of Comedy and followed all sorts of plots about agreeable mistakes (*gratis erroribus*)."

From *Donatus:* "Comedy is a tale containing various elements of the dispositions of town-dwelling and private people, to whom it is made known what is useful in life and what to be avoided."[1]

Let us rearrange the commonplaces from these ragbags of analysis into the shapes that evolved from them—the Jonsonian and Shakespearian forms of Comedy, the Satiric and the Romantic. *The Satiric* concerns a middle way of life, town dwellers, humble and private people. It pursues the principal characters with some bitterness for their vices and teaches what is useful and expedient in life and what is to be avoided. *The Romantic* expresses the idea that life is to be grasped. It is the opposite of Tragedy in that the catastrophe solves all confusions and misunderstandings by some happy turn of events. It commonly includes love-making and running off with girls.

The making of this distinction is neither wholly arbitrary nor original; something like it was formulated by Isidore of Seville (*c.* 560–636) in his *Etymologies*. He tells us that Comedies, by word and gesture, sing the doings of private people and portray the loves of courtesans and the rape of virgins (*Etymologies,* XVIII.xlvi). The Archbishop was evidently thinking of such pieces as Terence's *Eunuch* and uses the phrase *stupra virginum,* instead of Diomedes' milder *virginum raptus*: he also says (VIII.vii.6–7) that comic writers deal with cheerful matters (*rebus laetis*) but are of two kinds, the Old and the New. The Old excel in fun, as entertainers: the New, as Satirists who single out the vices for treatment.

I do not know of any other account or even mention of comic form until the twelfth century. Boethius had defined Tragedy but not Comedy. Unless I am mistaken, the next allusion to it occurs in the *Ars Versificatoria* of Matthieu de Vendôme (*c.* 1150). In true Boethian style he describes a vision of Philosophy, accompanied by Satire and Comedy; he also appears to discriminate between these two: Satire he says is sparing of silence, her brow

---

[1] *Comicorum Graecorum Fragmenta*, edidit Georgius Kaibel, vol. i, Fasc. Prior, Berlin (1899).

proclaiming the fear of wrongdoing, with eyes asquint, testifying to the oblique character of her mind; Comedy, in workaday dress, and with humbled head, gives no promise of rejoicing (*nullius festivitatis praetendens delicias*). This appears to imply happy endings unforeseen, for private people in their troubles, and so anticipates Vincent de Beauvais (*c.* 1250) who, in his *Speculum Maius* (vol. ii, bk. iii, p. 53), gives us at last a classic definition:

Commedia poesis exordium triste laeto fine commutans.

Comedy is a kind of poem which transforms a sad beginning into a happy ending. It was, in fact, exactly the opposite of Tragedy, as understood by the Middle Ages, for they were instructed by Boethius on this point.[2] Chaucer, commenting, renders the Boethian view of Tragedy as "a ditty of prosperity for a while that endeth in wretchedness."

The simple formula of Vincent de Beauvais is the true basis of Shakespearian Comedy—a tale of trouble that turns to joy. It is not so simple as it looks. The claim is that it not only is the shape of a human comedy, but also of ultimate reality. The story of the Universe is itself to be a Comedy, as defined, for those who deserve it; a *Divine Comedy*. So Dante saw it, and so he named his poem: starting in Hell, it moves upwards into Paradise, through Purgatory.

A prose lecture on this theme is to be found in the *Epistle to Can Grande,* sometimes attributed to Dante himself. It adds a further point, worth noting: ". . . Be it known that the meaning of this work is not single (*simplex*), indeed it can be called *polysemous,* that is of several meanings; for there is the first meaning to be had from the letter; another is to be had from what is signified by the letter. And the first is called the literal (meaning), and the second, the allegorical. . . ."

In these medieval descriptions of comedy we see a selection and an expansion of those hints thrown out by the fourth century that we have considered; what was

2 Bk. ii, prose 2.

satiric in them has remained underground, what was romantic has soared upward into divinity; love, mentioned by Diomedes as a theme, has become the center of all in the Beatific Vision. The more modest genius of Chaucer, however, was content to describe Comedy in purely human terms:

> As whan a man hath been in povre estaat,
> And clymbeth up, and wexeth fortunat,
> And there abydeth in prosperitee,
> Swich thing is gladsom, as it thinketh me.
> (*The Knight commenting on the Monk's Tale*)

This was his warm, earthbound but generous way of thinking about it.

The Renaissance view of Comedy was entirely different: suddenly the *Satiric,* after more than a thousand years of hibernation, sprang fully armed out of the ground and possessed the new theorists. For them the proper, the only, concern of Comedy was ridicule; it offered no necessary antithesis to Tragedy, it gave no suggestion, however rudimentary, of containing a narrative line (as did Vincent's definition). Punishment and deterrence were its business; Comedy should be an instrument of social ethics. A few quotations may stand for a host of critics:

George Whetstone, *Dedication to Promos and Cassandra,* 1578.
. . . For by the rewarde of the good the good are encouraged in wel doinge: and with the scowrge of the lewde the lewde are feared from euill attempts. . . .

Sir Philip Sidney, *An Apologie for Poetrie* (c. 1583, printed 1593).
. . . Comedy is an imitation of the common errors of our life, which he representeth in the most ridiculous and scornefull sort that may be; so as it is impossible that any beholder can be content to be such a one.

Sir John Harington, *Preface to the Translation of Orlando Furioso,* 1591.

. . . The Comicall, whatsoeuer foolish play-makers
make it (poetry) offend in this kind (i.e. by lewdness)
yet being rightly vsed, it represents them so as to make
the vice scorned and not embraced. . . .

Such, then, were the two theories of Comedy, the Romantic and the Satirical, of the Middle Ages and the
Renaissance respectively, that twinned out of the late Latin
grammarians to flower in Tudor times. Faced by a choice
in such matters, a writer is wise if he follows his temperament. Ben Jonson knotted his cat-o'-nine-tails. Shakespeare reached for his Chaucer.

II

It is true that he did not do so immediately. His first
thoughts in Comedy were for Plautus. Yet anyone (caring
for poetical form) who compares *The Comedy of Errors*
with its source in the *Menaechmi,* will find significant differences in the shape and content of these two plays. It is
not simply a matter of doubling the pairs of twins;
Shakespeare's play has a new beginning, a new end and
an infusion of tenderness; there is love in it. In fact he
medievalized the story, starting it off in trouble, ending
it in joy. It begins (daringly for a comedy) with a man
led seriously out to execution; it is *Egeon,* the father of
the Antipholus twins, a major character: this gambit is
not in Plautus. Execution on *Egeon* is deferred by the
Duke, but he remains (albeit offstage) under sentence of
death until the last scene. When, however, he is at last led
out once more to suffer, there emerges from an improbable
abbey, a more improbable abbess, who, most improbably
of all, is discovered to be his long-lost wife, the mother of
the Antipholi, and the means of his deliverance and their
reunion. She also is Shakespeare's invention, and turns
catastrophe to general joy. The scene gathers in the whole
cast and concludes in rejoicing, a model to all subsequent
comedy, with a stage crammed at the end with happy
people. The play-world has been led into delight, and
with it the world of the audience.

Although its main business is the fun of mistaken identity, *The Comedy of Errors* is given a touch of delicacy by the language of *amour courtois* (a thing unknown to Plautus) and the invention of a romantic subplot—the love affair between Antipholus of Syracuse and Luciana:

> Teach me deere creature how to thinke and speake:
> Lay open to my earthie grosse conceit:
> Smothred in errors, feeble, shallow, weake,
> The foulded meaning of your words deceit:
> Against my soules pure truth, why labour you,
> To make it wander in an vnknowne field?
> Are you a god? would you create me new?
> Transforme me then, and to your powre Ile yeeld. . . .

Thus could the fantasy of the Middle Ages transform the stolid fun of the world of Roman imagination; it was Shakespeare's earliest comedy;[3] his next, *The Taming of the Shrew,* was another venture with material not mainly romantic.

The Taming of the Shrew has often been read and acted as a wife-humiliating farce in which a brute fortune hunter carries all, including his wife's spirit, before him. But it is not so at all. True, it is based on the medieval conception of the obedience owed by a wife to her wedded lord, a conception generously and charmingly asserted by Katerina at the end. But it is a total misconception to suppose she has been bludgeoned into defeat. Indeed if either of them has triumphed in the art and practice of happy marriage, it is she.

Why is she a shrew? Shakespeare prepares us perfectly for this aspect of her character. She is a girl of spirit, forced to endure a father who is ready to sell his daughters to the highest bidder (as we see in the marriage-market scene, II.i) and who has made a favorite of her sly little sister. What choice has Katerina but to show her disdainful temper if she is to keep her self-respect?

Petruchio is a self-admitted fortune hunter, but he is also good-natured, vigorous, candid, humorous, and lik-

[3] I follow the chronology established by E. K. Chambers in *William Shakespeare*, vol. i.

able. No doubt whatever is left that he admires Katerina
for herself on sight. Though he is loudmouthed and swag-
gering, he is not contemptible; to Katerina he must have
seemed her one hope of escape from that horrible family,
against which she had developed the defensive technique
of shrewishness; it is this which Petruchio is determined
to break in her, not her spirit; and he chooses the method
of practical joking to do so.

At first she does not see the point; her shrew's armory
is put to its hitherto successful use against his Hotspur
manners; it has no effect whatever, except to draw his
praise of her gentleness. What is still more surprising, she
presently begins to sense in his boisterous behavior, an
element of affection; at first she resents it as hypocritical:

> And that which spights me more then all these wants,
> He does it vnder name of perfect loue.

It is not until he positively declares that the sun is the
moon that she sees it is all a joke, and how to handle it.
Her victory is found in a sense of fun as extravagant as
his own, and even able to outbid his in fantasy; when
commanded by him to address a totally strange old gentleman as if he were a beautiful girl, she rises to the occasion with:

> Yong budding Virgin, faire, and fresh, & sweet . . .

and when Petruchio whirls about once more with

> Why how now *Kate*, I hope thou art not mad,
> This is a man old, wrinckled, faded, withered,
> And not a Maiden, as thou saist he is

she reaches the top of her wit, out-joking her husband with

> Pardon old father my mistaking eies,
> That haue bin so bedazled with the sun. . . .

This line should, of course, be said, as I have heard Dame

Peggy Ashcroft, greatest of Katerinas, say it—though typography can barely indicate her sense of its fun, and the glance shot at Petruchio as she said it:

> That haue bin so bedazled with the—sun (?)

After that, victory is all the Shrew's, a shrew no longer, for she has no need to be; and like most of those wives that are the natural superiors of their husbands, she allows Petruchio the mastery in public. She has secured what her sister Bianca can never have, a happy marriage, by a solution not far from that imagined by Chaucer for Dorigen in *The Franklin's Tale*:

> Looke who that is moost pacient in love,
> He is at his avantage al above.

Neither of the two plays we have considered falls squarely into the "Romantic" class of comedy; yet in their troubled beginnings and happy endings and in their infusion of love, or at least of kindliness, they show Shakespeare's attraction to medieval form and content as opposed to the severities of Renaissance satire. They are, however, plays of "middle life." The kings and princes of his comedies are still to come.

III

As Shakespeare matured in Comedy, he was increasingly taken with the theme of love; he may be said to have come to see it as the core of that kind. As his tragedies end in multiple death, so his comedies end in multiple marriage; and they are all marriages of mutual love, or such as we are encouraged to hope may become so. His lovers, for the most part, love at first sight, like the Lover in the *Roman de la Rose*; and like him they are *"gentil,"* for love is essentially an aristocratic experience; that is, an experience only possible to natures capable of refinement, be they highborn or low.[4] In search of this refine-

---

[4] See *The Romaunt of the Rose*, in Chaucer's version, lines 2175–84.

ment, Shakespeare began to imagine and explore what we have come to call his "golden world," taking a phrase of his own from *As You Like It*. He found it chiefly peopled with princes and peasants, with Courtesy and Nature in their manners. It was a world of adventure and the countryside, where Jonson's was a world of exposure and the city. The greatest adventure was love; other adventures, and misadventures, were jealousies and ficklenesses, mistaken identities, wrongly reported deaths, separations and reunions, disguises of sex and all the other improbabilities that can be fancied, entangled and at last resolved into whole harmony by some happy turn of events. It is an Eden world, but the apples are still in blossom.

Two Gentlemen of Verona was the first experiment in this kind, not so great a success as the two comedies of "middle life" we have considered. There was, perhaps, no real model for what he was attempting. Then came *Love's Labor's Lost,* in its exuberance of language creating a new rhetoric for royalty in love, heavily loaded with conceits; it is the work of a young *avant-gardiste,* and full of daring novelties, such as the defying of expectation by bringing Death into the last moments of a farce, and by separating his lovers at the end for a year. He was standing comic form on its head, and he knew it:

> Our woing doth not end like an old Play:
> Iacke hath not Gill: these Ladies courtesie
> Might wel haue made our sport a Comedie.

He did not repeat the experiment, however, and in his next Comedy, *A Midsummer Night's Dream,* he returned to orthodoxy:

> Iacke shall haue Iill, nought shall goe ill,
> The man shall haue his Mare againe, and all shall bee well.

The definition of Comedy bequeathed to Shakespeare by the Middle Ages has a further aspect, as we have noted already, that was important to his imagination; it indicated a *narrative* structure—of adventures that would lead out of trouble into joy; this again distinguishes his Comedy from Jonson's, in whose work the story is not important; he places his characters in a situation that will display their "humors," which are like the *data* in a complex structure of argument, leading by their inner logic to some sort of Q.E.D. *Volpone* and *Epicene,* by dint of Jonson's stunning ingenuity, display their various humors in such a way as to form a story, but one can hardly say as much for *The Alchemist*; there is even less story in *Bartholomew Fair*; their powerful virtues must be found in other aspects of their composition. His characters (representing the humors indicated by their names) suffer no changes and offer no enigmas; nor should they, any more than x and y should change their values in an equation.

But Shakespeare's characters have to be changeable, for they are not fashioned to make possible a demonstration in morals, but to be credible in a world of freely imagined actions, where actions have motives other than those that fall neatly under the heading of a "humor." Let us consider, for instance, Antonio in *The Merchant of Venice*. One might think him at first to be intended as an embodiment of the humor of melancholy. But his is not the kind of affectation that is created to be ridiculed, like that of Morose in *Epicene;* it is more deeply seated, more secret and more to be compassionated.

Shakespeare has invested Antonio with this deep sadness because every aspect of the story that concerns him is unhappy to the last moment of the play. His is the "trouble" with which the Comedy begins; he will not say why he is troubled, but the reason (which we learn later) is that he is to lose his lover to a lady of whom he knows nothing, moreover he will have to pay for the wooing. That he loves Bassanio is not only necessary to the story, but clear from Solanio's remark in II.viii,

> I thinke he onely loues the world for him.

To make credible the turn in the plot by which Antonio must show himself willing to offer a pound of his flesh for the convenience of a friend, nothing less than a high homosexual affection, worthy of the *Symposium,* would

poetically suffice; it is an affection about which Shakespeare makes Antonio both conscious and shy. When
Solanio suggests, as a cause of his melancholy, "Why
then you are in love," he can only answer "Fie, fie." Later
we hear him say, giving no reason, for the reason is
obvious:

> I am a tainted Weather of the flocke,
> Meetest for death. . . .

But it is sadder still that his love does not bring out
the best side in Bassanio: that has to be reserved for
Portia. Antonio elicits a kind of falsity or bombast from
the young man; makes him protest too much:

> You know me well, and herein spend but time
> To winde about my loue with circumstance.

It is another bogus outburst when Bassanio (perfectly
safe himself) tries to encourage Antonio in the Trial
scene:

> Good cheere *Anthonio*, What man, corage yet:
> The Iew shall haue my flesh, blood, bones, and all,
> Ere thou shalt lose for me one drop of blood.

At the end of the play Antonio is odd man out. That
he recognizes his oddity and rejoices in his friend's happiness is well; but he is left alone, as the others move off
to their wedding beds, to find what consolation he can in
the safe return of his argosies. No wonder he is sad; it is
the first sounding of a note of melancholy, the first modi-
fication of Vincent's formula for comedy.

IV

We have seen that Dante, or his commentator, in the
Epistle to Can Grande, tells us that a comedy may be
"*polysemous,* that is of several meanings," and this seems
also true of certain of Shakespeare's comedies. He wrote

in an age when allegory was still a living force. *The Faerie Queene* was published within a year of the writing of *The Merchant of Venice;* it was an age that found no difficulty in accepting the *Song of Songs* as a figure for the love of Christ for His Church, and in thinking of human marriage as another allegory of that same reality.

Thinking in allegory is for us an unaccustomed exercise, but it will not be found difficult if we hold fast to the literal meaning and hear other meanings as simultaneous overtones of suggestion. An allegory should be attended to as we attend to a tune with a descant, that is: simultaneously, separately, and together. Each fortifies and enriches the other; they can, of course, be parted and heard one at a time, but that is not how they were designed to be heard. And just as the tune is always the important voice, so the literal meaning in an allegory is in dominance.

It is not always easy to know what the literal meaning is. We may again take *The Merchant of Venice* to serve us as an example relatively easy; others that have proved themselves more difficult of interpretation are *Measure for Measure, The Winter's Tale, Pericles,* and *The Tempest,* most difficult of all.

A director of *The Merchant of Venice* is faced by a seeming problem. It clearly has to do with an enmity between a Jew and a Christian. Is then its theme the racial and religious conflict of character? Should a producer take sides? if so, can he please himself as to which side he takes? The title page of the second quarto reads:

> The Excellent History of The Merchant of Venice.
> With the extreme cruelty of Shylocke the Iew towards
> the saide Merchant, in cutting a iust pound of his
> flesh. . . .

This announcement seems to justify an anti-Semitic slant; yet, if a producer attempts one, he finds himself presently faced with moments of dialogue utterly intractable to such interpretation:

Shylock. Shall I bend low, and in a bond-mans key
　　With bated breath, and whispring humblenesse,
　　Say this: Faire sir, you spet on me on Wednesday last;
　　You spurn'd me such a day; another time
　　You cald me dog: and for these curtesies
　　Ile lend you thus much moneyes.
Ant. I am as like to call thee so againe,
　　To spet on thee againe, to spurne thee too.　　　　(F)

Or

　　Hath not a *Iew* eyes? hath not a *Iew* hands, organs, de-
mentions, senses, affections, passions, fed with the same
foode, hurt with the same weapons, subject to the same
diseases, healed by the same meanes, warmed and cooled
by the same Winter and Sommer as a Christian is: if you
pricke vs doe we not bleede? if you tickle vs, doe we not
laugh? if you poison vs doe we not die?

The great speech from which these lines come—and there
are others like it—makes it impossible to carry through
an anti-Semitic presentation of the play; on the other hand,
to regard Shylock as the wronged hero of an oppressed
race falling with final grandeur to a verbal quibble, cannot be reconciled with the last Act, in which the agents
of his fall gather by moonlight for their joys in Belmont.
Is he to perish and are they to be rewarded?

If then the play will work neither as a Jew-baiter, nor
as its opposite, there is nothing to conclude except that
either Shakespeare did not know his business, or we have
misunderstood it. The latter is the more likely: the title
page of Quarto may have misled us. We must try again,
and seek a unifying theme that will include these opposites
of race and religion.

There is such a theme and it has a long tradition; its
best expression is in *Piers Plowman*. It is the theme of
Mercy against Justice. In that poem, Truth, who is God,
sent Piers a Pardon for the world. All in two lines it lay:

　　Et qui bona egerunt ibunt in vitam eternam
　　Qui vero mala in ignem eternum.

"Those who do well shall go into eternal life: but those indeed who do evil, into eternal fire." In what sense this is a pardon is hard to see, for it states an exactly proportionate requital, an eye for an eye, a tooth for a tooth, as the principle of reward and punishment; this may be justice but where is the pardon? Where is Mercy?

The poem leaves us unsatisfied of an immediate answer, but opens a labyrinth of inquiry that leads to the story of the Incarnation, the Passion, the Crucifixion, and Descent into Hell. And in Hell, in a great speech, Christ argues His own payment of man's debt:

> *Ergo,* soule shal soule quyte . & synne to synne wende,
> And al þat man hath mysdo . I, man, wyl amende.[5]

His payment on Calvary is available to all who acknowledge their debt, says the poet, and render their dues in confession and obedience; for to do this is to do well, and therefore to go into eternal life.

Now Christ's right to enter Hell and despoil the Fiend of his prey in this manner is formally debated in the poem by the Four Daughters of God, Mercy and Truth, Righteousness and Peace. Briefly their argument is this: under the Old Law, God ordained punishment for sin in Hell, eye for eye and tooth for tooth. But under the New Law of His ransom paid on Calvary, He may with perfect justice redeem "those that he loved," and this justice is His mercy. The New Law does not contradict, but complements the Old. Mercy and Truth are met together, Righteousness and Peace have kissed each other.

Almost exactly the same argument is conducted by the same four daughters of God at the end of *The Castle of Perseverance,* a morality play of the early fifteenth century. The protagonist, *Humanum Genus,* dies in sin and comes up for judgment. Righteousness and Truth demand his damnation, which the play would show to be just. Mercy and Peace plead the Incarnation, and *Humanum Genus* is saved.

---

[5] Therefore soul shall pay for soul and sin shall return to sin
And all that man has misdone, I, man, will amend.
                    Piers Plowman B xviii.338–9.

Now if we allow this Christian tradition of a former age to show us a pathway into Shakespeare, it will lead us to a theme that can make a unity of *The Merchant of Venice,* and solve our dilemma.

The play can be seen as a presentation of the theme of Justice and Mercy, of the Old Law and the New. This puts an entirely different complexion upon the conflict of Jew and Gentile. The two principles for which, in Shakespeare's play, respectively, they stand, are both inherently right. They are only in conflict because, whereas God is held to be absolutely just as He is absolutely merciful, mortal and finite man can only be relatively so, and must arrive at a compromise. In human affairs either justice must yield a little to mercy, or mercy to justice; the former solution is the triumph of the New Law, and the conflict between Shylock and Portia is an *exemplum* of this triumph. I do not wish to suggest that Portia or Shylock are allegorical figures in the sense that *Wikked-Tunge* or *Bialacoil* are in the *Romaunt of the Rose,* for these are only abstractions; but they are allegorical in the sense that they adumbrate, embody, maintain, or stand for these concepts, while remaining individuals in fullest humanity. Shylock, therefore, should seem a great Old Testament figure, a patriarch perhaps, standing for the Law; and he will be tricked, just as Satan was tricked by the Incarnation, according to the tradition of the Middle Ages. A *Bestiary* of the thirteenth century tells us that no Devil-hunter knew the secret way by which Christ the Lion came down and took His den on earth:

> Migte neure diuel witen,
> þog he be derne hunte,
> hu he dun come,
> Ne wu he dennede him
> in þat defte meiden,
> Marie bi name . . . [6]

And *Piers Plowman* has a like idea:

[6] No fiend was able to know, cunning hunter though he be, how he came down, or how he took his den in that deft Maiden, Mary by name.

> . . . the olde lawe graunteth
> That gylours be bigiled . and that is gode resoun
> *Dentem pro dente, & oculum pro oculo.*[7]

We must not, therefore, think the ruse by which Portia entraps Shylock is some sly part of her character, for it is in the tradition; besides she gives Shylock every chance. Thrice his money is offered him. He is begged to supply a surgeon. But no, it is not in the bond. From the point of view of the medium of theater, the scene is, of course, constructed on the principle of peripeteia, or sudden reversal of situation, one of the great devices of dramaturgy. At one moment we see Mercy a suppliant to Justice, and at the next, in a flash, Justice is a suppliant to Mercy. The reversal is as instantaneous as it is unexpected to an audience that does not know the story in advance. Portia plants the point firmly:

> Downe, therfore, and beg mercy of the Duke.

And, in a twinkling, mercy shows her quality:

> *Duke.* That thou shalt see the difference of our spirit,
> I pardon thee thy life before thou aske it:
> For halfe thy wealth, it is *Anthonio's,*
> The other halfe comes to the generall state,
> Which humblenesse may driue vnto a fine.

Out of this there comes the second reversal. Shylock, till then pursuing Antonio's life, now has to turn to him for favor; and this is Antonio's response:

> So please my Lord the Duke, and all the Court
> To quit the fine for one halfe of his goods,
> I am content; so he will let me haue
> The other halfe in vse, to render it
> Vpon his death, vnto the Gentleman
> That lately stole his daughter.

[7] The Old Law allows that those who use trickery should be tricked themselves; and that is good reasoning. A tooth for a tooth and an eye for an eye.

Two things prouided more, that for this fauour
He presently become a Christian:
The other, that he doe record a gift
Heere in the Court of all he dies possest
Vnto his sonne *Lorenzo,* and his daughter.

Evidently Antonio recognizes the validity of legal deeds as much as Shylock does, and his opinion on Jessica's relationship with Lorenzo is in agreement with Shakespeare's, namely that the bond between husband and wife overrides the bond between father and daughter. Cordelia and Desdemona would have assented. Nor is it wholly alien to Shylock who is himself a family man. For him to provide for Jessica and Lorenzo is not unnaturally harsh.

It is Antonio's second condition that seems to modern ears so fiercely vindictive. In these days all good humanitarians incline to the view that a man's religion is his own affair, that a religion imposed is a tyranny, and that one religion is as good as another, if sincerely followed.

But the Elizabethans were not humanitarians in this sense. Only in Utopia, where it was one of "the auncientest lawes among them that no man shall be blamed for reasonynge in the mayntenaunce of his owne religion" (and Utopia was not in Christendom) would such views have seemed acceptable. Whether we dislike it or not, Shylock had no hope, by Elizabethan standards, of entering a Christian eternity of blessedness; he had not been baptized. It would not have been his cruelty that would have excluded him (for cruelty, like other sin, can be repented) but the simple fact that he had no wedding garment. No man cometh to the Father but by me.

Shylock had spent the play pursuing the mortal life of Antonio (albeit for private motives) in the name of justice. Now, at this reversal, in the name of mercy, Antonio offers him the chance of eternal life, his own best jewel.

It will, of course, be argued that it is painful for Shylock to swallow his pride, abjure his racial faith, and receive baptism. But then Christianity is painful. If we allow our thoughts to pursue Shylock after he left the

Court we may well wonder whether his compulsory sub-mission to baptism in the end induced him to take up his cross and follow Christ. But from Antonio's point of view, Shylock has at least been given his chance of eternal joy, and it is he, Antonio, that has given it to him. Mercy has triumphed over justice, even if the way of mercy is a hard way.

Once this aspect of the Trial scene is perceived, the Fifth Act becomes an intelligible extension of the allegory (in the sense defined), for we return to Belmont to find Lorenzo and Jessica in each other's arms. Christian and Jew, New Law and Old, are visibly united in love. And their talk is of music, Shakespeare's recurrent symbol of harmony.

It is not necessary for a single member of a modern audience to grasp this study in justice and mercy by any conscious process during a performance, or even after-wards in meditation. *Seeing one may see and not perceive.* But a producer who wishes to avoid his private prejudices in favor of Shakespeare's meanings, in order that he may achieve the real unity that binds a poetical play, should try to see them and to imagine the technical expedients of production by which that unity will be experienced. If he bases his conception on the resolution of the principles of justice and mercy, he will then, on the natural plane, be left the freer to show Christians and Jews as men and women, equally endowed with such faults and virtues as human beings commonly have.

I now turn to *The Tempest* in which almost all critics have seen adumbrations of mystical meaning. I would first like to seize on what little there is in the way of fact to guide an inquiry that must be mainly subjective. What can we *know* that an Elizabethan audience understood in it?

First, that it is, at the start and at the end, a *Ship-play.* To an Elizabethan audience the stage imaginatively, and as I think to some extent visibly, changed into a ship, both in the first scene and during Prospero's Epilogue. The great bare apron was the main deck, the "inner stage" the cabin, the gallery above it the forecastle and the second gallery above that the masthead, rigging, or crow's nest. In the cabin were the royal party; above were the Master, the Boatswain, and his men. All this can be seen at once from the text of the dialogue in Act I, scene i. It makes it quite clear that the audience is looking at a stage representing *a ship that is going away from them*. I think it reasonable to suppose that this effect was visibly enhanced by the spreading of sails, ropes, and rigging above in the gallery, all of which at "We split! We split!" would collapse and disappear, together with the crew. Gonzalo says his last say and also disappears, drawing the curtains behind him, to close upon the King and his party at their prayers.

At the end of the play, when Prospero comes forth from his cell to speak the Epilogue, the sails are hoisted again; up goes the rigging with the mariners in attendance, and the curtains of the inner stage part to show the whole and happy company as a background to Prospero's speech

> Gentle breath of yours, my sailes
> Must fill, or else my proiect failes,
> Which was to please. . . .

If, with whatever scenic additions, the stage at the start and finish of the play represents a ship going away from the audience, we only now have to ask "where was it going?" and the answer must be, at the end of the play, *"Home."* It is a play about going home. Once this simple fact is apprehended it will be seen that all the action leads to it. "Home" in this case is called *Millaine* and it is associated in the mind of Prospero with the idea of being ready to die:

> Euery third thought shall be my graue.

In between these two ship scenes, we learn that Prospero has been expelled from his natural inheritance (together with his daughter), for having devoted himself too closely to a kind of knowledge that is itself forbidden, that is, to magical knowledge. And he has to abjure it before he can go home with auspicious gales. He has also to reconcile himself with the enemies he has made.

Now if we take such a story on the natural plane of meaning only, it is impossible to account for the deep impression made upon us by the play. Compared with any other play of Shakespeare the sequence of action from scene to scene is tenuously spun. The characters are less sharply observed; villains are merely villainous, comics are merely comic. Prospero himself is not psychologically recognizable in the sense that can be claimed for other male protagonists in Shakespeare. The natural plane of interpretation is insufficient to explain the effect the play produces.

What story then, familiar to Shakespeare and to his audience, does this *Tempest* story of a man and woman exiled from their natural inheritance for the acquisition of a forbidden knowledge resemble? An answer leaps readily to mind; it resembles the story of Adam and Eve, type-story of our troubles. *The Tempest* also contains the story of Prospero and his brother Antonio, that has something of the primal, eldest curse upon it, something near a brother's murder. There is in Genesis, as well as the story of Adam and Eve, the story of Cain and Abel. But in *The Tempest* there is also a turn in both stories by which there may be a repentance and a forgiveness, and a homecoming in harmony. This is the shape of the promise of the New Testament and of the Second Adam. There is the hope of a return to Paradise when we come to die. Trouble will turn to joy.

These simplest and most obvious elements in the Christian story, upon which (but literally and without allegory) the great medieval mystery cycles were built, are, at a distance, mirrored in the story of *The Tempest,* well enough at least to be worth pondering.

There are further suggestions of allegory that an Elizabethan might have grasped more instantly than we can. They believed that man was made of the four elements, the higher, air and fire; the lower, earth and water. It would be no great leap of intuition to see the two first in Ariel, whom Folio calls "an ayrie spirit" and who tells us

he "flam'd amazement" over the tempest-stricken ship.
Caliban, on the other hand, is first addressed as "Thou
Earth, thou," and is mistaken by Trinculo for a fish. If
it is a fanciful thought, the text suggests it; it is there to
be taken. That there is also some picture of the "Natural
Man" in Caliban, whom Folio calls "a saluage and deformed slaue," is not to be doubted; but when we consider
his relation to Ariel, two halves of a pair of servants to
Prospero, he corresponds to him very readily in terms of
the elements; his behavior in the play is a long rebellion
of grosser things; but he lives to repent and return to control under Prospero's will.

I do not wish to suggest any schematized or formal allegory: rather a kind of allegorical impressionism, dabs of
significant color that Shakespeare placed here and there
to excite further ranges of response and yet evade "this is"
and "this is not." It is tempting, for instance, to see in
Prospero the directing intellect, and in Miranda, the soul
he is guarding; their island, shortly to be relinquished for
ever, having for its only inhabitants (when they first came
to it) the elements that will be left behind at their departure, may seem to stand for his bodily life.

But we must hold fast to the literal story in these sym-
bolisms. Prospero has allowed his studies to take him
from his duties as a ruler, and misrule has resulted; his
faults have begotten greater faults in others, particularly
in his brother; his dedication to the bettering of his mind,
he says—

> Awak'd an euill nature, and my trust
> Like a good parent, did beget of him
> A falsehood in its contrarie, as great
> As my trust was. . . .

It takes a tempest to confront them now, across separating
seas and the twelve years that had intervened. It is Prospero himself who stirs these deeps, in a propitious hour,
to bring back into the foreground of consciousness the
guilty creatures that must be faced with their guilt and
then forgiven. His power summons these shadows from

"the dark backward and abysm of time"; he has designated Ferdinand for Miranda in advance; their union is to bind the whole reconcilement into harmony. And, at first sight, "they change eyes"; Prospero has indeed to delay them in their love, for fear the harmony may be too facile; there is a deep wound and it must be healed from below. He sends Ariel to accuse the consciences of his enemies, and the invisible voice reawakens in them the knowledge of their guilt:

> Methought the billowes spoke, and told me of it,
> The windes did sing it to me. . . .

But Prospero has also to make an abjuration; for the last time he uses his "rough magic" to summon "Some heauenly Musicke," the harmony in which he can confront and forgive his self-made enemies. The visual image of that reconciliation is the sight of Miranda and Ferdinand at chess.

After that, Stephano and Trinculo can return, chastened, and Caliban comes back to his sober senses to acknowledge his master and be accepted back into the order of things, into grace. Prospero has re-established his control over evil elements, whether or not they are reconciled, and restored degree in the world of the play.[8] Somehow the Old Adam has been mended by the New, through pardon, and a return to Paradise across the waters made possible. A deep kind of trouble ends in a grave kind of joy.

Yet Shakespeare has gone far beyond the formula of Vincent de Beauvais. Even in the "joyful" ending of *The Merchant of Venice,* Shylock and Antonio are left with their difficult lives to live; and as Shakespeare matured in Comedy, the hint of melancholy, of imperfect harmony, strengthened in almost every conclusion. Someone is left out of the sum of happiness; there is Jaques in *As You Like It* and Feste in *Twelfth Night,* which ends with his sad little song, and a stage empty of all but him; *Measure for Measure* ends in what (I think) we must take for rejoicing, hastily patched up as it may seem; but only after

[8] I owe this thought to Professor T. P. Dunning, in conversation.

long anxieties; Barnadine and Lucio make their chastened escape from the executioner. It is a play without cheerfulness.

In *The Tempest* there is less stark wickedness, and more entertainment; but there is a pervasive melancholy that strengthens towards the close. Though it is a play of homecoming, it is also one of farewell; the ship sails away from us. Prospero is not only going home, but to his long home, with every third thought. It has often been remarked that it is Shakespeare's farewell too, when, in another moment of allegorical impressionism, he seems to take leave of the stage for ever, "our revels ended." The play is indeed *"polysemous,"* as the author of the *Epistle to Can Grande* would have said—of many meanings, many allusions.

But the sadness is more than personal in its conclusion; however Prospero may declare his forgiveness, neither Sebastian nor Antonio have asked for it, nor do they show any sign of accepting it. There is nothing in the text that suggests a change of heart. It is for a director to interpret this as he can. If he sees their reconcilement as impossible, he must show them sullen and contemptuous to the end, as if they would be just as happy to be marooned as to go back with Prospero; but if not, he may gather them in, with some show of feeling in the last line of the play, on the colon provided in Folio:

> . . . My Ariel; chicke
> That is thy charge: Then to the Elements
> Be free, and fare thou well: *please you draw neare*.

I have italicized the cue; it may be made to refer particularly to them. How they respond is for the director to say. If they go back to Milan as treacherous and unreconciled as ever, they will at least be under control and observation. It is an imperfect world.

And that is the thought that seems to me to be at the heart of the melancholy of this play, a sense of the imperfection of things. It is her inexperience, more than her innocence, that makes Miranda exclaim:

O wonder!
How many goodly creatures are there heere?
How beauteous mankinde is? O braue new world
That has such people in't.

But the resigned, unillusioned answer of Prospero is more moving even than her exclamation; " 'Tis new to thee."

It is the Autumn of the Golden World; the apple trees have fruited in Eden and the fruit has been tasted. Evil and sorrow have entered it. It is true that the evil has been checked, and is still under control. The next generation will have to see to it; it is to be hoped it may do better. Ferdinand and Miranda are young and fresh and the world is still new to them. But it began a great while ago; and the time will come when, like the insubstantial pageant of their Wedding Masque, it too will fade and leave not a wrack behind.

RICHARD HOSLEY

Sources and Analogues of
The Taming of the Shrew

I

The problem of establishing the sources and analogues of Shakespeare's *Taming of the Shrew* is greatly complicated by the undecided question of the relationship of that play to the anonymous *Taming of a Shrew*.[1] The older theory that *A Shrew* is a source of *The Shrew*, though it dies hard,[2] is now generally rejected in favor of the theory that *A Shrew* is a "bad quarto"—that is to say, a memorial reconstruction. There is a sharp disagreement, however, about the play from which *A Shrew* is supposed to derive. Some scholars hold the theory that *A Shrew* is simply a bad quarto of *The Shrew*, albeit of an unusual type;[3] whereas others hold the theory that *A Shrew* is a bad quarto of a "lost Shrew play" which itself served as a source of *The Shrew*.[4] The issue has not been resolved,

From *The Huntington Library Quarterly*, XXVII (1963–64), 289–308. Reprinted by permission of the Huntington Library and the author.

[1] For *The Shrew* I have used the Folio text (1623) in the Yale facsimile edition (1954); for *A Shrew*, the quarto text (1594) in the Praetorius facsimile edition (1886).

[2] Artificial respiration is applied by John W. Shroeder, "The Taming *of a Shrew* and *The Taming of the Shrew*: A Case Reopened," *JEGP*, LVII (1958), 424–443.

[3] E.g., Peter Alexander, "*The Taming of a Shrew*," *TLS*, September 16, 1926, p. 614; J. Dover Wilson, ed. *The Taming of the Shrew* (Cambridge, Eng., 1928), pp. 104 ff.; E. A. J. Honigmann, "Shakespeare's 'Lost Source Plays'," *MLR*, XLIX (1954), 302–304.

[4] E.g., R. A. Houk, "The Evolution of *The Taming of the Shrew*," *PMLA*, LVII (1942), 1009–39; G. I. Duthie, "*The Taming of a Shrew* and *The Taming of the Shrew*," *RES*, XIX (1943), 337–356; W. W. Greg, *The Shakespeare First Folio* (Oxford, 1955), pp. 211–212.

yet the particular theory which we accept makes a big difference in our understanding of the sources. For example, if we accept the first bad-quarto theory, *A Shrew,* being derivative from *The Shrew,* does not enter the picture at all. On the other hand, if we accept the second bad-quarto theory, *A Shrew* is very much in the picture— not, to be sure, as a source of *The Shrew,* but as a reflection of the lost play which textual scholars have postulated as a source of *The Shrew.* Faced with this difficult situation, Kenneth Muir, in his general study of Shakespeare's sources, in effect threw up his hands: "The state of our knowledge is such that it would be unprofitable to discuss the question of sources."[5]

Muir's caution was in part motivated, one suspects, by an understandable reluctance to decide what eminent textual scholars have been unable to agree upon. But it may well have been motivated also by his tentative acceptance of the theory that *A Shrew* is a bad quarto of a lost Shrew play which served as a source of *The Shrew.* For how can we know the changes which Shakespeare assuredly would have made in the materials he took from X? And how can we know the changes which the author or authors of *A Shrew* would assuredly have made in the materials they also took from X? There is so much room for lost motion here that one can only agree with Muir that, if the textual situation is indeed as he tentatively supposes, discussion of the question of sources would be unprofitable. The situation has been rather less troublesome in what might be the parallel case of *Hamlet,* precisely for the reason that we do not have a bad quarto of the *Ur-Hamlet.*[6]

---

[5] *Shakespeare's Sources* (London, 1957), p. 259. Compare A. L. Attwater, "Shakespeare's Sources," in *A Companion to Shakespeare Studies* (Cambridge, Eng., 1941), p. 226n: "*The Taming of the Shrew* is excluded from this discussion owing to the doubt whether *The Taming of A Shrew* is to be regarded as a source play or a 'bad' quarto." Compare also J. Payne Collier's failure to include sources of *The Taming of the Shrew* in his *Shakespeare's Library* (London, 1843).

[6] Although *The Taming of the Shrew* did not escape the attention of the disintegrators, it is now generally assumed that the entire play is Shakespeare's uncollaborated work. Compare Ernest P. Kuhl, "The Authorship of *The Taming of the Shrew,*" *PMLA,* XL (1925), 551–618; and K. Wentersdorf, "The Authenticity of *The Taming of the Shrew,*" *SQ,* V (1954), 311–332.

When we turn to Geoffrey Bullough's treatment of the sources of *The Taming of the Shrew,* in his anthology of Shakespearean sources, we find a certain amount of confusion but not many sources or analogues.[7] Rejecting the generally accepted modern view that *A Shrew* is a bad quarto, Bullough returns to the older theory that *A Shrew* is a source of *The Shrew,* even suggesting that *A Shrew* may represent Shakespeare's early draft! His position on the text does not require comment, but it does need to be made clear in order that we may understand why he prints (and discusses) *A Shrew* as a source of *The Shrew.* Bullough prints also two other sources or analogues: Simon Goulart's version of "The Sleeper Awakened" in Edward Grimeston's translation, as representing a source or analogue (Heuterus) of the Sly-Lord action not in *The Shrew* but in *A Shrew;* and George Gascoigne's *Supposes,* as a source of the Bianca-Lucentio action in *The Shrew,* the assumption being that Shakespeare, though he used *A Shrew* as a source of the Sly-Lord action and of the Kate-Petruchio action, here abandoned *A Shrew* in favor of the *Supposes.* Thus Bullough prints only one generally acknowledged source (the *Supposes*), one representative version (Grimeston) of an acknowledged source or analogue (Heuterus), and one "source" (*A Shrew*) which practically all modern scholars would consider to be neither a source nor an analogue; and he fails to print or discuss a number of other possible sources or analogues, most prominent among them the ballad *A Shrewde and Curste Wyfe* which he seems to regard as merely an interesting example of the wife-beating tradition from which Shakespeare obviously departed.

II

Clearly the source problem in *The Taming of the Shrew* is intimately connected with the textual problem of the relationship between *The Shrew* and *A Shrew.* Can the textual problem be solved? Probably not, I suspect, at

7 *Narrative and Dramatic Sources of Shakespeare* (London, 1957–61), I, 55–158.

least not by the usual method of detailed comparison of texts—witness the impasse arrived at by the scholars of footnote 3 and those of footnote 4. One reason for the impasse is that any variation between *The Shrew* and *A Shrew* can be explained equally well by the one theory as by the other; and another is that, while the theory that *A Shrew* is a bad quarto of *The Shrew* lies open to the kinds of attack to which such theories are liable, the theory that *A Shrew* is a bad quarto of a lost Shrew play cannot be attacked at all since there is nothing there!

But if the problem will not yield to scholarly logic, it may yet yield to scholarly prejudice. We are offered two hypotheses; may we not opt for the one we prefer? Naturally we may, though most nonspecialist scholars hesitate to make a choice (in print) lest it later transpire that they have backed the wrong horse. I began my own study of the question by accepting the theory of a lost Shrew play. Gradually, however, I grew dissatisfied with the theory and in time came to believe that *A Shrew* is simply a bad quarto of *The Shrew*. My purpose is not to argue with the specialists who hold with the theory of an *Ur-Shrew*. It is, rather, to emphasize to nonspecialist readers that, since neither theory can be disproved conclusively, we may reasonably prefer one or the other theory without entering the wandering mazes of detailed textual comparison; and to point out, to them and to the specialists, three considerations which led me to my present opinion and which might conceivably lead them to a similar one.

The first is economy of hypothesis. (*Entia non sunt multiplicanda praeter necessitatem.*) There is no external evidence for the existence of a lost Shrew play. (Thus the situation is not to be compared, except conjecturally, with that of *Hamlet* and the *Ur-Hamlet,* for the existence of the latter play is attested to by several witnesses.) The theory of a lost Shrew play is merely a postulate by textual scholars designed to explain the unusual variations between Shakespeare's *Taming of the Shrew* and the bad-quarto text *The Taming of a Shrew*.

The second consideration is that the difficulties which have seemed to stand in the way of accepting the theory that *A Shrew* is simply a bad quarto of *The Shrew* are by no means insuperable. There are, in general, two such difficulties. The first is that there are, within a framework of basic similarities indicating a connection of some sort between the two texts, variations between them in language, structure, and characters greater than are usually to be observed in the comparison of corresponding "good" and "bad" texts. For example, the basic situation of *A Shrew* involves three sisters, whereas that of *The Shrew* involves only two; *A Shrew* lacks characters corresponding to Tranio and Gremio in *The Shrew* and provides the character of a page for Polidor (Hortensio in *The Shrew*); the induction to *A Shrew* is balanced by a "dramatic epilogue" in which we return to the story of Christopher Sly, whereas there is no dramatic epilogue to *The Shrew*—and so on. But such wide variations are not without distant analogues in other bad quartos. For example, the bad quarto of *Romeo and Juliet* contains a scene which, in language at least, varies widely from the corresponding scene in Shakespeare's text (II.vi). The bad quarto of *Henry V* omits one of Shakespeare's scenes (III.i) and reverses the order of two others (IV.iv and v). The bad quarto of *The Merry Wives of Windsor* has nothing to correspond to the first four scenes of Act V in Shakespeare's text, and the last scene of the play varies widely from Shakespeare's corresponding scene (V.v). The bad quarto of *Hamlet* shifts the nunnery scene from a point in III.i in Shakespeare's text to a point several hundred lines earlier, in a scene corresponding to II.ii; and it converts Shakespeare's scene in which Horatio receives Hamlet's letter about the England voyage (IV.vi) into a quite different scene in which Horatio gives Gertrude the information contained in that letter. These variations are not, to be sure, exactly analogous to the variations we are concerned with between *The Shrew* and *A Shrew,* but they do suggest that the authors of bad-quarto texts could, upon occasion, depart considerably from their sources in corresponding good texts. *The Taming of a Shrew* may well involve, upon a grander scale, comparable departures from its supposed source in

The Shrew, many of them undoubtedly originating in memorial error but some of them conceivably originating in conscious design. The other difficulty is posed by variant nomenclature. The names of characters in *A Shrew,* with the exception of Sly and Kate, vary in substance from those of *The Shrew*—for example, Grumio is called Sander in *A Shrew,* Petruchio Ferando, Bianca Philema, and so on; and the scene of *A Shrew* is Athens instead of Padua. Certainly the reporters could not have "forgotten" that the shrew-tamer's name was Petruchio or that the play was laid in Italy. But they might—for reasons that for the moment remain obscure—intentionally have altered the scene and most of the names in their reconstruction; and presumably such alterations would not have been out of keeping with the larger variations in language, structure, and characters which are observable between the two texts. To sum up: the theory of a lost Shrew play is of great convenience in explaining the two kinds of "difficulty" noted. Wherever the "gap" between *The Shrew* and *A Shrew* seems too large for a "normal" good- and bad-text relationship, we can explain the variation by postulating the influence of X. But the postulate is not strictly necessary. We may suppose *A Shrew* to be simply a bad quarto of *The Shrew* if we concede that it is of rather a different type from the bad quartos of other Shakespearean plays—an "abnormal" type, that is to say, which involves a good deal more conscious originality on the part of its author or authors than is usually to be observed in bad-quarto texts.

The third consideration follows from recognition of the artistic excellence of *The Taming of the Shrew.* Shakespeare's play (as preserved in the Folio text) had little appreciation during the two centuries from the Restoration to the Victorian period, as witness the long series of adaptations and "improvements" of which Garrick's *Catherine and Petruchio* (which dispenses with both induction and subplot) is perhaps the best known. Early critics occasionally express an appreciation of the play's excellence. Dr. Johnson, for example, admired the unity of the play proper: "Of this play the two plots are so well united, that they can hardly be called two without injury to the art with which they are interwoven. The attention is entertained with all the variety of a double plot, yet is not distracted by unconnected incidents."[8] Nor does it seem an exaggeration to suggest that the structural unity of main plot and subplot is comparable in excellence to that of such plays as *The Merchant of Venice* and *Twelfth Night*. But it has remained for quite recent critics—notably Donald A. Stauffer,[9] Maynard Mack,[10] and especially Cecil C. Seronsy[11]—to give proper emphasis to the brilliant threefold structure of induction, main plot, and subplot, unified as these elements are by the "Supposes" theme.[12] This thematic unity of a three-action play is perhaps all the more remarkable for being without parallel in Elizabethan drama. Now—to return to the relationship between *The Shrew* and *A Shrew*—if we concede the brilliance of the threefold structure of Shakespeare's *Shrew,* and if we postulate that *The Shrew* had a source in a lost Shrew play of which *A Shrew* is a bad quarto, we are assuming that Shakespeare was not responsible for the basic tripartite conception, for the essential threefold structure would have been present in the supposed *Ur-Shrew,* whence of course *A Shrew* would have derived its own essentially threefold structure. In this case we should be assuming, around 1593, the existence of a dramatist other than Shakespeare who was capable of devising a three-part structure more impressive than the structure of any extant play by Lyly, Peele, Greene, Marlowe, or Kyd. The assumption seems an unlikely one. Furthermore, in this case we should also be denying Shakespeare the powers of synthesis and invention which are so evident in plays like *The Merchant of Venice* and *King Lear,* especially when these are compared with their sources. Such a denial

[8] *Johnson on Shakespeare,* ed. Walter Raleigh (London, 1925), p. 96.
[9] *Shakespeare's World of Images* (New York, 1949), p. 46.
[10] "Engagement and Detachment in Shakespeare's Plays," in *Essays on Shakespeare and Elizabethan Drama in Honor of Hardin Craig* (Columbia, 1962), pp. 279–280.
[11] " 'Supposes' as the Unifying Theme in *The Taming of the Shrew,*" *SQ,* XIV (1963), 15–30.
[12] Interpretation along the same lines is proposed in my edition for the Pelican Shakespeare (Baltimore, 1964), pp. 24–25.

seems both unnecessary and undesirable. As M. C. Brad-
brook puts it, "It is unnecessary to postulate a lost source
play unless Shakespeare is held to be constitutionally
incapable of inventing a plot; for there is no sound external evidence for it."[13]

The reader, then, is invited to accept the following line
of argument. (1) *The Taming of the Shrew* has a structural and thematic unity which is peculiarly characteristic
of Shakespeare. Hence (2) we may reject the theory that
Shakespeare's play had a source in a lost Shrew play of
which *A Shrew* is a bad quarto. And hence (3) we may
accept the theory that *A Shrew* is simply a bad quarto of
The Shrew. Adopting this approach to *The Taming of a
Shrew*, we may approach the problem of establishing
Shakespeare's sources and analogues without the necessity
of considering either *A Shrew* or a supposed *Ur-Shrew*.
A small but important point will illustrate the advantages
of the position. Accepting it, we need not search for a
source or analogue necessarily involving three sisters (as
in *A Shrew*),[14] and we should be inclined to recognize the
special relevance, potentially, of a source or analogue involving two sisters (as in *The Shrew*).

III

As it happens, such a source has been under our noses
all along, in an anonymous verse tale printed by Hugh
Jackson about 1550 under the title *Here Begynneth a
Merry Jest of a Shrewde and Curste Wyfe, Lapped in
Morrelles Skin, for Her Good Behavyour*.[15] This is gen-
erally considered not to be a source of Shakespeare's play.

[13] "Dramatic Role as Social Image: A Study of *The Taming of the
Shrew*," *SJ*, XCIV (1958), 138. This article contains an excellent discussion of the shrew-taming theme in Elizabethan drama.
[14] E.g., the Jutland tale of the Three Shrewish Sisters; see Reinhold
Köhler, "Zu Shakespeare's *The Taming of the Shrew*," *SJ*, III (1868),
397–401. Nor need we search for a source of *A Shrew*, as John W.
Shroeder does in "A New Analogue and Possible Source for *The Taming
of a Shrew*," *SQ*, X (1959), 251–255.
[15] STC 14521. I have used the copy in the Huntington Library. The
poem was edited by Thomas Amyot for the Shakespeare Society (London,
1844); and by W. C. Hazlitt, in *Shakespeare's Library* (London, 1875),
IV, 415–448.

Bullough, for instance, who does not anthologize it, mentions it only in passing as an example of "the Shrew theme common in fabliaux from classical times." "*The Ballad of the Curst Wife Wrapt* [sic] *in a* [sic] *Morell's Skin* (*c.* 1550) given in *ShLib* iv.415ff., also shows the interest taken in unusual methods of taming" (p. 63). And Hazlitt, who did anthologize it, denied a relationship between the *Shrewde and Curste Wyfe* and Shakespeare's play. "The following humorous tale in verse has no special relation in its incidents to Shakespeare's 'Taming of the Shrew,' and consequently none to the older comedy [*A Shrew*] reprinted in the present work; but it is of a similar character, and has always been mentioned in connection with both: it is therefore appended, in order that the ancient materials existing in the time of our great dramatist, and most likely well known to him, may be at one view before the reader."[16] Since both writers regard *A Shrew* as a source of *The Shrew,* it is perhaps not surprising that they fail to see any particular relevance in the *Shrewde and Curste Wyfe:* a lion stands in the path. (As also in the path of believers in an *Ur-Shrew.*) Another reason (I would conjecture) for the position of these and other scholars who have seen no special relevance in the *Shrewde and Curste Wyfe* is an understandable distaste for the sadistic relish with which the husband of the ballad "tames" his truly "shrewde and curste" wife—a virago in the best tradition of medieval farce and *fabliau* (but not unchaste). He takes her down into the cellar and locks the door, tears off her clothes, beats her with birch rods till the blood runs on the floor and she faints, and then wraps her in the skin of an old lame plough-horse, Morel, killed and flayed especially for the occasion. Morel's salted skin quickly "revives" the wife, and the husband threatens to keep her in it all her life unless she yields him the mastership. At this threat the wife's "mood begins to sink": she calls for "grace," promises obedience, and becomes an exemplary wife. This Tudor Grand Guignol is

16 Hazlitt, IV, 415. Compare Israel Gollancz, ed. *The Shrew* (1896): "The nearest analogue in Elizabethan literature to *The Taming of the Shrew* is to be found in a popular poem . . . [the *Shrewde and Curste Wyfe*], but this poem cannot be considered the direct source of the play."

so far removed from Petruchio's "taming" of Kate (even if we accept the deplorable modern stage traditions of having him enter cracking a whip and later administer a spanking to Kate) that it is difficult to see, at first glance, how the *Shrewde and Curste Wyfe* can have any connection with *The Taming of the Shrew*.

Yet when we look closer we find parallels in the basic situation, the characterization, the development of the action, and the language. A man with a shrewish wife has two daughters. (Baptista. Shakespeare omits the mother, as in many of his other plays.) The younger daughter is the father's favorite, *"meek, and gentle"* (sig. Aii^r), sought after by many suitors. (Bianca. Compare Lucentio: "Maids *milde* behaviour.") Because she pleases him so, the father is reluctant to give the younger daughter in marriage. (Similarly Baptista, with a difference that tightly links main plot and subplot at their very beginning, refuses to permit the marriage of Bianca before that of Kate.) The older daughter is the mother's favorite and, like her, a shrew; she is "Sometime franticke and sometime *mad*" (sig. Aii^r); and she has no suitors. (Kate. Compare Tranio: "That wench is starke *mad*." Bianca: ". . . being *mad* her selfe, she's *madly* mated." Petruchio: "And thus Ile curbe her *mad* and headstrong humor.") Finally, however, a suitor appears who wishes to marry the older daughter. (Petruchio.) There is also a suitor for the younger daughter, but this couple drops out of the action and is not mentioned again. (Lucentio.) The father is willing to pay generously to get rid of his older daughter, but, "loth any man to beguile" (sig. Aii^r), he attempts to dissuade the suitor from marrying her: "Golde and sylver I would thee give:/If thou her marry by sweete Saynt John,/ But thou shouldest repent it all thy live" (sig. Aiii^r). (Similarly Baptista attempts to dissuade Petruchio from marrying Kate but offers a good dowry: "She is not for your turne, the more my greefe. . . . After my death, the one halfe of my Lands/And in possession twentie thousand Crownes.") Moreover, in warning the suitor against his shrewish daughter, the father likens her to a devil: "She is conditioned I tell thee playne,/Moste like a *Fiend,* this is no nay:/. . . It were great pitty, thou werte forlore,/With such a *devillishe Fende of Hell*" (sig. Aiii^v). (Compare Baptista: "thou Hilding of a *divellish spirit.*" Hortensio: "From all such *divels,* good Lord deliver us." Gremio: *"this fiend of hell."* Tranio: "Why she's *a devill, a devill, the devils damme."*) The suitor is unperturbed by the father's warning: "Me thinketh she is *withouten evell*" (sig. [Aiv]^r). (Compare Petruchio: "I know she is an irkesome brawling scold:/If that be all Masters, I heare *no harme."*) Accordingly the wedding goes forward: the bride and groom go to church, "And *after them* followed a full great *rout*" (sig. Biii^v). (Compare Gremio's report upon returning from the church: "and *after mee* I know the *rout* is comming.") At the wedding feast the father sadly reflects that his daughter is "as *angry* y wis as ever was *waspe*" (sig. [Biv]^v). (Compare Petruchio: "Come, come you *Waspe,* y'faith you are too *angrie."*) Removed to the husband's house in the country, the wife behaves very badly indeed, openly challenging the husband for the mastery, tyrannizing over the servants, reducing the household to a state of disorder, at one point refusing to provide dinner for the husband, and finally striking him: "And sodaynly with her fyst she did him hit" (sig. [Eiv]^v). (Similarly Kate, in the "wooing" scene, strikes Petruchio, for he says, "I sweare Ile cuffe you, if you strike againe.") At this the husband proceeds to "tame" the wife, by dint of birch rods and Morel's skin. At the end of the story the father, mother, and neighbors, entertained at a dinner, marvel at the wife's "good behavyour." (Similarly the guests at Lucentio's banquet marvel at the demonstration of Kate's obedience.) And in a jingling postscript the author or narrator makes a handsome offer to his readers or auditors: *"He that can charme a shrewde wyfe,/Better then thus:/*Let him come to me, and fetch ten pound,/And a golden purse" (sig. [Fiv]^v). (Compare Petruchio's challenge, in soliloquy, to the theater audience: *"He that knowes better how to tame a shrew,/*Now let him speake, 'tis charity to shew.") All of these details but the shrewish mother, the termagant behavior of a wife in the *fabliau* tradition (as opposed to the ill-tempered behavior of a spoiled young woman), and the brutal "taming" crop up, transmuted, in Shakespeare's play.

Petruchio "tames" Kate not by beating her but by bringing her to an awareness of her shrewishness and thus inducing her to mend her ways. Or, to put it differently, he "cures" her of chronic bad temper. And he effects the cure, as the more perceptive critics have noted, by behaving every bit as capriciously and exasperatingly as she does. More shrew than she, he kills her in her own humor; in fact, he out-Kates Kate. The business of driving out poison with poison, of fighting fire with fire, of driving out one nail with another, is typically Elizabethan—though Petruchio's particular use of the technique appears to be Shakespeare's original contribution to the literature of shrew-taming. And the business of "training" a wife to accept a viable social relationship to her husband, as one would teach a colt to go through its paces or a hawk to fly to the lure, is a commonplace of humanist discussions of marriage. One example seems especially relevant to *The Taming of the Shrew*.

This, which may be regarded as either a source or an analogue, is a colloquy of Erasmus anonymously translated into English as *A Mery Dialogue, Declaringe the Propertyes of Shrowde Shrewes, and Honest Wyves* (1557).[17] The persons of the dialogue are Xantippa, a young wife grown shrewish in response to her husband's habitual drunkenness and general bad behavior, and her friend Eulalia, a more experienced wife who counsels Xantippa to be patient and gently lead her husband to amendment.

> *Xantippa.* He his beyonde goddes forbode, he will never amende[.]
>
> *Eulalia.* Eye saye not so, there is no beest so wild but by fayre handling be tamed, . . . yet recken what paines ye toke or ye colde teache your paret to speake. (sigs. B5ᵛ, C1ᵛ)

17 STC 10455. I have used the copy in the British Museum. The analogue was noted by R. A. Houk, "Shakespeare's Heroic Shrew," *SAB*, XVIII (1943), 181–182.

(Earlier [sig. A6], Eulalia had compared the managing of her own husband to the taming of "Elephantes and Lyons or suche beastes that can not be wonne by strength.") Xantippa's situation has two aspects, both significant in the present context. She is a shrew who must cope with a male shrew. (Similarly Kate must cope with Petruchio.) But, being only shrewish in response to her husband's shrewishness, Xantippa is also a potentially "reasonable" wife who is advised to alter her customary behavior in order to induce her husband to mend his ways. (Similarly, the sexes being reversed, the "reasonable" Petruchio—in behaving like a shrew—alters *his* customary behavior in order to induce Kate to mend *her* ways.) These resemblances of situation are admittedly general, but their relevance is strengthened, I believe, by two specific verbal links with Shakespeare's play. In relating how her husband went to attack her after she had remonstrated with him for coming home drunk in the middle of the night, Xantippa says: "I gat me *a thre foted stole* in hand, and he had but ones layd his littell finger on me, he shulde not have found me lame" (sig. A3ᵛ). (Compare Kate's words to Hortensio: "But if it were, doubt not, her care should be,/To combe your noddle with a *three-legg'd stoole.*") The other verbal link (which crops up in Shakespeare only a few lines after the first) is found in an *exemplum,* narrated by Eulalia, which is itself an analogue to *The Taming of the Shrew,* containing several details which have general parallels in the play. It is the story of a young wife who had been brought up in the country by her mother and father to hunt and to hawk. Her husband "would have one that were unbroken, because he might the soner breake her after hys owne mind" (sig. A8ᵛ). He attempts to instruct his wife in learning, singing, playing, repetition of what she had heard at sermons, and "other things that myght have doone her more good in time to come."

This gere, because it was straunge unto this young woman which at home was brought up in all ydelnesse, and with the light communication of her Fathers servauntes, and

other pastimes, began to waxe grevouse and paynfull,
unto her. She withdrew her good mynde and dylygence
and when her husband called upon her she *put the finger
in the eye*, and wepte and many times she would fal
downe on the grounde, beatynge her head ageynst the
floure, as one that woulde be out of thys worlde.

(Compare Kate's sarcasm at Bianca's expense: "A pretty
peate, it is best *put finger in the eye*, and she knew why.")
At a loss, the husband takes the wife home to her father's
house, where he asks the father "to lay to hys hande in
amendinge his doughters fautes."

> her father answered that he had ones given him his
> doughter, and yf that she woulde not be rewled by
> wordes (a goddes name take Stafforde lawe) she was
> his owne. Then the gentylman sayd agayne, I know that
> I may do but I had lever have her amended eyther by
> youre good counsell or commaundement, then to come
> unto that extreme waies, her father promised that he
> woulde fynde a remedye. (sigs. B1ᵛ-2ʳ)

The father scolds his daughter, frightens her, and prevails
upon her to repent; and she proceeds to mend her ways.
The parallels with Shakespeare are the bad behavior of a
spoiled young woman (not a virago in the *fabliau* tradition), the return of husband and wife to her father's
house, and the husband's bringing about an amendment of his wife's bad behavior without resort to beating
her.

Two other contemporary discussions of marriage, both
by Princess Mary's tutor, Juan Vives, are neither sources
nor analogues to *The Taming of the Shrew* but do help
to define the humanist tradition of inducing a shrewish
wife to mend her ways, which Shakespeare evidently pre-
ferred to the *fabliau* tradition of wife-beating. The first is
The Office and Duetie of an Husband, translated by
Thomas Paynell.[18] In this, Vives advises the husband
never to proceed to the extreme of violence—so long as
his wife is chaste (sig. 2A5ʳ). ". . . the bow must not be

[18] London, ca. 1553, *STC* 24855 (copy in the Huntington Library).

broken with to muche bendynge therof" (sig. 2A5ᵛ). Rather, the husband should seek to "purge" his wife of a vice (sig. 2B2ᵛ). And Vives, like Erasmus, uses the image of training an animal:

> The Breaker of horsses that doeth use to ride and to pace theym, doeth handle the rough and sturdy colte with all crafte and fearcenes that maye be, but with it that is more tractable, he taketh not so greate payne. A sharpe wyfe must be pleased and mitigated with love, and ruled wyth Majestye. . . . (sig. N7ᵛ)

(Similarly Petruchio compares, at some length, his "taming" of Kate to the training of a hawk.) The other discussion of marriage by Vives is in *A Very Fruteful and Pleasant Boke Callyd the Instruction of a Christen Woman,* translated by Richard Hyrde in about 1529.[19] A significant passage deals with the relation of the wife to the husband:

> The woman is nat rekened the more worshipfull amonge men, that presumeth to have maystrye above hir housbande: but the more folysshe, and the more woorthy to be mocked: yea and more over than that, cursed and unhappy: the whiche turneth backewarde the lawes of nature, lyke as though a souldiour wolde rule his capitayne, or the mone wolde stande above the sonne, or the arme above the head. For in wedlocke the man resembleth the reason, and the woman the body. Nowe reason ought to rule, and the body to obey, if a man wyll lyve. Also saynte Paule sayth: The head of the woman is the man. (foll. 71ᵛ–72ʳ)

(Compare Kate's long speech on the proper subordination of wife to husband: "Such dutie as the subject owes the Prince,/Even such a woman oweth to her husband. . . .") And another significant passage suggests the paradox (sometimes emphasized in modern productions by an

19 I have used the edition of 1541, *STC* 24858 (copy in the Huntington Library).

ironic delivery of Kate's speech on subordination of the wife) that she who is ruled can also rule:

> But on the other partie, if thou by vertuous lyvyng and buxumnes, geve hym cause to love the, thou shalte be maistres in a mery house, thou shalte rejoyse, thou shalt be gladde, thou shalt blesse the daie that thou were maryed unto hym, and all them that were helping there unto. The wyse sentence saieth: *A good woman by lowely obeysaunce ruleth hir husbande.* (fol. 64)

At least three elements of the main plot of *The Taming of the Shrew* have identifiable sources or analogues. The first is the episode of Petruchio's rating the Tailor for cutting Kate's gown in fantastical fashion (IV.iii). A source or analogue of this episode appears in Gerard Legh's *Accedens of Armory* (1562), a discursive dialogue on the science of armorial bearings.[20] Legh relates the following anecdote about Sir Philip Caulthrop, a knight of Norwich in the time of Henry VII. Sir Philip brought some fine French tawny and commissioned his tailor to make it into a gown. John Drakes, a shoemaker, happened to see the cloth at the tailor's, was pleased by it, and asked the tailor to make him a gown of the same material and in the same fashion as the knight's. During a fitting the knight noticed the second gown and, when apprised of the situation, commanded that his own gown be "made as full of cuts as thy sheres can make it." Both gowns, of course, were so treated, and Drakes was furious when he discovered the state of his. "I have don nothing quoth the Tailor, but that you bade mee, for as sir Philip Caltrops is, even so have I made yours. By my latchet quoth John Drake, I will never were gentlemans fashion againe" (fol. 112).

The second is the episode of Kate's agreeing with Petruchio in his assertion of what is palpably untrue, to the consternation of Vincentio whom they have met on the road (IV.v). An analogue of this episode occurs in *El Conde Lucanor,* a collection of stories made by Don Juan

20 I have used the edition of 1568, *STC* 15389 (copy in the Huntington Library).

Manuel, Infante of Castile, in 1335–1347.[21] Vascuñana, the wife of Don Alvar Fañez, is a paragon, and accordingly he treats her very well. His nephew criticizes him as uxorious. Shortly thereafter Don Alvar and the nephew go on a journey together, and Don Alvar sends for his wife. While they are waiting they see a herd of cows which Don Alvar calls mares. The nephew protests. When Vascuñana arrives she supports her husband, maintaining that the animals are indeed mares, even though she knows perfectly well that they are cows. She behaves similarly in the case of a herd of mares which Don Alvar calls cows, and in that of a river which he insists is flowing toward its source. The nephew is confounded, and Don Alvar lectures him on the satisfactions of having an agreeable wife.

And the third is the wager which Petruchio, Lucentio, and Hortensio make on their wives' obedience (V.ii). An analogue of this episode occurs in *The Book of the Knight of La Tour-Landry,* a collection of stories made by the Angevin knight Geoffrey de la Tour-Landry in 1372–1373 and translated into English by Caxton (who printed his own translation in 1484).[22] Here three merchants wager a jewel, to be won by him whose wife obeys best. Each will order his wife to jump into a basin set before her. The first and second wives in turn refuse to obey, and each is in turn beaten by her husband. The merchants then pass to the house of the third merchant, where he entertains them at a dinner. Before being put to the test, the third wife misunderstands her husband to say jump on the table ("Sayle sur table") when he is only calling for salt ("Sail" or "Sel sur table"). She obeys his supposed command, making a frightful mess of the food, wine, and tableware, and this so amuses the others that

21 *Count Lucanor,* trans. James York (London, 1898), Ch. v. The analogue was noted by J. O. Halliwell, ed. *The Shrew* (1856). A direct connection with Shakespeare has been (rightly) denied by M. Alcalá, "Don Juan Manuel y Shakespeare: Una Influencia Imposible," *Filosofía y Letras,* X (1945), 55–67.

22 STC 15296. I have used the edition by G. B. Rawlings, *The Booke of Thenseygnementes and Techynge that the Knyght of the Towre Made to His Doughters* (London, 1902). A variant translation in manuscript has been edited by Thomas Wright for the EETS (Oxford, 1868). The analogue was noted by Albert H. Tolman, "Shakespeare's Part in *The Taming of the Shrew,*" *PMLA,* V (1890), 238–239.

they judge her husband to have won the wager and do not require the test of the basin. Points of contact with *The Taming of the Shrew* are the wager and the obedience test won by the third wife, the merchant's dinner table (compare Lucentio's banquet table), and the Knight's closing comment on the impropriety of beating a wife of gentle station (compare Petruchio's forbearance in this regard).

The source of the subplot of *The Taming of the Shrew* is generally acknowledged to be Ariosto's *Suppositi*, or rather Gascoigne's English translation of Ariosto, the *Supposes* (1573; printed by Bullough). Shakespeare's debt to the tradition of Renaissance romantic comedy (whether English or Italian) is generally recognized in his suppression of Polynesta's promiscuity and pregnancy,[23] as also in his giving Bianca a much larger share in the action than Polynesta (who comes on stage only twice, and then to speak in only one scene). Other significant aspects of Shakespeare's handling of the story are perhaps less widely recognized. Chief among these are the shift of the story from the retrospective to the progressive mode of drama (and Ariosto's skillful conformance to the unities, incidentally, is itself deserving of praise); the provision in Hortensio of a second undercover wooer for Bianca, with the result that the girl exercises choice between competitive suitors who have secret access to her; and the addition of a "stolen marriage"—not strictly necessary for the conduct of the plot (since the arrival of the true Vincentio would itself untie all knots) but expressive of the romantic-comedy principle (as in *The Merry Wives of Windsor*) that true lovers should proceed to marry whom they like, without regard for their parents' wishes. The character type of the sympathetic rival suitor (Hortensio, as opposed to the aged suitor Gremio or the fake suitor Tranio) and the device of the stolen marriage, since these occur neither in Roman comedy nor in the *Supposes,* evidently came to Shakespeare from the tradition of Renaissance romantic

---

[23] Compare H. B. Charlton, *Shakespearian Comedy* (London, 1938), Ch. iv. This essay is especially useful in relating *The Taming of the Shrew* to traditions of the *commedia erudita.*

comedy—perhaps specifically from the *commedia erudita*. Hortensio serves also to link main plot and subplot, and since his character as suitor is essentially sympathetic (though gently mocked) he is matched with the Widow— a sort of *madonna ex machina*—at the end of the play.

Shakespeare took the names *Petruchio* and *Litio* (Hortensio's alias) from the names of servants in the *Supposes*. The former is of course a phonetic spelling (with vocalic "i") of *Petrucio* or *Petruccio* (with nonvocalic "i") and should never be given the vulgar pronunciation *Petrukio*. A short textual note may be advanced about the latter. In the Folio text (1623) the name is spelled *Litio* at II.i.60, III.i.54, and III.ii.146, *Lisio* at IV.ii.1, 15, 16, and 49. The Second Folio (1632) reads *Licio* at II.i.60, and Rowe (1709) and subsequent editors read *Licio* throughout (whence occasionally the mispronunciation *Leech-io* or *Leech-o*). But *Litio,* the form in the *Supposes,* is a spelling variant of *Lizio,* the form in Ariosto's verse version of the *Suppositi* (*Lico* in the prose). The name is apparently a joke in the New Comedy tradition of significant names, for *lizio* is an old Italian word for garlic (Hoare's *Italian Dictionary*; the word does not appear in Florio's *World of Words*). Since *Lisio* appears to be a phonetic spelling of *Litio,* an editor may justifiably read *Litio* throughout a normalized old-spelling text, *Litio* or *Lizio* throughout a modern-spelling text. One other, rather puzzling, aspect of Shakespeare's text may be mentioned. In Gascoigne (and Ariosto) the fake father is a merchant. The corresponding character in Shakespeare is also a merchant, though this does not seem to have been generally noticed: "For I have bils for monie by exchange/ From Florence, and must heere deliver them." Yet he is invariably called a Pedant in the stage directions and speech-headings! Apparently Shakespeare chose the wrong profession from the alternatives which, in the dialogue, he himself put into Biondello's mouth: "Master, a Marcantant [i.e., *mercatante*], or a pedant, I know not what."

Shakespeare's names *Tranio* (connoting "revealer, clarifier") and *Grumio* (connoting "clodhopper") have sources in the *Mostellaria* of Plautus, as do also the contrasting characters of clever servant and thickheaded one.[24] (But the two types of slave are generally characteristic of Roman comedy.) Grumio's beating at Petruchio's hands is paralleled in the *Mostellaria,* and the Tranio of that play (like Shakespeare's Tranio and Ariosto's Dulipo) deceives the father of his young master. Two devices of the plot which came to Shakespeare from the *Supposes* have ultimate origins in Roman comedy: the exchange of identity between servant and master, in *The Captives* of Plautus (where, however, the context of the device is not amatory); and (as Bullough points out) the "lock-out," in the *Amphitruo* of Plautus (where the context of the device is amatory), already used by Shakespeare in *The Comedy of Errors.* Ariosto followed Plautus (*The Captives*) in providing an end-of-the-play "recognition" of Dulipo as Cleander's long-lost son. By this token Shakespeare's Tranio should turn out to be Gremio's son—but perhaps Shakespeare (who in any case did not give Gremio Cleander's strong motivation to get a son and heir) wished to avoid an additional complication of his last scene, even at the expense of seeming to leave both Tranio and Gremio out in the cold. For that matter, the curious treatment (in the last scene) of Tranio as Lucentio's equal in rank may well be a fossil of Dulipo's "recognition" in the *Supposes.*

At least one element of the subplot of *The Taming of the Shrew* has an identifiable analogue. This is the device of Lucentio's wooing of Bianca under the guise of construing a Latin text (III.i). The analogue occurs in R.W.'s play *The Three Lords and Three Ladies of London* (1590).[25] In Simplicity's directions for the punishment of Fraud we are again in the classroom—though in a lower form from that to which Bianca, in reading Ovid's *Epistolae heroidum,* has attained:

O Singulariter *Nominativo,* wise Lord *pleasure: Genetivo*
bind him to that poste, *Dativo.* give me my torch,

[24] *Mostellaria,* ed. Edwin W. Fay (New York, 1902), pp. 63–64.
[25] *STC* 25783 (copy in the Huntington Library). The analogue was noted by Gollancz, ed. *The Shrew* (1896).

Accusat. For I say he's a cosener. *Vocat.* O give me
roome to run at him. *Ablat.* take and blind me. *Plur-
aliter, per omnes casus.* Laugh all you to see mee in my
choller adust to burne and to broile that false *Fraud*
to dust. (sig. 13ᵛ)

But the general conception of Shakespeare's scene may
have a source or analogue in some example of the *commedia erudita* in which an *innamorato* disguises himself as
a *pedante* in order to gain access to a *donzella*.

Finally, the induction to *The Taming of the Shrew* has
a generally acknowledged source in the story of "The
Sleeper Awakened" (ultimately from *The Arabian Nights*),
either in the version contained in a letter from Vives to
Francis Duke of Béjar,[26] in a lost collection of stories
compiled by Richard Edwards and printed in 1570,[27] or
in the *De rebus burgundicis* of Heuterus (1584). The
story in Heuterus was translated into French by Goulart,
in his *Thrésor d'histoires admirables et mémorables de
nostre temps* (1600); and Goulart's version was translated into English by Grimeston (1607). (Bullough prints
Grimeston.) The version in Heuterus (as represented by
Grimeston) is suggestive since the viewing of "a pleasant
Comedie" is included in the entertainment of the deluded
artisan who corresponds to Shakespeare's Sly. In all narrative versions of the story we are told of the return of
the artisan to his original condition before elevation to
high rank. But in Shakespeare's dramatic version (the
first in which the story is used as introduction to an actual
play) Sly drops out of the action after the first scene of
the play proper and is (apparently) forgotten. This fact
and the appearance of a "dramatic epilogue" in *The Taming of a Shrew* have led some scholars to suppose that the
Folio text of *The Shrew* is defective in omitting a dramatic
epilogue by Shakespeare. However, as I have suggested
elsewhere,[28] there would have been a number of reasons

26 See Foster Watson, "Shakespeare and Two Stories of Luis Vives,"
Nineteenth Century, LXXXV (1919) 297–306.
27 Thomas Warton records having seen the book in his *History of
English Poetry* (London, 1775), Sec. LII.
28 "Was There a 'Drámatic Epilogue' to *The Taming of the Shrew?*"
SEL, I (1961), 17–34; ed. *The Shrew* (1964), p. 24.

for Shakespeare's apparent failure to provide a dramatic epilogue: a desire to avoid the anticlimax which would result from a return, at the end of the play proper, to the different fictional situation of the induction; a desire to present, not (as in *A Shrew*) Sly's learning of a lesson in shrew-taming (Shakespeare's Sly seems not to have a wife), but Sly's being persuaded by the Lord to accept a new personality (for exactly so will Petruchio persuade Kate); and a desire to facilitate the Elizabethan theatrical practice of doubling parts of the induction with parts of the play proper—for an awkward pause would have been necessary to enable actors on stage at the end of the play to return to the costumes of their roles in the induction.

From the present study there emerges an understanding of Shakespeare's *Taming of the Shrew* as a synthesis of many sources and traditions.[29] The induction derives from the story of "The Sleeper Awakened," perhaps as told by Heuterus in *De rebus burgundicis*. The basic situation of the play proper is taken from the anonymous ballad of *A Shrewde and Curste Wyfe*. The main plot is animated, however, not by the *fabliau* tradition of beating a virago into submission but by the humanist tradition of inducing a spoiled young wife to mend her ways—perhaps specifically by the *Shrewd Shrews and Honest Wives* of Erasmus. The basic situation of the play proper is filled out with a subplot derived from Gascoigne's *Supposes,* and both actions are embellished with episodes taken from traditions represented by analogues in Gerard Legh's *Accedens of Armory,* Don Juan Manuel's *Conde Lucanor, The Book of the Knight of La Tour-Landry,* and R.W.'s *Three Lords and Three Ladies of London.* Two names come from the *Mostellaria* of Plautus, and much of the spirit and technique of the play comes from Roman comedy in general, much also from romantic comedy of the Renaissance—perhaps specifically from the *commedia*

29 A story (viii.2) in Straparola's *Piacevoli notti* (1560), though suggested as an analogue by Halliwell, ed. *The Shrew* (1856), and subsequent editors, seems to have no particular connection with *The Taming of the Shrew*.

erudita. Further search should turn up additional sources and analogues, certainly of details, possibly of major elements in the three actions of the play.[30]

[30] It is a pleasure to record my indebtedness to the Director and Trustees of the Henry E. Huntington Library for a fellowship grant which made possible the research on which this article is based.

HAROLD C. GODDARD

from *The Meaning of Shakespeare*

I

Richard III proves that *double entendre* was a passion of the youthful Shakespeare, and both *The Two Gentlemen of Verona* and *Love's Labor's Lost* illustrate the fact that he was fond of under- and overmeanings he could not have expected his audience as a whole to get. But it is *The Taming of the Shrew* that is possibly the most striking example among his early works of his love of so contriving a play that it should mean, to those who might choose to take it so, the precise opposite of what he knew it would mean to the multitude. For surely the most psychologically sound as well as the most delightful way of taking *The Taming of the Shrew* is the topsy-turvy one. Kate, in that case, is no shrew at all except in the most superficial sense. Bianca, on the other hand, is just what her sister is supposed to be. And the play ends with the prospect that Kate is going to be more nearly the tamer than the tamed, Petruchio more nearly the tamed than the tamer, though his wife naturally will keep the true situation under cover. So taken, the play is an early version of *What Every Woman Knows*—what every woman knows being, of course, that the woman can lord it over the man so long as she allows him to think he is lording it over her. This interpretation has the advantage of bring-

From *The Meaning of Shakespeare*. Chicago: University of Chicago Press, 1951, I, pp. 68–69, 71–72. Reprinted by permission of the University of Chicago Press.

ing the play into line with all the other Comedies in which Shakespeare gives a distinct edge to his heroine. Otherwise it is an unaccountable exception and regresses to the wholly un-Shakespearean doctrine of male superiority, a view which there is not the slightest evidence elsewhere Shakespeare ever held.

II

We must never for a moment allow ourselves to forget that *The Taming of the Shrew* is a play within a play, an interlude put on by a company of strolling players at the house of a great lord for the gulling of Christopher Sly, the drunken tinker, and thereby for the double entertainment of the audience. For the sake of throwing the picture into strong relief against the frame—as in a different sense in the case of *The Murder of Gonzago* in *Hamlet*—the play within the play is given a simplification and exaggeration that bring its main plot to the edge of farce, while its minor plot, the story of Bianca's wooers, goes quite over that edge. But, even allowing for this, the psychology of the Katharine-Petruchio plot is remarkably realistic. It is even "modern" in its psychoanalytical implications. It is based on the familiar situation of the favorite child. Baptista is a family tyrant and Bianca is his favorite daughter. She has to the casual eye all the outer marks of modesty and sweetness, but to a discerning one all the inner marks of a spoiled pet, remade, if not originally made, in her father's image. One line is enough to give us her measure. When in the wager scene at the end her husband tells her that her failure to come at his entreaty has cost him a hundred crowns,

> The more fool you for laying on my duty,

she blurts out. What a light that casts back over her previous "sweetness" before she has caught her man! The rest of her role amply supports this interpretation, as do the hundreds of Biancas—who are not as white as they are painted—in real life.

Apart from the irony and the effective contrast so obtained, there is everything to indicate that Kate's shrewishness is superficial, not ingrained or congenital. It is the inevitable result of her father's gross partiality toward her sister and neglect of herself, plus the repercussions that his attitude has produced on Bianca and almost everyone else in the region. Kate has heard herself blamed, and her sister praised at her expense, to a point where even a worm would turn. And Kate is no worm. If her sister is a spoiled child, Kate is a cross child who is starved for love. She craves it as a man in a desert craves water, without understanding, as he does, what is the matter. And though we have to allow for the obvious exaggeration of farce in his extreme antics, Petruchio's procedure at bottom shows insight, understanding, and even love. Those actors who equip him with a whip miss Shakespeare's man entirely. In principle, if not in the rougher details, he employs just the right method in the circumstances, and the end amply justifies his means.

* * *

The Taming of the Shrew, by slighting certain things like the tamer's begging for a kiss, is undeniably susceptible of the traditional rowdy interpretation whereby Petruchio becomes a caveman and Kate a termagant. It has been so acted down the years and there is little doubt that it was so acted in Shakespeare's time. Poets are under no obligation to spoil the popular success of their plays by revealing their secrets, even to stage directors. But unless *The Taming of the Shrew* is frankly taken as sheer farce, the primitive interpretation of it is utterly offensive to our sensibilities, saved only by its wit from being as brutal a spectacle as a bearbaiting. Indeed, the analogy that dominated the Elizabethan mind throughout must have been that of the taming of the female hawk. If, then, without distortion, the text is susceptible of another construction that both satisfies us better and at the same time deepens the psychological complexity and truth of the main characters, what, pray, is the authority of tradition that shall prevent our adopting it? If I find a key that fits a treasure chest and am about to open it, but am suddenly confronted with indisputable evidence that it is a key to an entirely different chest several hundred years old, I may defer to the authenticity of the historical documents that have proved the fact, but what a fool I would be not to go ahead in spite of them and open the chest! A work of art exists for what it says to us, not for what it said to people of its "own" day, not even necessarily for what it said, consciously, to its author. A work of art is an autonomous entity. So long as we do no violence to it, we may fit it to our experience in any way we wish.

MAYNARD MACK

from *Engagement and Detachment in Shakespeare's Plays*

Finally, toward the beginning of Shakespeare's career, we have Sly in *The Taming of the Shrew*. Even in the anonymous play *A Shrew,* but much more in Shakespeare's version, we confront in Sly's experience after being thrown out of the alehouse what appears to be an abstract and brief chronicle of how stage illusion takes effect. Sly, having fallen briefly into one of those mysterious sleeps that Shakespeare elsewhere attributes to those who are undergoing the power of a dramatist, wakes to find the identity of a rich lord thrust upon him, rejects it at first, knowing perfectly well who he is ("Christopher Sly, old Sly's son, of Burtonheath. . . . Ask Marian Hacket, the fat alewife of Wincot, if she know me not"), then is engulfed by it, accepts the dream as reality, accepts also a dressed-up players' boy to share the new reality with him as his supposed lady, and at last sits down with her beside him to watch the strolling players put on *The Taming of the Shrew*. Since Sly's newly assumed identity has no result whatever except to bring him face to face with a play, it is tempting to imagine him a witty paradigm of all of us as theatergoers, when we awake out of our ordinary reality of the alehouse, or whatever other reality ordinarily encompasses us, to the

From *Essays on Shakespeare and Elizabethan Drama in Honor of Hardin Craig,* edited by Richard Hosley. Columbia, Missouri: University of Missouri Press, 1962, pp. 279–280. Reprinted by permission of the University of Missouri Press. Copyright © 1962 by the Curators of the University of Missouri.

superimposed reality of the playhouse, and find that there (at any rate, so long as a comedy is playing) wishes are horses and beggars do ride. Sly, to be sure, soon disengages himself from the strollers' play and falls asleep; but in Shakespeare's version—the situation differs somewhat in *A Shrew*[1]—his engagement to his identity as a lord, though presumably broken when the play ends, stretches into infinity for anything we are ever told.

This way of considering Sly is the more tempting in that the play as a whole manipulates the theme of displaced identity in a way that can hardly be ignored. For what the Lord and his Servants do in thrusting a temporary identity on Sly is echoed in what Petruchio does for Kate at a deeper level of psychic change. His gambits in taming her are equally displacements of identity: first, in thrusting on himself the rude self-will which actually belongs to her, so that she beholds what she now is in his mirror, and he (to quote his man Peter) "kills her in her own humor" (4.1.174); and second, in thrusting on her the semblance of a modest, well-conducted young woman—

> 'Twas told me you were coy and rough and sullen,
> And now I find report a very liar,
> For thou art pleasant, gamesome, passing courteous—
> (2.1.237–39)

so that she beholds in another mirror what she may become if she tries, in the manner of Hamlet's advice to his mother:

> Assume a virtue, if you have it not.
> That monster, custom, who all sense doth eat
> Of habits evil, is angel yet in this,
> That to the use of actions fair and good
> He likewise gives a frock or livery
> That aptly is put on.
> (3.4.161–66)

---

1 In *A Shrew*, Sly wakes up resolved to try out what he has gleaned of the play's purport before falling asleep, and tame his own shrew at home.

Petruchio's stratagem is thus more than an entertaining stage device. It parodies the idolatrousness of romantic love which, as Theseus says, is always seeing Helen in a brow of Egypt; but it also reflects love's genuine creative power, which can on occasion make the loved one grow to match the dream. Lucentio, possibly because identity for him is only skin-deep, as the nature of his disguises seems to show, takes the surface for what it appears to be (like Aragon and Morocco in *The Merchant of Venice*), and though he wins the girl discovers he has not won the obedient wife he thought. In Geoffrey Bullough's words, he falls victim to "the last (and richest) 'Suppose' of all."[2]

[2] *Narrative and Dramatic Sources of Shakespeare* (1957), p. 68.

Suggested References

The number of possible references is vast and grows alarmingly. (The *Shakespeare Quarterly* devotes a substantial part of one issue each year to a list of the previous year's work, and *Shakespeare Survey*—an annual publication—includes a substantial review of recent scholarship, as well as an occasional essay surveying a few decades of scholarship on a chosen topic.) Though no works are indispensable, those listed below have been found helpful.

1. Shakespeare's Times

Byrne, M. St. Clare. *Elizabethan Life in Town and Country.* Rev. ed. New York: Barnes & Noble, Inc., 1961. Chapters on manners, beliefs, education, etc., with illustrations.

Craig, Hardin. *The Enchanted Glass: the Elizabethan Mind in Literature.* New York and London: Oxford University Press, 1936. The Elizabethan intellectual climate.

Joseph, B. L. *Shakespeare's Eden: The Commonwealth of England 1558–1629.* New York: Barnes & Noble, Inc., 1971. An account of the social, political, economic, and cultural life of England.

Nicoll, Allardyce (ed.). *The Elizabethans.* London: Cambridge University Press, 1957. An anthology of Elizabethan writings, especially valuable for its illustrations from paintings, title pages, etc.

Shakespeare's England. 2 vols. Oxford: The Clarendon Press, 1916. A large collection of scholarly essays on a wide variety of topics (e.g., astrology, costume, gardening, horsemanship), with special attention to Shakespeare's references to these topics.

Tillyard, E. M. W. *The Elizabethan World Picture*. London: Chatto & Windus, 1943; New York: The Macmillan Company, 1944. A brief account of some Elizabethan ideas of the universe.

Wilson, John Dover (ed.). *Life in Shakespeare's England*. 2nd ed. New York: The Macmillan Company, 1913. An anthology of Elizabethan writings on the countryside, superstition, education, the court, etc.

2. Shakespeare

Barnet, Sylvan. *A Short Guide to Shakespeare*. New York: Harcourt Brace Jovanovich, Inc., 1974. An introduction to all of the works and to the traditions behind them.

Bentley, Gerald E. *Shakespeare: A Biographical Handbook*. New Haven, Conn.: Yale University Press, 1961. The facts about Shakespeare, with virtually no conjecture intermingled.

Bradby, Anne (ed.). *Shakespeare Criticism, 1919–1935*. London: Oxford University Press, 1936. A small anthology of excellent essays on the plays.

Bush, Geoffrey Douglas. *Shakespeare and the Natural Condition*. Cambridge, Mass.: Harvard University Press; London: Oxford University Press, 1956. A short, sensitive account of Shakespeare's view of "Nature," touching most of the works.

Chambers, E. K. *William Shakespeare: A Study of Facts and Problems*. 2 vols. London: Oxford University Press, 1930. An invaluable, detailed reference work; not for the casual reader.

Chute, Marchette. *Shakespeare of London*. New York: E. P. Dutton & Co., Inc., 1949. A readable biography fused with portraits of Stratford and London life.

Clemen, Wolfgang H. *The Development of Shakespeare's Imagery*. Cambridge, Mass.: Harvard University Press, 1951. (Originally published in German, 1936.) A temperate account of a subject often abused.

Craig, Hardin. *An Interpretation of Shakespeare*. Columbia, Missouri: Lucas Brothers, 1948. A scholar's book designed for the layman. Comments on all the works.

Dean, Leonard F. (ed.). *Shakespeare: Modern Essays in Criticism*. New York: Oxford University Press, 1957. Mostly mid-twentieth-century critical studies, covering Shakespeare's artistry.

Granville-Barker, Harley. *Prefaces to Shakespeare*. 2 vols. Princeton, N.J.: Princeton University Press, 1946–47. Essays on ten plays by a scholarly man of the theater.

Harbage, Alfred. *As They Liked It*. New York: The Macmillan Company, 1947. A sensitive, long essay on Shakespeare, morality, and the audience's expectations.

————. *William Shakespeare: A Reader's Guide*. New York: Farrar, Straus, 1963. Extensive comments, scene by scene, on fourteen plays.

Ridler, Anne Bradby (ed.). *Shakespeare Criticism. 1935–1960*. New York and London: Oxford University Press, 1963. An excellent continuation of the anthology edited earlier by Miss Bradby (see above).

Schoenbaum, S. *Shakespeare's Lives*. Oxford: Clarendon Press, 1970. A review of the evidence, and an examination of many biographies, including those by Baconians and other heretics.

————. *William Shakespeare: A Compact Documentary Life*. New York: Oxford University Press, 1977. A readable presentation of all that the documents tell us about Shakespeare.

Smith, D. Nichol (ed.). *Shakespeare Criticism*. New York: Oxford University Press, 1916. A selection of criticism from 1623 to 1840, ranging from Ben Jonson to Thomas Carlyle.

Spencer, Theodore. *Shakespeare and the Nature of Man*. New York: The Macmillan Company, 1942. Shakespeare's plays in relation to Elizabethan thought.

Stoll, Elmer Edgar. *Shakespeare and Other Masters*. Cambridge, Mass.: Harvard University Press; London: Oxford University Press, 1940. Essays on tragedy, comedy, and aspects of dramaturgy, with special reference to some of Shakespeare's plays.

Traversi, D. A. *An Approach to Shakespeare*. Rev. ed. New York: Doubleday & Co., Inc., 1956. An analysis of the plays beginning with words, images, and themes, rather than with characters.

Van Doren, Mark. *Shakespeare*. New York: Henry Holt & Company, Inc., 1939. Brief, perceptive readings of all of the plays.

Whitaker, Virgil K. *Shakespeare's Use of Learning*. San Marino, Calif.: Huntington Library, 1953. A study of the relation of Shakespeare's reading to his development as a dramatist.

3. Shakespeare's Theater

Adams, John Cranford. *The Globe Playhouse*. Rev. ed. New York: Barnes & Noble, Inc., 1961. A detailed conjecture about the physical characteristics of the theater Shakespeare often wrote for.

Beckerman, Bernard. *Shakespeare at the Globe, 1599–1609*. New York: The Macmillan Company, 1962. On the playhouse and on Elizabethan dramaturgy, acting, and staging.

Chambers, E. K. *The Elizabethan Stage*. 4 vols. New York: Oxford University Press, 1923. Reprinted with corrections, 1945. An indispensable reference work on theaters, theatrical companies, and staging at court.

Gurr, Andrew. *The Shakespearean Stage 1574–1642*. Cambridge: Cambridge University Press, 1970. On the acting companies, the actors, the playhouses, the stages, and the audiences.

Harbage, Alfred. *Shakespeare's Audience*. New York: Columbia University Press; London: Oxford University Press, 1941. A study of the size and nature of the theatrical public.

Hodges, C. Walter. *The Globe Restored*. London: Ernest Benn, Ltd., 1953; New York: Coward-McCann, Inc., 1954. A well-illustrated and readable attempt to reconstruct the Globe Theater.

Kernodle, George R. *From Art to Theatre: Form and Convention in the Renaissance*. Chicago: University of Chicago Press, 1944. Pioneering and stimulating work on the symbolic and cultural meanings of theater construction.

Nagler, A. M. *Shakespeare's Stage*. Tr. by Ralph Manheim. New Haven, Conn.: Yale University Press, 1958. An excellent, brief introduction to the physical aspect of the playhouse.

Smith, Irwin. *Shakespeare's Globe Playhouse*. New York: Charles Scribner's Sons, 1957. Chiefly indebted to J. C. Adams' controversial book, with additional material and scale drawings for model-builders.

Venezky. Alice S. *Pageantry on the Shakespearean Stage*. New York: Twayne Publishers, Inc., 1951. An examination of spectacle in Elizabethan drama.

4. Miscellaneous Reference Works

Abbott, E. A. *A Shakespearean Grammar*. New edition. New York: The Macmillan Company, 1877. An examination of differences between Elizabethan and modern grammar.

Berman, Ronald. *A Reader's Guide to Shakespeare's Plays.* Chicago: Scott, Foresman and Company, 1965. A short bibliography of the chief articles.

Bullough, Geoffrey. *Narrative and Dramatic Sources of Shakespeare.* 5 vols. Vols. 6 and 7 in preparation. New York: Columbia University Press; London: Routledge & Kegan Paul, Ltd., 1957–. A collection of many of the books Shakespeare drew upon.

Campbell, Oscar James, and Edward G. Quinn. *The Reader's Encyclopedia of Shakespeare.* New York: Thomas Y. Crowell Co., 1966. More than 2,700 entries, from a few sentences to a few pages on everything related to Shakespeare.

Greg, W. W. *The Shakespeare First Folio.* New York and London: Oxford University Press, 1955. A detailed yet readable history of the first collection (1623) of Shakespeare's plays.

Kökeritz, Helge. *Shakespeare's Names.* New Haven, Conn.: Yale University Press, 1959; London: Oxford University Press, 1960. A guide to the pronunciation of some 1,800 names appearing in Shakespeare.

————. *Shakespeare's Pronunciation.* New Haven, Conn.: Yale University Press; London: Oxford University Press, 1953. Contains much information about puns and rhymes.

Linthicum, Marie C. *Costume in the Drama of Shakespeare and His Contemporaries.* New York and London: Oxford University Press, 1936. On the fabrics and dress of the age, and references to them in the plays.

Muir, Kenneth. *Shakespeare's Sources.* London: Methuen Co., Ltd., 1957. The first volume, on the comedies and tragedies, attempts to ascertain what books were Shakespeare's sources and what use he made of them.

Onions, C. T. *A Shakespeare Glossary.* London: Oxford University Press, 1911; 2nd ed., rev., with enlarged addenda, 1953. Definitions of words (or senses of words) now obsolete.

Partridge, Eric. *Shakespeare's Bawdy.* Rev. ed. New York: E. P. Dutton & Co., Inc.; London: Routledge & Kegan Paul, Ltd., 1955. A glossary of bawdy words and phrases.

Shakespeare Quarterly. See headnote to Suggested References.

Shakespeare Survey. See headnote to Suggested References.

Smith, Gordon Ross. *A Classified Shakespeare Bibliography 1936–1958.* University Park, Pa.: Pennsylvania State University Press, 1963. A list of some 20,000 items on Shakespeare.

Spevack, Marvin. *The Harvard Concordance to Shakespeare*. Cambridge, Mass.: Harvard University Press, 1973. An index to Shakespeare's words.

Wells, Stanley, ed. *Shakespeare: Select Bibliographies*. London: Oxford University Press, 1973. Seventeen essays surveying scholarship and criticism of Shakespeare's life, work, and theater.

5. *The Taming of the Shrew*

Brown, John Russell. *Shakespeare and His Comedies*. London: Methuen & Co. Ltd., 1957.

Charlton, H. B. *Shakespearean Comedy*. London: Methuen & Co. Ltd., 1938.

Child, Harold. "The Stage History of *The Taming of the Shrew*," in the Cambridge edition of *The Taming of the Shrew*, ed. by Sir Arthur Quiller-Couch and John Dover Wilson. London: Cambridge University Press, 1928, 1953.

Craig, Hardin. *An Interpretation of Shakespeare*. New York: Citadel Press, 1948.

————. "*The Shrew* and *A Shrew*: Possible Settlement of an Old Debate," in *Elizabethan Studies and Other Essays in Honor of George F. Reynolds*. Boulder, Colorado: University of Colorado Press, 1945, pp. 150–154.

Crane, Milton. "Shakespeare's Comedies and the Critics." in *Shakespeare 400*, ed. James G. McManaway. New York and London: Holt, Rinehart, and Winston, 1964, pp. 67–73.

Evans, Bertrand. *Shakespeare's Comedies*. Oxford: The Clarendon Press, 1960.

Frey, Albert R. *The Taming of the Shrew*. The Bankside Shakespeare, New York, 1888. Prints *A Shrew* and *The Shrew* on opposite pages, so arranged as to call attention to identical and similar passages. A long introduction summarizes a good deal of evidence, and many older opinions, about the plays, and argues for Shakespeare's authorship of *A Shrew*.

Hickson, Samuel. "The Taming of the Shrew," *Notes and Queries*, I, No. 22 (March 30, 1850), 345–347. First to argue that *The Shrew* is the prior play and that *A Shrew* is an imitation of it.

Huston, J. Dennis. " 'To Make a Puppet': Play and Play-Making in *The Taming of the Shrew*," *Shakespeare Studies*

9, ed. J. Leeds Barroll III. New York: Burt Franklin & Co., Inc., 1976.

Leggatt, Alexander. *Shakespeare's Comedy of Love.* London: Methuen & Co. Ltd., 1974. Salingar, Leo. *Shakespeare and the Traditions of Comedy.* Cambridge: Cambridge University Press, 1974.

Stauffer, Donald A. *Shakespeare's World of Images,* New York: W. W. Norton & Co., Inc., 1949.

Tillyard, E. M. W. *Shakespeare's Early Comedies.* London: Chatto & Windus, 1965.

The SIGNET Classic Shakespeare

(0451)

- [ ] **ALL'S WELL THAT ENDS WELL, Sylvan Barnet**, ed., Tufts University. (516575—$1.75)
- [ ] **ANTONY AND CLEOPATRA, Barbara Everett**, ed., Cambridge University. (514114—$1.95)
- [ ] **AS YOU LIKE IT, Albert Gilman**, ed., Boston University. (516672—$1.75)
- [ ] **THE COMEDY OF ERRORS, Harry Levin**, Harvard. (511638—$1.50)
- [ ] **CORIOLANUS, Reuben Brower**, ed., Harvard. (515765—$1.95)
- [ ] **CYMBELINE, Richard Hosley**, ed., University of Arizona. (512685—$1.50)
- [ ] **HAMLET, Edward Hubler**, ed., Princeton University. (514157—$1.75)
- [ ] **HENRY IV, Part II, Norman H. Holland**, ed., M.I.T. (514017—$1.95)
- [ ] **HENRY V, John Russell Brown**, ed., University of Birmingham. (515757—$1.75)
- [ ] **HENRY VI, Part I, Lawrence V. Ryan**, ed., Stanford. (510321—$1.75)
- [ ] **HENRY VIII, Samuel Schoenbaum**, ed., Northwestern University. (512464—$1.50)
- [ ] **JULIUS CAESAR, William and Barbara Rosen**, eds., University of Connecticut. (514300—$1.75)
- [ ] **KING JOHN, William H. Matchett**, ed., University of Washington. (513991—$1.95)
- [ ] **KING LEAR, Russel Fraser**, ed., Princeton University. (516230—$1.75)
- [ ] **LOVE'S LABOR LOST, John Arthos**, ed., University of Michigan. (514289—$1.95)
- [ ] **MEASURE FOR MEASURE, S. Nagarajan**, ed., University of Poona, India. (514432—$1.95)
- [ ] **MACBETH, Sylvan Barnet**, ed., Tufts University. (515544—$1.75)
